CERTAIN KINDS OF LOVING

NANCY ZAROULIS

IVY BOOKS • NEW YORK

Ivy Books
Published by Ballantine Books
Copyright © 1986 by Nancy Zaroulis

Library of Congress Catalog Card Number: 86-2053

ISBN 0-8041-0162-0

This edition published by arrangement with Doubleday & Company,
Inc.

Manufactured in the United States of America

First Ballantine Books Edition: November 1987

Lily and David waited up for her; Peaches and Thomas had wanted to, but they were too tired and so shortly after nine they went to bed.

She was glad, now, that she had said goodnight to Neal in his car. He had not attempted to kiss her, a restraint for which she was grateful. She did not want to kiss him, not yet. The idea of falling in love was still too new, really too alarming. She had not intended to fall in love ever again; had not wanted to. Or not, at least, for a long time — until the children were older.

Falling in love, maintaining a love affair, took a good deal of energy; for so long now she had given all the energy she had to her children that she could not imagine where she would find more for a man . . .

CERTAIN KINDS OF LOVING

"This subtle chronicle of the intrusion of love into the lives of people who thought they were getting along quite nicely without it is a delight — full of feeling and forgotten truths."
Elizabeth Forsyth Hailey

"An utterly delightful, thoroughly mature love story for adults."
The Cleveland Plain Dealer

For Alex

Acknowledgments

I am grateful to my daughters, who are unfailingly generous with help and advice, to Winthrop A. Burr, Michael Simon, Susan Simon, and Frederick G. Whoriskey, M.D., for their specialized information; to Roz Brezenoff for being in the right place at the right time; and particularly to my husband, my best reader and critic, my constant support.

1

❧❧❧❧

LILY SAW THE ENEMY THE MOMENT SHE REACHED the top of the tree. She peered through the branches, not minding the scrape on her leg. She was looking for the scouting party from the wagon train. Instead she saw a man climbing down from a red van labeled ENERGY-WORKS in black letters, parked in the driveway behind her mother's dark green Volvo station wagon.

The others clustered at the base of the tree, awaiting her instructions.

"Are they coming?" called Thomas, much too loud.

David shushed him. Lily heard their soft, tense exchange; then she heard Peaches giggle.

"Wait," she called softly. "Just wait a minute." She held to the tree with one hand while she adjusted her paper headband with its three crayoned paper feathers, one red, one blue, and one yellow; the blue one had bent so that it drooped over her right eye, obscuring her vision.

The enemy had gone up the flagstone path, up the steps to the front porch. He was a stocky man with brown hair; he wore chino pants and a light blue shirt. He carried a clipboard.

Lily heard movement below. She looked down. David's head appeared through the branches beneath her feet. He had discarded his paper feathers; perspiration dribbled down this thin, flushed face.

"Come on," he said. "You've got to see them or Peaches says she'll go inside. They've got to attack us right away so we can beat them in time for lunch."

Lily looked back to the house. The man had not reappeared; her mother must have let him in. Although Lily was a good distance away from the house, at the top of the tree, she felt shut out and vaguely anxious for her mother.

"No," she said. "I don't see them anywhere."

"Maybe they fixed the axle. Maybe they've started up again. Come on—we can surprise them at the pass." David's voice was eager, intense. He was a throwback to an earlier time: he loved this game more than any other, more than any space age game in which he had to play a robot or carry a laser gun or pretend to be from another galaxy.

"No," said Lily. "They aren't there." The heat pressed down on her. She wanted to go home and get a drink of orange juice; she wanted to sit on the porch and read Judy Blume.

She wanted to see the enemy up close.

"Watch out," she said. "I'm coming down." The paper feathers annoyed her. She pulled them off and dropped them. They caught on a branch.

"*Lily*—"

"Watch *out*," she said. "It's no good today. Peaches was right. We should have played Star Wars." She felt with her foot for the next branch down. David scrambled beneath her; he dropped to the ground and picked up his bow and the quiver of arrows which he had propped against the trunk of the tree. It was a real bow, not just a piece of string tied to a branch, and a real imitation leather quiver. Their grandfather—their mother's father—had given them to him last Christmas.

Peaches and Thomas watched them. Lily climbed all the way down without jumping and straightened her pink alligator shirt where it had hitched up around her waist. "Come on," she said; and then, seeing Thomas' crestfallen expression: "We'll try again tomorrow. There's always a new wagon train coming through."

"I *told* you we should have played Star Wars," said Peaches. She spoke pleasantly, without malice; she was making an observation rather than censuring the older ones' judgment.

"Listen," said Lily, watching Thomas struggle with his disappointment. "I didn't see the wagon train. But I did see a man come to the house—you can't see his truck from here—and we can pretend he came to kidnap us, only when he finds out we're not there he holds Mom hostage or something. We can sneak up and look in the window—"

"And then we can call the police!" said Thomas, his face brightening. "Or we can hold *him* hostage—"

"Come on," said Peaches. "We need to get a good description."

Lily led the way down the wooded hill and along the tall shrubbery to the gap that led to their back garden. They went single file, Indian-style, cautious, stealthy. Lily, at eleven, was the eldest; she usually led them wherever they went but sometimes she let David, who was ten. Peaches, eight, and Thomas, six, almost never led; once, earlier in the summer, when Lily and David had given Thomas a chance to lead them on an exploration into the Amazon to hunt for buried treasure, he had taken them through a patch of poison ivy and they had all itched for days.

Lily paused when she reached the opening in the

hedge. "We shouldn't go in right away," she said. For Thomas' sake she spoke in a stage whisper.

"Let's go on the back porch and look in the window," said David. Lily could tell from the way he spoke that he wasn't playing seriously; he was humoring her as she had humored Thomas.

"Somebody should get the license number of the truck," said Peaches, remembering a Safety Day at school. "Miss Bronson said if a man comes in a car and asks you to get in, always get the license number if you can. But don't get in, she said, that's the main thing."

"Will you do that?" said David. "Get the number? While we look in the window?"

"I can't remember license numbers. And besides, I want to stay with you."

"All right," said Lily. "Never mind. Let's just make a run for it to the porch. But stay bent down. And *be quiet.*"

In a moment they were across the hot, sunny lawn. Cautiously Lily opened the screen door to the back porch and motioned them on ahead of her. Still crouching, they tiptoed to a window that gave onto the dining room. They peered in. They saw no one.

"Maybe they're in the living room," said Peaches.

"If he's a robber, he'll take the silverware," said Thomas. "The silverware is in the dining room."

"In the sideboard," said David. "It's a service for twelve."

"And a teapot and sugar bowl and stuff," said Peaches.

"I think the teapot's just plate."

"What's plate?" said Thomas.

"It means it isn't real silver. The knives and forks are real silver."

"If he just wants to take the silverware, then maybe he won't want to kidnap Mom," said Peaches.

"Do you think he'll do that?" said Thomas. "Do you think he'll kidnap Mom?"

Lily heard the fear in his voice. "No," she said. "He's not going to do that."

"But he *might*. He's a strange man, and she let him in, didn't she? Why does she tell us never to let a strange man in, if she does it?" Tired of crouching, Thomas sat down on the porch floor. "Remember when she got mad when the man came that time and David almost let him in?"

"She wasn't mad. She was upset. Afraid."

"I remember that," said Peaches. "He came back when she was home and she opened the door and talked to him but she didn't let him in. He was from Greenpeace, or Save the Whales, or something."

A movement within the house caught David's eye. "Sssssh," he hissed. Still crouching, they looked in; Thomas stood up and looked over their shoulders. Their mother and the stranger were standing just inside the dining room door. The window was open; they were talking about heat loss.

Lily ducked and sat on the porch floor and the others followed her example.

"What should we do?" mouthed Peaches. She was grinning, hugely enjoying herself.

Lily shook her head. "Nothing. Wait."

"Call the police?" said Thomas.

"No. Not yet."

"He looks pretty big," said David. He was still holding his bow, the quiver slung over his shoulder. "He could pick Mom up and put her in the truck easy as anything."

Thomas made as if to bolt. "I'm going to the Laffertys' to call the police," he said, too loudly. Lily could see that he was really frightened, that he had forgotten that it was only a game. They all forgot, from time to time: you got so involved in watching for the wagon train or finding the secret treasure that you had to stop and think for a moment before you remembered that you were Lily Merrill and you lived with your mother and your three younger brothers and sister and you were going into the sixth grade. "No, Thomas. Wait. It's only a game."

"I'm going to," he said. His voice trembled, but it was still too loud. "I'm going to, right now!"

"What are you going to do right now, Thomas?"

They looked up. Their mother and the strange man stood just inside the window looking out.

Lily felt herself blush. Their mother knew and did not mind that they played their games—she was glad that they did, Lily thought—but she might not be glad to have herself and this stranger, whoever he was, included. Lily stood up and the others followed. The two adults peering out were hard to see in the dim light of the shaded room, but Lily could imagine clearly enough her mother's expression: a blend of love and affection and mild curiosity which would, Lily knew, quickly turn to alarm if she thought anything was wrong. If Thomas was frightened, for instance.

Thomas stood mute.

"Nothing," said David. "We were just— Nothing."

Margaret Merrill stared out at her children: her precious little quartet, her lifeline to the world. If it were not for them, she often thought, she would simply crawl into bed and not get up. Ever. But they kept her going; and if she went long enough, far enough—

She turned to the man standing beside her. "Sorry," she said. "About the windows—?"

He was not looking at the children. He was examining the window—large, too large, the sash loose in the frame, a big expanse of glass, no doubt the original glass. The storm windows installed by the previous owner, cheap and badly fitted, were hardly better than nothing at all against the winter cold.

"As I was saying," he said. "You could replace two or three of these windows every year with thermals. And for now you can put weather stripping around. Or you could just put in a better quality storm window. You have a tremendous amount of heat loss through these large panes."

"Yes," she said. As they moved back through the dining room to the hall, she was conscious of the children standing on the porch, watching. They were probably hungry, she thought. She would hurry with this man. Although he was here because she had called his company for an estimate, she felt now that he was an intruder. She wanted him gone.

She led him upstairs, and then up another flight to the third floor. The heat under the roof was stifling now, in August, but in winter these rooms were so cold that they were uninhabitable.

He walked through, looking, taking a flashlight from his utility belt to peer at the ceiling and the base of the walls where they were in shadow. She could not remember his name. He seemed pleasant enough, and one of her neighbors had been pleased with the work that his firm had done. "You'll save half your heating bill the first year," the woman had said. "And insulation's a big plus if you sell."

But she would not sell: not this year, anyway, and probably not next. They would manage somehow. The children loved this house, this neighborhood, their school; she would not uproot them. Not yet.

He clattered down the stairs and she followed him. She felt oddly defensive: I know it's a big old drafty uninsulated pile, a house built a hundred years ago when fuel was unlimited and cheap and servants were on hand day and night to bring it in. There were fireplaces in the living room and the dining room and three of the bedrooms on the second floor. Firewood was as expensive as oil now—more so, in fact—and so they had fires only very rarely, taking the wood piece by precious piece from where it was stacked in the carriage house.

He stopped to examine the big stained-glass window at the back of the second floor hall. "Nice," he said. "Did it come with the house?"

"My husband found it in the cellar."

Before he left us, she might have added, but of course she did not. This man was not interested in her personal life. Moreover, she had discovered long ago that such declarations were easily misinterpreted as invitations—to sympathy if not to sexual advances. She wanted neither. Divorced women were looked upon by many men as fair game; Margaret had learned, therefore, to neuter herself when she dealt with men: to not smile too much, to ignore innuendos when they came (as they invariably did, for she was a pretty woman, gentle and sweet-tempered, and a natural target, therefore, for men of all kinds). She understood that men who made advances to her were not trying to harm her but were simply trying to approach her, albeit clumsily; nevertheless she did not want their approaches, did not want their advances, and so she had learned to adopt a dull, protective coloration.

The man went into one of the bedrooms on the second floor and stopped and cocked his head to listen. There was a small bathroom between this and the next bedroom. He looked in. It was the original bathroom, claw-foot tub, pull-chain toilet, wide marble sink with tall brass taps. One faucet was leaking, and the toilet was running, the flush ball in the mahogany tank high up on the wall not seated properly. Both were simple matters to fix. If he'd had a ladder he could have fixed the toilet in five minutes.

Often he visited houses like this, old houses inhabited by single women either widowed, or divorced, or sometimes groups of women living together. Very few of them were handy; they let little things go until they became big things. Big, expensive things.

He caught her eye and looked away. Sometimes women asked him to fix the little things; long ago he had learned not to mention them, but sometimes the women asked anyway. Nice to have a man around the house. But not him.

He moved past her out of the bedroom into the hall and into another bedroom. A girl's: pink ruffled bedspread and curtains, a doll house. Here on the second floor, as on the first, the paint and wallpaper looked relatively new.

"All right," he said. "I'll just look at the basement."

She nodded. She seemed distracted. Shy, he thought. A little anxious. Not likely to ask him to fix the toilet.

"In the kitchen," she said, and followed him down the stairs. The kitchen had been renovated: butcher-block and brick-colored counter tops, hanging plants at the windows, a semisphere French pot rack hung with copper pots. Like the living room, which was sparsely furnished with plump-pillowed modern furniture, it did not match the house. On the center island was a plate of fresh-baked chocolate chip cookies. She did not offer him one.

"Down there," she said, nodding at the door that led to the cellar. "You don't need me, do you?"

"No," he said, and went down. In a few moments he was back. She had taken out a loaf of bread and a bowl of tuna fish salad and was making sandwiches.

He put his clipboard on the island across from her and released an Energyworks flier.

"This house is about a hundred years old, right?" he said.

"Yes."

"You're lucky. The fieldstone walls in the basement are in good shape. The house has never been insulated, and that makes it easier for us. We'd work from outside, since your paint and paper look in good shape and we'd have to drill holes in the walls every sixteen inches. So we'd go from outside, take shingles off, and you wouldn't have too much mess. We'd put in fiberglass, it's better material than cellulose, it won't settle, won't hold moisture if it gets wet. Those pipes in the basement ought to be wrapped, cold water as well as hot. Keep them from freezing. Your heating plant is in good shape, that's the most important thing." He wrote his name in the blank space at the bottom of the flier: Neal Donovan. His handwriting was almost printing, she noticed: a large, clear, bold script.

"You can wrap the piping relatively inexpensively," he went on. "It's a pre-molded wrap, closed cellular foam. Either we can do it, or you can buy it from us and do it yourselves."

She glanced at him and then away. "No," she said. "You people had better do it. I'm not very handy."

So the husband who had found the stained glass was no longer there.

"Either way," he said. "I'll leave this with you and you can get back to us if you want to go ahead."

"That'll be fine." She had put tuna fish on five slices of bread. Now she tore off pieces of lettuce from a freshly washed head and topped each slice with that. Her hands were small, slim, the fingers a little bony. Her hands looked more competent than she did. She put second slices of bread—whole wheat, but not the hard-looking kind—on the lettuce.

"I assume if you'd want the work done you'd want it done before the cold weather," he said. "Say, before November."

She put each sandwich on a plate and cut it into four triangles. She paused for a moment and looked up at him as if she were thinking for the first time about what he was saying. "Yes," she said. "Yes, I would. That's right."

"So if you get back to us in a couple of weeks, we'd be able to schedule you in. This is our busy season."

"Yes," she said. Her eyes were wide and blue; her face was a little pink on the cheeks, framed by very curly blond hair. He couldn't tell if either the cheeks or the hair were natural. "Yes," she said again. "I'll let you know right away."

Seeing the sandwiches and the cookies had made him hungry. He would stop for lunch before going back to the office, he thought.

She followed him to the front door. "Thanks very much," she said. He opened the screen door—old and wooden, like the house—and went out across the porch into the broiling day.

And, for a moment, his heart stopped.

The children were waiting for him. They were lined up steplike along the walk, tallest to shortest. The shortest one, a boy, wore a headdress made of leafy twigs; one of the middle ones, a girl, wore a battered cowboy hat that was too large for her head; the bigger boy trained an arrow on him, the string on his bow drawn back, ready to shoot. They stood silent, not moving: watching him.

He walked steadily on. Although he knew perfectly well where he was, he heard a voice—his voice?—

screaming at him from somewhere deep in his brain, deep in the past: *"Donovan! Gooks!"*

Suddenly, with a wordless cry, the littlest one lunged toward him. In an instinctive movement, Neal dropped to a half crouch and reached for his grenade. It was not there. Instead his fingers closed on the handle of his utility knife in its sheath. *Little fucker—!*

The child stopped. He was about ten feet away. He looked very frightened. No one spoke; no one moved.

Neal recovered first. He straightened and took a deep breath. Then he walked on.

In three seconds he was past them. He felt embarrassed. He wondered if they would laugh at him. They did not. He should have smiled at them, should have made some cute remark. But no words had come to him—or, rather, no words that he could have uttered here, in this pleasant suburban landscape, in this pleasant suburban town, a peaceful, prosperous town inhabited by peaceful, prosperous people untouched by war.

His knees shook as he climbed into the high seat of the van. He did not look toward the children but he saw them from the corner of his eye. They stood motionless, astonished, still watching him.

He backed out of the driveway; he started down the street.

He had seen children in the war: small, yellow, black-haired children, fragile like little birds, thin hungry children watching the big American boys. Sometimes the children begged; sometimes they stood silent and simply watched.

And sometimes they were rigged up with grenades, and they were then not simply small hungry children but miniature killers, sent to kill him.

Once, on a very bad day, a day when his unit had

taken heavy losses, one of his comrades, seeing such a child come toward them at a run, had killed it.

He pulled over at the corner, out of sight of the house, and sat breathing deeply until his heart beat normally again, until his hands were steady enough to hold the wheel.

Then he drove on.

2

LATER—MUCH LATER, AROUND NINE O'CLOCK—
Neal closed his office and drove to The Rising of the
Moon on Mass. Ave. in Cambridge and had two roast
beef on ryes and three Heinekens and listened to Jason
Goodrich talk about the movies. Or, as Jason liked to
say, "films." Or better yet, "cinema." Tonight it was
The Marriage of Maria Braun."

"It's a paradigm of postwar Germany," Jason said.
He sat next to Neal and twisted the upper part of his
body toward him, leaning his right elbow on the bar.
He was drinking dark beer. "I mean, it's just absolutely perfect. Death and resurrection. Defeat and
triumph and ultimate regeneration of the spirit per-
ceived through the persona of a beautiful woman. She
embodies—if I may use that word—she embodies the
entire Teutonic myth. She's a twentieth-century Val-
kyrie. And the ending—well, I won't tell you the ending, you have to see it for yourself. It's coming to the
Harvard Square. Or it's on tape if you have a machine. I
urge you to see it. As your friend and adviser, I beg you
not to miss this one. You'll never understand Double-
yew Double-yew Two if you don't see *The Marriage of
Maria Braun*."

"I still don't understand the war I was in," said

14

Neal. "How am I supposed to understand one I wasn't?"

"You have to," said Jason. "You can't understand the twentieth century, for Christ's sake, if you don't understand the Big One."

Jason taught at Boston University. When Neal had asked him, once, what he taught, Jason had said "creative writing." Neal had asked him if anyone taught uncreative writing. Jason, to his credit, had laughed. Neal thought it was odd that although Jason taught writing, he never talked about writing; he talked about the movies.

"Right," said Neal. He glanced around as someone bumped into his other side, a dark-haired young woman who hadn't bothered to say "excuse me." It was after ten, the place was filling up. He turned his attention back to Jason. They had met one evening two years ago in this same bar; although they had seen each other from time to time in other places, this was still their usual spot.

"On the other hand," said Jason, "if you're in the mood for it, *Diva* is rather amusing. It has a bitter undertone, a kind of high-tech ambiance, a counterpoint of major *tristesse*, but it's a stunning film. And don't forget, *The Big Sleep* is coming next week, the *original Big Sleep*. The finest flowering of *film noir*."

Neal nodded. The noise level was rising. Soon some homesick colleen would get up and take the small stage and sing about the Rising and the Easter martyrs. Often he stayed for these performances and even enjoyed them, but tonight he would not.

"The best film of all is still *The Children of Paradise*," said Jason. He spoke quite loud now against the noise. "It has such life, such *soul*."

Neal felt a momentary surge of irritation. "Why do

you say *films*?" he said. "We always called them
movies."

"Because, dear boy, a film is a work of art. A movie
is commerce."

On another evening Neal would have said, "For instance?" But tonight he did not. He was suddenly tired
of Jason, tired of the noisy bar which as the evening
progressed would become more and more vocally, defiantly Irish. Although he was Irish himself, sometimes
the blatant ethnicity bothered him.

He reached for his wallet and took out a ten and
three ones and put them on the counter, at the same
time easing himself off the barstool.

"Goodrich, you're a mine of information," he said.
"I don't see how your students put up with you."

"You going?" said Jason. "It's early yet." He looked
disappointed, Neal thought.

"It's my busy season," he said. "I'll catch you tomorrow night if I have time."

Jason nodded. "Better yet, go to see *The Third
Man*. It's at the Brattle."

"I don't like to go to movies by myself." He said
"movies" on purpose.

"You don't have a date? I met a girl last week. She's
just your type."

Neal laughed. "What type is that? No, don't tell
me. I'll let you know when I feel like going out and
maybe you can fix me up." He touched Jason lightly
on the upper arm and turned and worked his way out
of the crowded bar.

It was a warm night. His car, a year-old Nissan, was
parked a block down Mass. Ave. He walked quickly in
the bleak illumination of the street lights, feeling suddenly really tired now, not just bored with the crowd at
the bar. He would get up at five-thirty tomorrow to go
over the accounts with his partner before setting out at

eight to get to Lynn for a nine o'clock appointment.
The busy season.

He drove home in silence, no music, no talk shows.
Home was a four-room apartment on the second floor
of a house in Dorchester. He owned that house and
two others. He parked in the driveway behind the
Toyota and sat for a moment in the quiet night. The
first-floor tenants—owners of the Toyota, a young
couple with two children—were asleep: no lights.
They were good tenants, prompt payers of the rent. So
were his others. He was lucky; some people had trouble.

He got out of the car, closed the door as quietly as
possible, and went in. On the way he took the mail
from his box. Telephone bill, Wilderness Society, *The
New Yorker*, a letter whose return address was indeci-
pherable.

His apartment was stuffy. He switched on the hall
light, went into the bedroom, and turned on the air
conditioner. Its low purring seemed to fill some of the
room's emptiness. Bed, bureau, night table, small television on a stand, narrow overladen bookcase near the
window. Freshly painted when he bought the place two
years ago, but nothing on the walls: no pictures, no
posters. Because he visited so many homes he was
aware that his was badly decorated: was not, in fact,
decorated at all but merely a repository for odd pieces
of furniture. No color scheme, no careful selection of
accessories—no personality. In the living room were a
brown sleep sofa, a green easy chair, a maple rocker
with faded, flowered pads on the seat and back, a
scarred fruitwood coffee table, two tall bookcases
crammed with books, a turntable and two speakers, a
stack of records beside one of them. On the floor was
a brown rug curling at the edges. A stranger coming in
would have been hard put to know him from his living

quarters. Except for the books. You could make something of them, he supposed.

He went into the kitchen and dropped the mail on the table. It was an old gate-legged table that he had bought for five dollars; rather than refinish it he simply kept it covered with a fabric-backed red-and-white-checked vinyl cloth. He opened the refrigerator and took out a glass container of coffee; he put ice cubes in a glass and a spoonful of sugar and then poured the coffee and added a little milk. Caffeine at night didn't bother him.

He sat at the table and picked up the letter. He didn't recognize the handwriting. The coffee refreshed him: cold, not too sweet. He tore open the envelope. In addition to a single badly typed sheet there was a photograph of a young man and woman and a little boy about two, he guessed.

Dear Neal,
You may be surprised to hear from me but I was up your way last week and tried to call you. I didn't leave a message on your machine because I thought you wouldn't remember me. I was in the hospital when you were in with shrapnel in your gut. I was the bad burn case, the next bed to yours. It took me a year after you left to get better. They sent me over here so it wasn't like I never got home again. Then I met Corinne and we got married and I got a job at her father's. He has a hardware store here and one in Dayton. Things have been going pretty good. The son turned two in June. His name is Kevin Michael.
     Well take care Neal, and drop me a note sometime. Hope all is well with you and hope

you've found a good woman to keep you out of trouble.

The letter was signed Michael Halloran. At the bottom was a return address in Columbus, Ohio.

Neal finished his iced coffee. The clock on the wall said eleven forty-seven. He took the glass to the sink, rinsed it, and took the letter and *The New Yorker* into the bedroom. It was cooler there now and he turned the air conditioner to low. He took a quick shower and put on his pajama bottoms and lay on the bed flipping through the magazine looking at the cartoons. He read. "The Talk of the Town." There was a long piece on El Salvador but he was too tired to start it.

Michael Halloran? He slipped the photograph out of the envelope and studied it. Like most snapshots it was taken too far back and the faces were indistinct. He had no idea who this person was who had written to him.

But that, he thought, was fair enough. You passed by a lot of people in your life and you could not be expected to remember all of them. No: the point was not that he did not recognize this person; it was that he did not care about recognizing him. He hadn't the faintest interest. Michael Halloran and his little family and his contentment with his life meant nothing to him.

So I wish you well, Michael, he thought, but I don't intend to follow up.

He turned off the light and stretched out on the bed. Although he was not cold he pulled the sheet up because he liked the feel of it.

The shrapnel had been bad, but not as bad as many other injuries might have been: not as bad as amputation, or blinding, or the burns this fellow had had.

Not as bad as death.

His last image before he went to sleep was of a row of children: white children on a suburban lawn. They did not speak to him, they did not rush toward him; they merely watched him, their faces guarded, hostile, as if they were waiting for him to make a wrong move.

And then, if he did, they would go after him.

3

❧❧❧

MARGARET AND HER FORMER HUSBAND, RICHARD, had bought the house during the first year of their marriage. The down payment had been an inheritance from Richard's grandfather and an equal sum as a wedding present from Margaret's father. Richard had viewed the house as a challenge: he had painted the woodwork and wallpapered and learned how to carpenter in a semiprofessional way. He had sanded and refinished the floors, replaced rotting cellar steps, made new screens for the porch. With the help of a friend who was a small contractor, he had redone the kitchen. Somehow he had never gotten around to the basics: insulation, new wiring and plumbing, an efficient furnace, waterproofing the cellar. Margaret had had the new furnace put in the year after he left.

The house had been built in 1885, and it reflected its era: there was a turret, and a pantry; there were fireplaces, and several leaded glass windows; there was much wasted space, tall ceilings, claw-footed bathtubs, an inglenook. Save for the addition of the inefficient storm windows, none of it had been touched since the 1920s, when a "modern" kitchen had been put in. Slowly, painstakingly, Richard had worked at it. Sometimes she had thought, I should be jealous of this

21

house. He cares more about it than he does about me. And then, in the end, there had been another woman after all, and on the evening after Thomas' second birthday party he had told her that he was leaving. It seemed to hurt him more to part with the house than with her.

But she loved the house, too, and so there had never been any question of moving. With what Richard sent her, and occasional help from her parents which they could well afford ("You'll have it all in any case," her father had said, "so why not have some of it now?"), she had enough to live on; the mortgage payments were less than what an apartment would cost to rent now. The children were happy in their school, the neighbors were kind and friendly. Her parents had advised selling, not because of financial need but because "there's always something needing to be fixed in a place like that," her mother had said. "A house like that needs a man."

Margaret had expected her to finish the thought: "just as a woman does." But those words had been left unsaid. Her parents had not liked her husband—had never really trusted him to care for her properly, she thought—and had not been unhappy to see him go. In the four years since, however, they had been waiting for her to find someone else. They had not nagged her, of course, for they were not the kind of people who nagged, but she understood their concern. Once— only once—her mother had tried:

"How was the Sampsons' party the other night?"

"All right."

"Many people there?"

"Quite a few, yes."

"Anybody interesting?"

"I talked for a while to a woman who'd just come back from Nigeria. She's a doctor. She'd been working there for two years." She watched faint disappointment cloud her mother's eyes.

"Anybody else?"

"No, Mother. Nobody else. No eligible men, if that's what you mean."

"I was only asking."

"I know. And I'm answering."

"You know I don't mean to pry. But it's hard to be alone, Margaret. Especially with children. I don't have to tell you that."

"Not as hard as it is to be unhappily married. That's the hardest thing of all."

"I know. I know. But I hate to see you struggle by yourself. I was always lucky. I had only you, and yet if I'd lost your father I don't know what I'd have done."

"You'd have survived. We all do, one way and another."

"I'm not so sure."

Her mother was a small, plump woman with perfect, pink-and-white skin, short, curly gray hair, and wide, trusting blue eyes. At fifty-five she was still very pretty. She was devoted to her husband, and he to her. They were, in fact, the happiest couple Margaret knew, and she had sometimes thought that their happiness had in a curious way led to her own sorrow. She had grown up never hearing a harsh word between them, and despite the evidence all around her—her friends' parents, her parents' friends—she had thought that her marriage would be happy, too. To be married was to be content, secure—settled. Her parents had objected to her leaving college after her sophomore year, but at last they had given in; perhaps they, too, had been deceived by their own success. They were, she thought, a remarkably unworldly couple. Her father had inherited a good deal of money from his parents. He was a professor of English. He had spent his life comfortably tenured, sheltered from the realities of life, harsh and otherwise, living in the world of books and scholarship. The books, of course, told tales of sorrow and struggle; but one could always close the book, marking the page, and go home to a good hot dinner lovingly prepared by one's loving wife. Unlike Margaret, her mother had graduated from college— Wellesley—but then had promptly married and begun to be happy.

The man from Energyworks had come in mid-August, and by Labor Day Margaret had still not made up her mind about having the work done. She knew that she should have another estimate, but she had not done that either. Winter seemed far away during these last hot days of summer, despite her efforts to call up memories of the long months when to save money they kept the bedrooms cold and gathered in the evenings in the living room like a family in Colonial times.

When the children start school, she thought; I'll deal with it then. Thomas was going into first grade: her last chick out of the nest. He had gone to kindergarten, but that was different. First grade was a milestone—for her as well as for him, since she would have more free time and therefore a sense of needing to fill it in some constructive way. Returning to college was the obvious thing, but she did not want to return to college. There was nothing that she wanted to study. She wanted to take care of her children. Possibly, sometime in the distant future, she wanted to marry again. Unlike many women of her generation, the postwar generation, she did not want a "career." She had never wanted one: she had wanted a husband and family. Some women, she supposed, would have called that choice a career, too, but she had never thought of it that way. It had been, simply, her life.

Well: she had the family, at any rate.

From time to time the man who had been her husband reappeared, although even at such times she saw very little of him. He had moved to California; twice a year or so he returned to visit the children. The last time had been in late June, at the beginning of their summer vacation. He had said then that he would come back in August, but he had not done so. Both she and the children had learned that such a promise, from him, was more of an attempt to fend off questions than an expression of intent. He would arrive, as he always did, when he pleased; she should be grateful, she supposed, that he came at all, and especially from such a distance.

The important thing, everyone said, was to let the children know that even though she and her husband were divorcing each other, they were not divorcing the children. She had explained this to them on several occasions; she thought that Lily and David understood, but she was not sure about Peaches and Thomas.

For a long time she had worried that the children might be irreparably scarred by the breakup of her marriage, but in the past year or so she had come to believe that that was not the case. They had survived it, even as she had.

She had no idea what she would have done if they had not.

At the birth of each of her children she had had a sense of taking one more step toward the completion of a predestined plan: her life's plan. Each time she had thought, This is right, this is the way my life is supposed to unfold. The plan called for four children, a number that she and her husband had agreed on. After Thomas' birth, therefore, she had had her fallopian tubes tied; four was the number, five would have been too many.

She knew some women who, no matter how they tried to conceal it, were disappointed by motherhood —bored by its confinement, or frustrated by its tedium, or, worst of all, shocked by the realization that, having tried motherhood, they wanted now to try something else.

Margaret had never felt that way. She had loved it all, even the nausea and heartburn of pregnancy, the pain of labor, the night nursing, the endless feeding and diapering—everything. It had seemed to her that each of her children had brought with it into the world a new richness for her own life. Such an attitude was, she supposed, selfish. On the other hand, because of her delight in them, she had been, she thought, a good mother. Every day brought new joy, something for her to treasure: Lily suddenly understanding how to tell time; Thomas' face as he studied a particularly intricate pattern of frost on a windowpane; all their elation, one March, at seeing the first tiny shoots of green from the crocus bulbs planted in the fall.

Margaret had given up trying to explain her happiness in her children, even to her own mother. When she tried to put it into words it sounded trite, saccharine—even stupid. Once, hugely pregnant with Thomas, she had talked to a woman at a party who was working her way up the corporate ladder at a large law firm. Margaret was then twenty-five; the other woman was perhaps thirty. She had talked to Margaret a little about her work—complicated litigation that Margaret did not understand. Then, politely, the woman had given Margaret a chance to expound a little on her own life. In a burst of self-exposure that even then she had known to be unwise, Margaret had told the woman about Lily's learning, that very morning, to tie her shoe laces. The woman had smiled in a condescending way and moved on to more challenging conversational partners. The incident had not lessened Margaret's pleasure in such little triumphs, but it had made her more cautious about talking about them.

All of the children except Peaches (née Patricia) looked like their father: they had his straight brown hair, his wide-set hazel eyes, his height. Peaches was like Margaret: smaller-boned, blue-eyed, with Margaret's curly blond hair and happy disposition. The others were more serious. Margaret remarked these things about her children dispassionately, even as she noted that Peaches had difficulty with numbers, that Thomas was prone to colds, that David was as sloppy as Lily was neat. Loving them as she did, she understood that they were not without fault. Just as she knew mothers who were disappointed in their offspring, so she also knew mothers who would admit no fault in their children. Margaret was not like that: despite her joy, despite her pride in them, she knew that like everyone else they were only human and therefore imperfect. She did not ask for perfection; she asked only that they continue to love her as she loved them.

4

~~~~~

ON THE SUNDAY OF LABOR DAY WEEKEND, MARgaret took the children to a concert at the Hatch Shell on the Esplanade on the bank of the Charles. The New Boston Jazz Band was playing. Someone had told her once that "jazz" used to be an obscenity in the black subculture.

She had made a picnic supper; they sat on a blanket on the grass and ate it while they waited for the sun to go down and the music to begin. There was a large crowd. The sun hung low in the West, but the heat was still intense. They had cold fried chicken and deviled eggs and potato chips and chocolate cupcakes and cans of Coke and root beer. After they finished eating they packed the remains back into the wicker basket and settled down to wait. Margaret lay on her back and looked at the sky as its color ebbed toward night. Lily began a round of "The Minister's Cat.":

"The minister's cat is an *adorable* cat."

"The minister's cat is a *big* cat." (David)

"The minister's cat is a *cute* cat." (Peaches)

Pause. Thomas was too young, Margaret thought; he had an insufficient vocabulary and his knowledge of the alphabet was insecure. She lifted her head a little and he scrambled over on his hands and knees to lean down to her.

"Dumb," she whispered.

Relief flooded his face.

"The minister's cat is a *dumb* cat!" he shouted, whereupon several people nearby turned to stare and Lily shushed him.

They went through the alphabet with only a minimum of cheating (*k* and *x* and *z* were always difficult), and then they began a game of Twenty Questions. The sun went down; the stars began to come out. Lily took the foil-wrapped insect-repellant pads from the picnic basket and handed them around and they all wiped themselves down. Margaret sat up. The crowd was greater now, people pressing in on all sides, parents with children and foursomes of grown-ups and couples young and not young. As the light faded and darkness came on the audience would lose its separate identities and become one, facing the lighted band shell.

"Mom—"

Thomas had flopped over onto his side, his hands pressed to his abdomen.

"I feel sick," he said. "I think I'm going to throw up."

"Not on the blanket," said David. "Get up—come on!"

Thomas moaned, but he managed to scramble up.

At once Margaret was on her feet beside him. She was aware that her knees were trembling. Their illnesses always frightened her far more than they should. She seized his hand. "Come on," she said. She hurried him through the obstacle course of blankets and outstretched legs to the edge of the lawn. He stopped, retched, and vomited. She held his head.

"All right?" she said.

He leaned against her. She felt him shake his head.

"More?"

"Yes." And he vomited again, standing splay-legged while she held him. Dear God, she thought, please don't let it be anything serious.

A man had approached. "Can I help?" he said.

She looked up. She recognized him but she couldn't remember from where.

"I think—he seems all right now," she said. Thomas leaned against her, trembling. She felt his forehead; it was wet. No fever, or at least not much.

"Here," said the man, offering a canned drink; she could not tell what it was. "Maybe he'd like to rinse his mouth."

Never accept anything from strangers.

Thomas took the can, drank, and spat. Margaret realized that the man was staring at her. "Mrs. Merrill?"

"I don't—"

"Neal Donovan. Energyworks."

"Oh. Yes." She hadn't called him back. No matter. She was too concerned about Thomas to be embarrassed. Through the gloom she saw Lily approaching. The stage lights in the band shell had come on.

"Mommy?" Lily's eyes flicked over Neal Donovan but she did not acknowledge him. "Is he all right?"

"I don't know." Thomas handed the can to her— ginger ale, she saw—and now she felt his arms go around her waist. "I think perhaps we should go." She bent toward him. "All right, Thomas? Shall we go home?"

She felt him nod.

Neal Donovan took the can of ginger ale from her. "Do you have a car?"

"No. We came on the trolley. It's quite near to the house." She heard her voice; it sounded odd, high and tense. "Go tell them," she said to Lily. "Get the basket and the blanket and we'll meet you around on the path."

Don't let them get lost, she prayed: but they never did.

"Well—" Neal Donovan did not seem to know what to say. "I'm sorry you have to miss the music."

"It doesn't matter. We can come another time."

"Yes. Well, so long, then."

As she led Thomas away she was aware that Donovan stood watching her; and then, as she found her children in the darkness, she helped them arrange their things to carry them the easiest way and she forgot him. She was glad that none of them complained about leaving; possibly, she thought, they hadn't wanted to come in the first place and had done so only to humor her.

Neal Donovan went back to his date. Her name was Enid. He had met her several weeks ago; he had not yet made up his mind whether she was attractive or not. They settled back on the blanket. The band trooped onto the stage. They played one selection and then another. Neal found that he could not concentrate; the music annoyed him. During the applause for the fourth selection he put his mouth close to Enid's ear and said: "Have you ever heard of Maria Braun?"

Enid shook her head. "Nope. Who's she?"

He pulled back. "Never mind." For reasons that he could not have explained, he felt cheated.

5

❦❦❦❦

MARGARET PUT THOMAS TO BED AS SOON AS THEY got home. She told Lily and David and Peaches that they could stay up to watch the nine o'clock movie. Thomas' forehead was cool, and so she decided not to call the doctor.

"I'm just tired," said Thomas, and turned on his side and promptly went to sleep. She touched his silky brown hair. Her first sharp panic had vanished, leaving her with only her familiar worry, the worry about all four of them that she carried with her constantly: Don't take candy from strangers, don't get your feet wet, be careful crossing the street, wash your hands.

She turned off the lamp on the table beside his bed and sat for a moment in the dark. She could hear the sounds of the movie from downstairs. *Don't take candy from strangers.* Every time you turned on the television set you let strangers into your home. Except that sometimes they became friends, and that was a little scary when you stopped to think about it. Her husband had been an avid television watcher. Often, when she had tried to talk to him during one or another of his favorite programs, he had become annoyed.

She stood up, fighting her sudden fatigue, and went out and pulled the door half shut. She wanted to go to bed, but of course she would not do that until the other three were settled for the night. She went downstairs and retrieved her book from the kitchen and went into the den with the others.

She sat in the overstuffed chair and put her feet on the ottoman and read a bit and dozed. After a while Peaches fell asleep on the sofa. Lily and David were wide awake. Toward ten o'clock Margaret roused herself and went upstairs to look at Thomas. He was sleeping on his side exactly the way she had left him. She put her hand on his forehead. No fever. She went downstairs again.

Very late, toward eleven, the telephone rang. For a moment Margaret was alarmed—no one ever called this late—but then even before she answered it she decided that it must be a wrong number, and her alarm subsided. The phone was in the kitchen. She reached it on the third ring.

"Mrs. Merrill?"

"Yes."

"Neal Donovan."

"Who?"

"Neal Donovan. I saw you earlier at the concert. I'm just calling to see how your boy is doing."

"Oh—oh, yes, I—he's all right. He's sleeping."

"I hope I didn't wake you."

"No. No, you didn't. He's—I think it was just a temporary upset. He seems fine."

"Good. Well—I just wanted to check."

She had no idea what to say to him. She sank onto the window seat and held the receiver and felt as awkward as she had felt the first time a boy ever called her, when she was fourteen.

"Thank you," she said. "It's good of you to call." She remembered that this man had wanted to sell storm windows and insulation to her. Surely he would not mention them now?

He made no reply, and so to fill up the silence (but why should she feel compelled to talk, when he had initiated the call?) she said, "How was the concert?"

She was annoyed with herself for saying it—for saying anything, for feeling that it was her responsibility to keep the conversation alive.

"It was all right. If you like that kind of music. A friend of mine plays drums. I try to catch him every now and then."

The sound of the television suddenly stopped. Lily and David appeared in the doorway. They stared at her, curious about the telephone call.

She put her hand over the mouthpiece. "Go on up. I'll be up in a minute."

"Peaches is asleep on the sofa," said David.

"I know. I'll bring her up."

Neal Donovan was saying something but she missed it. "What? I'm sorry, the children—"

"I said, have you ever heard of Maria Braun?"

"You mean in the movie?"

"That's right. Some people call it a film."

"Yes," She smiled, hearing the sarcasm in his voice. "Yes, I've heard of it. It's German."

"That's right." What he said next surprised them both. "Do you—would you like to see it?"

Lily had obeyed her; David had not. He still stood in the doorway, watching. Listening.

"Go on up," she said, not troubling to put her hand on the mouthpiece this time. He went.

"Sorry," she said into the receiver. "I didn't hear that last—" Not true: she had heard it. She wanted a moment to deal with it.

"I was wondering if you'd like to see it. A friend of mine said it's pretty good."

She still did not know how to deal with it. "Ah—well, I don't—"

"Tell you what. It's at the Harvard Square. Tomorrow's the last day. I'll wait outside, and if you feel like coming, I'll meet you. In front of the theater. Six o'clock."

Don't talk to strangers.

"Ah—well, I doubt it. I really don't think so. But thanks—"

"Harvard Square Theater," he said. "Six o'clock." His voice was brisk—brusque, even—and yet not unfriendly. He hung up before she did. She heard the harsh buzz of the dial tone. Carefully she replaced the receiver and sat for a moment in the dark kitchen.

She felt as though she—all of them—had been invaded: not by an enemy, necessarily, but by someone who, more from curiosity than desire, had decided to come into their safe little world.

It was easy enough, she understood, to counter that invasion; she had only to say no, and the intruder would go away.

6

❦❦❦

"OF COURSE THE CHILDREN CAN COME FOR SUP-
per," said Ellen Lafferty when Margaret called her the
next morning. "We never go anywhere on Labor Day.
Have them come in the afternoon if they want and
they can go for a dip in the pool. Do you want them to
spend the night? What's up?"

Ellen Lafferty was that kind of friend—had always
been, since the days when they were college room-
mates. Her Mary and Peaches were best friends, but
even if Ellen had had no children, she would have volunteered to take Margaret's.

"Nothing much. I'm just going to a movie."

"Uh huh." Ellen did not press for details; she was
that kind of friend also. "Well, bring them when you
like, and have them bring their pj's so if they decide to
stay over they'll be all set. I could lend Peaches some,
of course, but the others would be a problem." Ellen
had one other child, a two-year-old girl.

"I should tell you that Thomas threw up last night."

"But he's all right this morning?"

"Yes. Fine."

"So we won't worry about it. I'll see you later, all
right?"

Margaret had no idea why she had decided to accept an invitation to go to a movie with a man she hardly knew. Correction: she did not know him at all.

Don't talk to strangers.

If he was an ax murderer, could he murder her in the movie theater? No. Not, at least, without great difficulty. Afterward? But she was driving there herself. She would drive herself home. He could, of course, follow her home and murder her with his ax as she walked from her car to her house. Or he could follow her into the empty house—assuming she didn't go to Ellen's and pick up the children—and murder her in the kitchen.

"Mother of Four Found Slain..."

She knew that her life was too sheltered. She knew that she had few opportunities to meet men. She did not want to meet men. She wanted to live her life with her children and keep them all safe. Including, of course, herself. Occasionally she imagined an automobile accident in which she was killed. Her parents, of course, would take the children: at her mother's urging, she had made a will and named them as guardians. But Richard could put up a fight for them if he wanted to. She did not think he would want to, but you never knew. She did not want him to bring up the children. No matter that he was their father, she did not want him to bring them up. Therefore she must stay alive until they were grown. Once or twice in the past few years she had declined to drive any great distance to see friends—to Cape Cod, to New York— because she had been afraid that she would be killed on the highway by a drunk driver.

"Police Hunt for Clues in Ax Murder..."

"Mrs. Lafferty has invited you over later this afternoon, all right?" she said to the children at lunch.

"Are you going?" said David.

"No."

"Why not?"

"I'm going out for a while."

"Where?"

"To a movie."

"Who with?"

"Barbara Kimball."

Another friend: a free spirit, twice divorced, who lived in fact not far from Harvard Square. She was currently in England, due back on Friday.

"All right?" she said again. "Take your pj's in case you want to stay over. You can put your bathing suits on here. And don't forget towels."

No matter how conversationally you spoke, she thought, you always sounded like a boot-camp sergeant.

As she thought about the children going to Ellen's, having a swim, eating supper on the Laffertys' big screen porch, she began to envy them. She wished that she were doing that, too. But now, of course, she could not.

On the other hand she did not have to go to meet Neal Donovan, either. She could go to another movie by herself. She could come home after dropping off the children and, after an appropriate length of time, return to Ellen's and pick them up. She could drive around for three hours.

Since all of these possibilities seemed slightly ridiculous, she decided to go to *The Marriage of Maria Braun*, if for no other reason than to teach herself a lesson: *Don't talk to strangers*.

With any luck, she thought, he would stand her up.

7

❧❧❧❧

As it turned out, she did not like *The Marriage of Maria Braun* very much. She was in many ways an old-fashioned woman and she had a fondness for plot.

She arrived at the theater just a few minutes before six, so that they had no time for more than a brief greeting. He had bought two tickets: a small extravagance, a possible loss of money if she hadn't come.

Afterward they walked to a quiet bar on Mount Auburn Street. He could have taken her to The Rising of the Moon, but he did not want to.

"What did you think?" he said. "Did you like it?"

"Not particularly."

"Did you understand it?"

"I think so."

"Good. Then you can explain it to me."

Because she was driving, and because she was not much of a drinker in any case, she ordered a Coke. She was glad that he did not object; some men would have.

He was smiling, but she sensed his animosity.

"Well—it's just about this very Germanic woman, and she's trying to survive, and she does, except that she marries the wrong man—"

"And in the end none of it means anything."

"I think it's *supposed* to mean something, though. I think it's supposed to symbolize what happened to Germany during that war. And after."

He was annoyed. Nine dollars to see a movie he didn't understand. He was annoyed further because she did. He did not know at whom he should be more annoyed: Margaret, or Fassbinder the filmmaker.

"'Supposed' isn't good enough," he said.

"No. I agree."

Perversely, he was annoyed at that, too. Their drinks came; his was a Heineken. He had almost ordered something more exotic, so as to impress her, but he had decided against it. If she was the kind of woman who was contemptuous of a Heineken—or impressed by a beer whose name she did not know—she was not worth his time.

"What do you do when you're not at the movies?" he said.

"I take care of the children."

"No job?"

"No." *Yes*, she wanted to say: the children are a "job." But she knew better than to say it.

"You're divorced?"

"Yes."

It was his habit, when he was getting to know a woman, to question her for a while in his blunt way; it saved time, and the woman's reaction told him almost as much as her answers. Margaret's reaction was calm, gentle, polite, almost as if she was humoring him.

"What did you do before you were married?"

"I went to college. I dropped out after my sophomore year."

"Where?"

"Mount Holyoke."

"And you haven't gone back?"

"With four children? Hardly."

"Anywhere. Most women, when they get divorced, want to go back to school for a degree, or a master's, so they can get a better job."

She shrugged; she sipped her Coke.

"Mind if I ask how old you are?" he went on.

"Thirty-two."

"A lot of women these days are having big careers. Thirty percent of the medical students nowadays are women."

She smiled: a gentle, polite, dismissive smile.

"I'm not very aggressive. I like mothering."

"'Parenting,' they say nowadays."

"Whatever."

Ordinarily he did not like aggressive women; he did not like the kind of woman who went to law school or medical school or took an M.B.A. But now he found that he did not like this woman's passivity, either. He himself had a good deal of gumption, and he liked to see it in other people as well.

For instance: after a certain point, he liked a woman to ask him a few questions of her own. Not asking them, he thought, meant that he had failed to arouse her interest. This one seemed to have no interest in him at all.

He was silent. She looked away from him, at the other people in the bar. Most of them were talking: some quietly, some with animation. She did not mind his questions, at least not as long as they did not become too personal. But he seemed for the moment to have satisfied his curiosity, and so she felt that it was only good manners to respond in kind.

"What about you?" she said.

A little too late, he thought.

"What about me?"

"Well—how did you get into the insulation business?"

"Friend asked me to come in."

"Do you like it?"

"It's not bad. Yes. I do."

She nodded; she seemed to have no other questions, and that, too, annoyed him. He decided that he would talk about himself whether she wanted him to or not.

"I drifted for a couple of years after I got out of the service. Before I went in I did two years at Northeastern. I didn't see much point in going back. Nothing made much sense for a while after I came home."

"From—"

"The war."

She nodded. She kept her eyes fixed on his face, attentive, polite.

"I grew up not far from here," he went on. "North Cambridge. Some of the guys I knew in high school were killed. Some were wounded worse than I was. I was lucky."

"Yes."

She had heard that men who had been in the war did not like to talk about it.

"So when I came back I found that my old man had had cancer for six months. He died not long after."

"I'm sorry."

"There was no love lost between us. I never once talked to him for as long as I'm talking to you now. He gave my mother hell for almost thirty years and she gave it right back to him."

She flushed slightly, unnerved—as he had known she would be—by his frankness.

He wanted to jolt her out of her good manners, and so he continued: "I suppose that's why I haven't married. Afraid I'll wind up the same way."

She nodded politely.

He persisted: "Also, I never met a woman I didn't like—that's a paraphrase of Will Rogers, you know? —but I also never met one I'd want to live with for the rest of my life."

"Marriage is difficult."

"I guess you know that better than I."

She gave no sign that he had touched a nerve. No, he thought, he really did not like her. He did not like her good manners, her reticence.

"My parents were very happily married," she said. "They still are. I had a wonderful childhood with them. I can hardly remember an unhappy day."

He felt a pang of envy. His childhood had simply been something to escape.

"I thought—I wasn't prepared for anything different from what they have," she went on. "And so I thought my children would have what I had."

"What went wrong?"

She shrugged. He sensed that he was getting too close now, too personal, and so he persevered. He wanted to make sure that he was right to dislike her; he wanted her to continue to talk about herself so that he could be certain.

"Money?" he said.

"No."

Suddenly her polite face was gone; she looked close to tears.

"Booze?"

She shook her head.

He reminded himself never again to ask a woman out on impulse.

He liked a woman to be able to stand up to his questions; if he touched a nerve, as he so obviously had with this one, he wanted the woman not to flinch too hard, but to come back at him.

He waited for her reply, but she made none; after a time she changed the subject. He went along; he did not think that he cared enough about her to go on with his questions.

Both of them, shortly afterward, were glad to leave. He walked her to her car, which was parked on Brattle Street. To Margaret's relief, he did not suggest that they see each other again.

As Margaret drove home she realized that the worst thing about the evening was that now she would have to find some other company to insulate her house, since obviously it would be awkward to deal with Energyworks.

It was not late, just past ten o'clock. She drove to Ellen Lafferty's. It seemed a long time since she had seen the children; she missed them very much. She did not want to spend the night without them. She wanted them safe with her, in their own beds, in their own house: the five of them together. A family.

8

❦

"YOU SAW IT?" SAID JASON. "*MARIA BRAUN*? TER-rific! You like it?"

"Nope."

"Why not?"

"This place closes in three hours. That's not long enough to tell you."

"Neal, I'm disappointed. I really am. I know—I *know* that you are an intelligent human being. I even know you're a *thinking* human being, which is something else again. In fact, I know your secret. You're a closet reader. So you have something going on up there in that handsome head of yours. Now no intelligent thinking *reading* human being can see that film—"

"Movie."

"*Picture*—and not like it. Impossible. Did you see it alone?"

"Nope."

"A date? Why didn't you let me fix you up?"

"Because you've fixed me up before."

Jason was short, thin, myopic, and not handsome. Therefore he had an endless supply of woman friends, none of whom were interested in him romantically, whom he shared with his men friends. Neal had decided, however, that Jason's taste in women was on a par with his taste in movies: they were incomprehensible, pretentious, and dull.

"Who was she? Did she understand it?"

"A Mount Holyoke dropout. Yes, she understood it. She didn't like it either."

Jason looked crestfallen.

"Maybe we should try it the other way around," said Neal. "When you tell me you hated a movie—or when you call it a movie and not a film—then I'll figure it's something I'll like."

"Sorry, kid. I really thought, this time—what can I say? How was the date?"

"Nine dollars and a couple of Cokes."

"You like her?"

"I'd have liked her better if she hadn't understood the damned movie."

9

❧❧❧

THE NEXT MORNING, AS HE OCCASIONALLY DID when he awakened very early, Neal drove to the Esplanade and jogged along the river for a while before going to work. He put his clean clothing in the car; he would shower and shave at the office.

There were a few other joggers, but mostly he had the riverbank to himself. It was a mild morning; mist hovered in patches over the water, and even so early the sun was warm. The buildings across the river looked artificial, two dimensional, like a painted frieze between the pale sky and the darker expanse of the river.

As he always did on such outings—he was not a regular jogger—he tried to clear his mind and not think of anything except the feel of his feet hitting the narrow asphalt path, the feel of his lungs taking the air in and out, his heart pumping: old reliable.

He was in good physical condition. Unlike most of his contemporaries, he was not particularly concerned with his body. He belonged to no gym; he participated regularly in no sport. People exhausted themselves with exercise because they wanted to live longer. Having been close to death in the war, Neal had no fear of it now that he was home; or, rather, no sense that it was near. He would live long enough, however long that was.

His concern was with his mind—which was, he had been told, a muscle like any other. He was, as Jason had said, a closet reader. He was not sure why this was so except that he had, apparently, been born with more than the normal amount of curiosity. Or perhaps every child was born so, and most of them had it stamped out as they grew and went to school. Or perhaps—and he admitted the possibility to himself—his curiosity was a kind of arrogance: he, too, wanted to be able to say that he had read *War and Peace*. Or *The History of the Decline and Fall of the Roman Empire*.

He knew that there was a certain body of work that was generally acknowledged to be important—certain books, certain works of art and music that were the province of educated men.

He, too, wanted to be educated. He did not want to return to school, which was a different thing entirely: a matter of credit hours and degrees that produced a kind of union card that he did not need. He simply wanted to be educated—to educate himself, in his own way, at his own pace.

And so, gradually, he was reading his way through Western civilization. Not methodically, but with a certain system. One thing led to another. Eventually he hoped to get to Eastern civilization as well.

He read mostly history and literature: first history, to find out what had happened; then literature, to find out what certain men had made of it. From time to time he went to the museum. He observed that the objects there looked different to him every time he went—presumably, he thought, because each time he brought something different, something more, to them.

One of the reasons—perhaps the main reason—he

had so disliked *The Marriage of Maria Braun* was that
it had been a waste of time. There would never be
enough time, he felt, to learn everything he wanted to
learn.

On the other hand, he understood that his dislike
showed that his self-education was having some effect.
Several years ago he would not have trusted his reaction—would not have liked the movie, perhaps, but
would not have known why. Or would have been reluctant to admit, even to himself, that he disliked it.

So his response was a sign of progress: he was learning something after all.

The Marriage of Maria Braun made him think of
Margaret Merrill. In retrospect he regretted the way
he had behaved with her. He realized that he would be
embarrassed to call her to follow up on the sale.

Forfeit it, he thought. And don't make the same
mistake again.

10

A FEW DAYS AFTER BARBARA KIMBALL RETURNED from England she went to see Margaret. As they had done so often, they sat together in Margaret's kitchen over cups of coffee and told each other their news. Since Margaret had little to report, Barbara did most of the talking.

"So then I went to Bath," she said. "And do you know they've discovered something poisonous in the water, so you can't take the baths any more? I could have cried. But it all turned out for the best." She smiled in a way that Margaret recognized: she knew what Barbara would say next. A few years older than Margaret, talented and hard-working, Barbara made a good living as a graphic designer. Some time ago she had formed her own company; it had thrived to the point where she now employed two designers and a girl-of-all-work, thus freeing her from time to time to take vacations. Usually, on these jaunts, she had a romantic encounter; and indeed, this time had been no different.

But why not? thought Margaret. Barbara was a beautiful woman, with sleek, dark red hair and a perfect figure and a gleam in her hazel eyes that signaled irresistibly to every man she met. Why shouldn't Barbara enjoy herself?

Margaret admitted that she granted her friend a freedom that she herself was both unwilling and unable to take. Barbara went through men like a casting agent looking for the perfect face. Each time she emerged seemingly unscathed. Although Margaret knew of at least two men who had been devastated by Barbara's breaking off with them, Barbara herself had never shown a sign of regret. "When it's done, it's done," she said. "No point in prolonging the pain."

Despite her two marriages, neither of which had produced children, Barbara refused to admit that she was searching for Mr. Right. "Both of those marriages were a triumph of hope over good sense," she said. "Both times, I was hoping for a relationship that we didn't have. I thought that the wedding ring would make the relationship happen. It didn't, of course. So now I know better. The relationship has to happen first. Then, perhaps—who knows? The worst of it is, I always get *bored*. I look at these people who stay married for twenty, thirty years—fifty years, for Heaven's sake—and I think, how do they stand it? How many surprises can be left after fifty years?"

Margaret, who had had a very unpleasant surprise indeed from her husband after only eight years of marriage, thought that a reasonably happy arrangement with no surprises was not such a bad thing. She made no comment, however. She understood what Barbara meant; she understood that Barbara was a free spirit.

Now, smiling at her friend over the rim of her coffee mug, glad to see her again, she waited for the revelation that she knew would come. Barbara laughed (a little self-consciously, Margaret thought); her eyes were bright with the excitement that, for Barbara, only a new man could bring.

"In *Bath*," Barbara said. "Of all places."

But why not Bath? thought Margaret. Barbara had met men in Boston and New York and Atlanta; in the subway; in the Oyster Bar and the Top of the Mark; thirty thousand feet up on the way to Los Angeles and in the middle of the Caribbean on the way to Aruba...

"I was simply devastated," Barbara went on. "About not being able to take the waters, I mean. Isn't that quaint? Not being able to take the waters? That's what they say. I was walking across the bridge—a little bridge with shops, the way London Bridge used to be —and he came up beside me and said, 'Shall we try Baden-Baden?' How's that for an approach? He had heard my conversation with the attendant in the pump room, and he followed me out. It was like something in Jane Austen. Don't laugh, Margaret. It *was*."

"I know Jane Austen was a genius of sorts," said Margaret, "but even she couldn't have worked you in. She couldn't possibly have imagined you, not in a thousand years."

"That's all right," said Barbara. "I can't imagine her, either. Can you think what it must have been like, living then?" She shuddered a little, her face suddenly blank with the thought, but then she brightened again as she remembered what she had to tell. "He's from Boston, can you imagine? He lives right here—in town, I mean—and he's getting back next week. We spent three days together in England before he had to leave for France. Oh, Margaret, he's divine. I mean really *divine*. His name is Craig McCarren. He started a computer company five years ago and already he's— well. I don't want to sell him to you on the basis of money, but he's made a fortune. And he's not exactly good-looking, but—well—he's *interesting*-looking. You'd spot him in a crowd. He's a little over six feet, and he has—oh, sort of wind-blown brown hair and a—a *weathered* face. Very strong-looking."

"The Marlboro Man," suggested Margaret.

"Well, yes, in a way—oh, Margaret, don't laugh."

"I'm not. What's he like?"

"He's wonderful. Simply wonderful. He's bright and funny and he's not threatened by me, not at all."

This, Margaret knew, was an important point. Barbara had frightened away more than one attractive man simply by virtue of what she was: talented, aggressive, successful.

"I am what I am," Barbara had said, more than once. "I'm not going to change just to accommodate some insecure male. If a man backs off he's doing me a favor. Better sooner than later."

"Does he know what there is to be threatened by?" Margaret said now. For it was possible, she knew, for Barbara to so dazzle a man at first that he did not take into account her drive, her determination to succeed so that she need not be dependent on anyone—certainly not on him.

"Oh, yes. When I told him how much I made last year he was impressed, I admit, but it didn't bother him. It was a lot, but it was much less than what he made."

What if it had been more, Margaret wondered. That was the sticking point for a lot of men; they didn't like women who made more money than they did. Something to do with the masculine ego: money was power, and like Samson without his hair, a man without money (or more money, at least, than his woman) felt intolerably weak.

But she said nothing; she let Barbara go on, smiling at her friend's ebullience, hoping for a happy outcome to this new episode in Barbara's life.

At last Barbara fell silent. A faint smile lingered on

her face. Then, abruptly, as if she was conscious of having been bad-mannered, she said, "But what about you? What's been going on here?"

"Oh—nothing much." Margaret felt herself smile. She realized, as Barbara perhaps did not, that "nothing much" was good news. A placid, uneventful life was all she asked: no crises, no upheavals. "Thomas has started first grade. And I'm thinking about having the house insulated. At last."

"Uh-huh." Barbara nodded encouragement; she was a good friend, and if insulating the house was Margaret's most exciting news, then she would be interested in that. "And—?"

"That's all."

Barbara's expression had suddenly become animated; she understood that it was not all. "I don't believe you," she said. "You look like the cat who swallowed the canary."

Margaret laughed. "Uncomfortable?" she said. "With feathers coming out of my mouth?"

"No. Just a little secret satisfaction that shows in your eyes. You're keeping something back. I can tell."

Now Margaret felt herself flush, and she laughed again to try to cover her discomfiture.

Barbara beamed at her. "Well? Come on. You can tell Auntie Barbara. You've met a man." It was not a question but a statement of fact.

"He's not a *man*, for Heaven's sake," said Margaret.

"What is he? A hermaphrodite?"

They laughed together then while Margaret flushed a deeper, more incriminating red.

"I mean, I didn't meet him as a man. He came to see about the insulation."

"Ah-hah. And?"

"And then I ran into him when I took the children to a concert at the Hatch Shell."

"And?"

"One thing led to another. More or less."

"Is he nice? Do you like him? How many times have you been out with him? Are you going to see him again?"

To all of this Margaret simply threw up her hands and denied that anything of interest had happened. "Just one date, that's all. I don't think you could call it a success. And now I'll have to find someone else to do the insulation."

"Was it that bad?"

"Not bad, exactly. Just—" Margaret remembered Neal's hostility (had it been that? or had she misunderstood him?) as she sought for a way to explain the situation to Barbara. "Just a bit awkward. I don't think he liked me very much."

"Then he's an idiot," said Barbara cheerfully. "And so now you feel that you can't call him back to do the insulation because he'll think you're trying to get him to ask you out again, when all you want is a good job of work on the house."

"Yes," said Margaret.

"Call back," said Barbara. "It's almost harder, these days, to find a decent *work*man than it is to find a decent *man*."

Which, thought Margaret, was a singularly depressing observation.

11

❧❧❧❧

Two weeks later, when the children had settled in at school and she saw that Thomas was taking well to the first grade, Margaret called the Energyworks office and asked them to send someone to do the measurements and give her an estimate. Although she did not want to see Neal Donovan again, she was beginning to worry about having the work done. She had called two other companies for estimates; one said that no one could come for three weeks, and the other made an appointment that they did not keep.

The Energyworks secretary said that someone would come along on Friday if that would be convenient. Margaret hoped that it would not be Neal.

"Afternoon," she said. "I'll be here after one."

As she occasionally did, she had invited several people for dinner that evening. She planned to make a chocolate Bavarian cream pie—a tedious and lengthy operation—and osso buco, which needed a long cooking time, and a first course of cold cucumber soup, and a spicy raw eggplant appetizer.

There had been a period of time when she no longer liked to cook, but in the past year or so she had come to enjoy it again. She stood at the center island and sliced eggplant and chopped it. She did not have a

Cuisinart—did not want one. Cuisinarts symbolized an ease and affluence that a divorced woman with four children could not expect. She was lucky enough to be able to stay in this house; she could not hope for luxuries.

She put the eggplant in a bowl and sprinkled it with lemon juice. She made a pie crust and arranged it in her good earthenware pie plate and pricked it thoroughly before putting it into the oven. She put the veal shanks into a marinade.

Then she went into the dining room and took the pale blue tablecloth and napkins from the sideboard and began to set the table. They would be six: the Laffertys, the Olsens, and Joe Brown. Ellen Lafferty's husband was a laywer with a big firm in Boston. Ingrid Olsen was also a laywer with a big firm in Boston. Her husband was an architect. They had no children. Instead they had a Lifestyle: a Jaguar for him and a Saab for her and a twenty-five-foot sailboat for both of them and an annual trip abroad. Nevertheless Margaret liked them: their consumption was conspicuous but not offensive, and they had not dropped her (as some people had) after her divorce. Joe Brown was an account executive at an advertising agency. He could hardly be considered her date, since she did not have dates, Neal notwithstanding. No matter: he was amusing and nice and she liked him. In the weeks and months after her husband had left her, Joe had been a great comfort, frequently calling in to see her, keeping tabs on her, not with any intention of moving in on territory that her husband had vacated, but simply to be kind.

She put out her silverware and the good Lenox china. She took a cut-crystal bowl into the kitchen; there were still flowers in the garden that she could use for a centerpiece. It was two o'clock. In half an hour the children would be home. She wished that the man from Energyworks would come so that he would be through in time for her to give the children their supper and then take a half hour for herself, to shower and dress.

She took the lightly browned pie shell from the oven and then she went out to cut the flowers. There was still abundant phlox and two or three late roses, pink and white, and spiky blue ajuga. She carried the flowers inside and stood at the center island to arrange them in the crystal bowl. The front screen door slammed: the children. They all went to the same school, five blocks away; they walked back and forth in a group picking up several others in the morning and dropping them off in the afternoon. She was glad that Lily and David were still part of the group now that Thomas had started first grade.

They trooped into the kitchen to find her, first thing, as they always did. Lily took four glasses to pour milk; while they drank it and ate oatmeal cookies they gave her their news: a new girl in Peaches' class, a movie in David's, a permission slip for Margaret to sign for a field trip by Lily's class to the Museum of Science.

Then they went their separate ways and Margaret took out the dark chocolate squares to melt for the pie.

Still no one from Energyworks. She would have to call another company after all. She wondered if Neal had canceled the appointment personally.

She blended milk and egg yolks and gelatin into a double boiler with the chocolate; when the chocolate had melted she put the bowl in the refrigerator for the mixture to thicken. She chopped vegetables. She sliced a loaf of French bread, buttered each slice lightly, sprinkled them with garlic powder, re-formed the loaf, and wrapped it in tinfoil.

It was four o'clock.

The doorbell rang. David went to answer. He did not admit whoever it was, but came to report to her. "It's that man."

"What man?"

"The one who was here before."

So he had come after all. Well: she would simply have to deal with it. With him.

"All right. Ask him to come in."

David went to obey. He felt more than a little ridiculous. He had not thought that he would ever see this man again. He wished that they had not ambushed him that bright hot day. He opened the door so that the man could come in, but he did not look at him. Immediately he went upstairs to report to the others, all except Peaches who had gone to see her friend Mary.

"Who's here?" said Lily. She was stretched on her bed reading *Anne of Green Gables*.

"That guy with the red truck that came before, remember?"

She nodded. She was not in the mood for games today; she was not looking for the enemy. And besides, it seemed that the man had come a long time ago. He wasn't important anymore; and besides that, she wanted to keep on reading. She was at the point in the book where Anne dyes her hair green; she had read it several times before and she knew how it came out but she always enjoyed reading it again.

David went on to Thomas, who was watching his tropical fish. The tiny, delicate forms rippled and shimmered in the water like pieces of supple, iridescent glass.

"Who's here?" said Thomas.

"That guy with the red truck that came before. I think you're giving them too much food."

"Why?"

"Because they haven't eaten it all. See? On top? Look at the one floating. He's dead."

"No he isn't."

"Yes he is. You gave him too much food and now he's dead."

"No he *isn't*. He's just sleeping."

"All right." David shrugged and turned to leave; he didn't feel like arguing. "He's just sleeping."

Downstairs Margaret greeted Neal politely, but she kept on with her work, which now involved preparing the children's dinner as well as the one for company. Because he could see that she was busy he greeted her politely in turn and said that she needn't trouble herself, he would be done in a jiffy. He had not intended to make this call; he had told the secretary to assign it to his partner, but his partner had been held up and so Neal had come after all. A job was a job.

As he went upstairs he saw the boy who had let him in; he was standing in the doorway of a bedroom, watching. On guard? Neal went along to the third floor. He measured the windows there and then on the second-floor front, the north side; then downstairs.

In half an hour he was done. He returned to the kitchen. Margaret was whipping a bowl of cream and keeping on eye on the veal shanks which were browning in a big pot on top of the stove.

"All set," he said. "We can schedule you in for the last week in October."

She nodded. "That'll be fine." She did not look at him; she concentrated on what she was doing. She took a bowl from the refrigerator and blended a spoonful of the whipped cream into its contents; then, wielding a spatula with one hand and turning the bowl with the other, she folded the chocolate mixture into the rest of the whipped cream.

He watched her. His mother had not been a very good cook.

"What's that?" he said.

"Chocolate Bavarian cream pie."

She scraped the mixture into the cooled pie shell. Then, surprising him, she handed him the empty bowl. "Want a taste? It's very good." He saw that there were a few dollops of chocolate left in the bowl. He scraped one up with a finger.

"Right. It is." It was slightly bitter, the way good chocolate should be.

She put the pie into the refrigerator and took out a head of lettuce. She paid no attention to him, and so, once again, he began to feel slightly irritated with her.

"What's on the stove?" he said.

"Osso buco."

He had seen the table set for six in the dining room.

"Company?"

"Yes."

There was of course no reason why she should not have company, but the idea gave him a sense of being left out. It had been a long time since anyone had invited him to dinner.

"Special occasion?"

"No. Just friends I like to see every now and then."

He found a space on the crowded counter and began to fill in figures on his specification form.

Thomas appeared in the doorway. "Mommy," he said. Instantly she knew that something was wrong.

"What?"

"One of the Tiger barbs died."

"Oh, Thomas. I'm sorry."

She wiped her hands on a stray paper towel and went to him and gave him a hug.

"I want a box to put him in," said Thomas, his voice

muffled against her shoulder. "And I want to bury him."

"Yes. Ask David to look in my closet. There are some boxes on the high shelf."

She watched him as he ran through the hall and up the stairs. Then the phone rang and she came back into the kitchen to answer it. It was Peaches, calling from Mary's house to ask if she could bring Mary to supper and to stay the night.

"Yes," said Margaret. "But come along quickly if you want to see the funeral. One of the fish died and Thomas is burying it."

She realized that Neal was watching her. It was no use trying to explain, she thought. Either you understood what it was like, having children, or you did not.

By the time Peaches arrived with her friend, Thomas and David had arranged the corpse in a nest of cotton balls and secured the tiny cardboard coffin with two rubber bands. Margaret said that they could dig the grave at the edge of the flower bed where the ground was soft, but she warned them not to trample the plants that were still in bloom. Lily and David attended the ceremony, too; afterward David found a large rock to put over the grave so that the neighborhood dogs would not dig up the box.

Margret watched them from the window as she prepared their supper: hamburgers (which they much preferred to osso buco), green beans, fruit salad.

When they trooped in they saw that their meal was ready, and so they took turns washing their hands at the sink and then slid into their places at the table. They did not acknowledge Neal's presence.

It was after five o'clock: the half hour that Margaret had allotted to shower and dress. She was aware that Neal seemed to have settled in. She decided to be polite but firm.

"All set?" she said.

"All set."

He understood that she was pressed for time: the children to attend to, company coming, last-minute tasks to perform. He understood that she wanted him to go so that she could perform them. She would, no doubt, have a pleasant evening with her friends. He thought of The Rising of the Moon and Jason Goodrich.

He wondered what her friends were like. Much like her, probably; very different from him. Not born and brought up in a three-decker in North Cambridge. They would be polite and pleasant, as she was; but every now and then, particularly from the men, there would be that flicker of condescension that signaled a gulf between him and them: of class, of caste, of taste, of profession. It would not please her, he thought, to have to introduce him to them.

He decided to stay.

The children finished their meal. Still, none of them spoke to Neal, but Margaret saw that they glanced at him off and on; she could tell from the way Peaches giggled that Peaches was ever so slightly showing off. They took their plates and glasses to the sink, where Lily rinsed them and put them in the dishwasher. Then Lily returned upstairs to her book; Peaches and Mary went to play makeup; David took Thomas across the street to play in the neighboring boy's tree fort. Suddenly the kitchen was very quiet.

"Well," Margaret said in what she hoped was a sufficiently brisk and businesslike way. "Thank you very much." She took a step toward the front door, but Neal did not follow her and so she felt constrained to stop.

"Look," he said, "about that movie—"

She did not want to be reminded of Maria Braun.

"That's all right," she said. "Just let's forget it, shall we?"

He smiled at her: a friendly, open, forthright smile that almost succeeded in eliminating her embarrassment. "Right," he said. "But I don't want you to hold it against me."

"I don't."

The pungent odor of the simmering veal filled the kitchen. "How can I tell?" he said.

"Because I say so. Really, it was nothing."

Not quite nothing, he thought, but he let it pass. "We could try again," he said.

"I don't think—"

"If you wanted to."

She hesitated, and so he pressed his point. Charmingly, she thought later: it was his unexpected charm that disarmed her.

"You could, for instance, invite me to stay for dinner."

That surprised her; a little flustered, she laughed.

"Unless you think your friends wouldn't approve," he went on. He spoke in a friendly way, smiling, but she heard the challenge—the threat?—of what he said, and she felt that she had to meet it.

And so, almost as much to his surprise as to hers, she asked him to stay.

Knowing that she wanted him to refuse, he accepted.

12

BY THE TIME DAVID AND THOMAS RETURNED THE
guests had arrived. They ducked into the living room
to say hello, as Margaret had taught them to do, and
then they retreated upstairs to report to the others that
one of the guests was the man from Energyworks.

Because they were intelligent children they had,
each of them, understood very early that the ways of
adults were arbitrary, mysterious, and immutable. It
was the task of each child born into the world to survive until he or she was grown, at which time it would
be his or her task to impose adults' rules on the next
generation of children.

Since whatever their mother did was right, they did
not condemn her for inviting the stranger to the party.
But they felt a slight anxiety, a small but nagging
awareness that something was amiss.

And so while they did not organize themselves
against him as they had done before, they stayed on
the alert, as if they were on guard, watching for the
enemy: the invader.

At length, however, tired from their busy day, one
by one they fell asleep until only David remained
awake. He lay wide-eyed in his bed, straining to hear
the rise and fall of the conversation downstairs, the

occasional burst of laughter. Such sounds had always
comforted him; they let him know that all was well,
that he could safely go to sleep and that when he
awoke in the morning the world would be as it had
been the night before, familiar and secure.

But tonight, aware of the newcomer, even able to
distinguish his deep, rather harsh voice, David was not
reassured. He assumed that the younger ones had
dropped off (unless Peaches and her friend had stayed
awake giggling, which was not unlikely); Lily might
still be reading, but David was too comfortable to get
up to see.

He was, in fact, very tired; he wished that his
mother's guests—including the man from Energyworks—would hurry up and go home. He felt himself
sliding into sleep. He was conscious of struggling to
stay awake, and aware that he could not.

The last sound that he remembered hearing was the
stranger's laugh, not terribly loud, but louder than the
other's: confident, distinctive. As if he felt right at
home.

13

TO NEAL'S SURPRISE, AND ALMOST TO HIS DISAP-
pointment, he enjoyed himself. The Olsens and the
Laffertys were civil at first, and then, as they adjusted
to his presence, cordial and even friendly. Joe Brown
was an enigma, but a disarmingly pleasant one. He and
Margaret seemed to be old friends; they laughed and
joked and even flirted a bit, but Neal could see that it
was not serious flirting. It was the way they dealt with
each other; it was not put on to impress him.

For their part, the Olsens, the Laffertys, and Joe
Brown were all mildly surprised to see the extra guest,
but after their initial curiosity and concern—who was
this man? would he help Margaret or hurt her?—they
relaxed a bit and allowed themselves to get acquainted
with him. All of them had stayed by Margaret during
her divorce, gathering around her protectively, fearing
that she would do very badly on her own. At last,
when the divorce was final, when they realized that
Margaret would be all right, that her children, through
their need of her, would keep her well, they had
stopped worrying about her and settled back into
steady friendship.

From time to time Ellen Lafferty or Ingrid Olsen
would encounter a stray man; their first thought,

always, was, "Would he be good for Margaret?" Often
he was not; occasionally, when he was, they had gone
so far as to ask Margaret whether she would like to
meet him.

Invariably her answer was no. She felt that she was
managing her life, and those of her children, very well;
she was not ready to add the complication of a man.

She understood that like her mother, these friends
had only her best interests at heart. They sincerely believed that she needed a husband (or, at the very least,
a lover) in order to survive. She did not resent that
belief, but she did not share it. Not yet, she thought:
we are keeping our equilibrium very nicely just as we
are.

"Mother of Four Rocks Boat: All Drown . . ."

Now, watching her friends adjust to Neal Donovan's
presence, she was amused. At last, all on her own,
without their help, she had acquired—for the evening,
at least—a man; and if he was not as "eligible" as one
they might have chosen, then neither was he a complete disaster. He had, she noted, no difficulty in
keeping up his end of the conversation; indeed, he was
quite a good talker, eloquent, perceptive of others'
viewpoints, quick to supply a graceful, pointed anec-
dote. She admitted to herself that she was surprised at
this: he was very different, tonight, from the rather
brusque and not particularly charming man who had
taken her to *The Marriage of Maria Braun.*

She could even see, after a while, that the men, at
any rate, liked him; the women were a little wary. She
watched them watching him; she realized that they
were not so quick, tonight, to join the general discussion but rather were content to let the men do the
talking so that they could sit back and observe.

She knew that sooner or later she would have to
deal with her friends' interest. The first question came

between the cucumber soup and the osso buco, when she had carried the soup plates into the kitchen and was ladling the stew onto the serving platter. Ellen followed her, her face alight with curiosity.

"Where'd you find him?" she said.

Although Margaret had anticipated the question, she was momentarily flustered. "Oh—he just turned up one day."

"Seriously."

"Seriously."

"Margaret, I know you. You're not the kind of lady for whom men just 'turn up.'"

"*Damn.*" The juice had splattered; Margaret had not put on an apron, and now she dabbed at a spot on the skirt of her pale blue dress.

"Here," said Ellen, offering a damp sponge. Margaret scrubbed the spot until it was gone and then, as they both understood very well, proceeded to be very busy serving the meal while deliberately neglecting to answer her friend's question. It was not, she thought, a question that could be answered easily in any case, and certainly not in brief snatches in the midst of running a dinner party.

But Ellen was not so easily put off; at the next opportunity (the removal of the dinner plates and the making of the coffee) she followed Margaret again into the kitchen and whispered, with a conspiratorial smile, "He's cute."

Margaret thought the word singularly inappropriate, but she made a grimace of acknowledgment. Rather than cute, she thought, he was clever. Having intruded himself into the evening, he was showing her that she need not have feared to include him. Throughout the evening he ignored her, rather pointedly, she thought. He concentrated instead on the others, with such success that around midnight, when

the time came to say good night, she could see that
they were all reluctant to go; they would gladly have
stayed into the small hours, listening to his stories,
being charmed by him. She realized that he was, for
them, a slightly exotic figure, the kind of person they
seldom encountered and almost never had a chance to
talk to at length.

There was an unspoken but quite clear agreement
among them that Neal would be the last to go. He
stood on the porch with Margaret in the soft, warm,
quiet night.

"Thanks for dinner," he said; but it was not the
meal for which he was grateful, and they both understood that. He was not, in fact, grateful at all, and they
both understood that as well. Rather, he was—in a
very amiable, noncensorious way—saying something
to her on the order of, "Your trust in me, and in your
own instincts, was rewarded. I did not misbehave, I
did not disgrace you, I used the correct fork, I did not
spill my wine or drink too much of it."

"You're welcome," she said dryly.

They both laughed, then, and he said good night
and left.

14

AND SO SHE WAS NOT SURPRISED WHEN HE CALLED her the following week to invite her to dinner, and he was not surprised when she accepted.

He took her to a sleek, expensive restaurant on the top floor of one of the city's new skyscrapers. The tables were arranged on rising terraces so that each had the view over the harbor—a dramatic, breathtaking view that justified, at least in part, the dramatic, breathtaking prices on the menu.

He had admitted to himself that he wanted to impress her. He succeeded.

"Fancy," she said, smiling.

"It's all right."

"Who are all these people?" she said. She often had the sense that the world was passing her by: that even though she had taken refuge of her own free will in a small, quiet corner of it, she was, inevitably, being left behind while the world went on.

"Just people. Like you and me."

"Not like me," she said. "This is the big business crowd."

The waiter was very pleasant. "They'll fire him as soon as they find out he's not arrogant enough," said Neal.

71

They ordered drinks: a frozen daiquiri for her, a vodka martini for him. In answer to Neal's question, Margaret said that she would have wine with the meal, and the waiter brought a wine list as thick as a small telephone book. They ordered the food which the menu listed under the headings, *hors d'oeuvres, potage, entrées, legumes,* and *salades.* Neal had a little Saigon French; Margaret had her high school and Mount Holyoke Spanish which was no help at all. He handled the ordering very well, she noticed; he behaved as though he ate in such restaurants all the time, although she had to assume that he did not.

In fact, the restaurant, the famous view, the decor, the menu, the other diners—none of these held any terror for him. He had survived the war; he could survive the Bay Tower Room.

After the waiter went away again she settled back to watch, alternately, the view and the other customers. In her five-year-old blue silk dress she felt slightly out of date and uncomfortable in this elegant room; on the other hand, she felt entirely comfortable with Neal. She understood that on their previous date, the evening of *Maria Braun,* he had been testing her: her patience, her tolerance, the extent to which she was firmly rooted in her social class. She understood the country's great myth: that it was a classless society. On the contrary, it was a society made up of infinite gradations of class and caste, not so blatant, perhaps, as those in other countries but existing all the same. She had often thought how difficult it must be for a foreigner, coming here, to know how—and where—to fit in. She remembered a friend from college who had married and had two children and whose husband had become seriously ill. He had lost his job; their families could not—or would not—help them; the friend had done secretarial work at miserable pay; they had lived in poverty. And yet their values, their tastes, had remained what they were before, so that their children and Margaret's had much in common despite the fact that they lived in a dingy apartment in Somerville and had no decent clothing, no car, no anything. But the children, thanks to the public library, read what Margaret's children read; they watched, on their small, snowy black-and-white television screen, the same programs that Margaret's children watched; their values, thanks to their parents, remained largely the values of Margaret's children. They were as different from their equally poverty-stricken neighbors as if they had dropped from another planet.

And so "poor" did not necessarily mean alien; and "well-to-do" often meant ignorant and crass, alien beyond recognition. She had tried to explain this to her children, but she was not sure that she had succeeded.

The *hors d'oeuvres* arrived: *pâté de canard* for Neal and shrimp cocktail, trite though it was, for Margaret.

As they ate, they talked easily; he was not, tonight, in an abrasive mood.

The *potage* arrived: gazpacho for Neal and vichyssoise, trite though it was, for Margaret.

They talked desultorily, amicably: politics, real estate (it seemed everyone, these days, talked about real estate), even—despite *Maria Braun*—the movies. It began to be obvious to her, as it had not been before, that he was well read, that he knew far more than she did about more things.

After the soup plates had been taken away, but before the *entrées* arrived, he told her that coming to this restaurant had not been his idea. "I have a friend named Jason Goodrich. He's a real man of the world. Knows what's the best, whether it's cars or restaurants or wine—or even movies, although I gave him hell about that damned German thing. But generally he knows. So I asked him where he'd go if he had a special date. He gave me three: one Italian, one Chinese, and this place."

He spoke so curtly, so matter-of-factly, that it was a moment before Margaret realized what he had said. She took her time with it; she let his words settle into her consciousness and come to rest there. She was aware that in that moment everything had changed. It was as if she had suddenly been given new sight: everything—the restaurant, her fellow diners, Neal himself —had suddenly shifted into a new, sharp-edged perspective, and where before they had looked rather ordinary (even the famous view), now they looked fresh and sparkling, wonderfully appealing.

She smiled at him, then—a gentle, luminous smile that she could feel as it welled up from some place deep inside her, a place long asleep where she had laid to rest those nonmaternal emotions which, she thought, she would not need soon again. Now they surfaced. She recognized them; she made room for them.

It was as if an angel, stopping by, had absentmindedly plucked her heartstrings; and she listened now to the first faint tremor of their music resonating through her soul.

Of course she knew what was happening to her: she was falling in love.

15

LILY AND DAVID WAITED UP FOR HER; PEACHES AND Thomas had wanted to, but they were too tired and so shortly after nine they went to bed.

There was a not too fine distinction between waiting up in bed and waiting up downstairs in the den with the baby-sitter. In bed, at least for the older children, was frowned upon but permissible; downstairs was out of bounds.

Margaret, discovering them there with the placid, sensible teenager, did not want to spoil the evening by ending it scolding her children. She never scolded in any case; never needed to. An occasional mild reprimand, a look of disapproval from time to time, and the younger ones' emulation of the older two were sufficient. They were good children; she understood very well how lucky she was to have them.

But she was glad, now, that she had said good night to Neal in his car. He had not attempted to kiss her, a restraint for which she was grateful. She did not want to kiss him, not yet. The idea of falling in love was still too new, really too alarming. She had not intended to fall in love ever again; had not wanted to. Or not, at least, for a long time—until the children were older. Falling in love, maintaining a love affair, took a good deal of energy; for so long now she had given all the energy she had to her children that she could not imagine where she would find more for a man.

She paid the baby-sitter, who lived around the corner and could walk back and forth, not needing to be driven: a great convenience. She saw her to the door. When she returned to where Lily and David were sitting, the television still turned on, she refrained from shooing them upstairs. Instead she sat with them, perching on the edge of a wing chair badly needing reupholstering.

They observed her. All of them were conscious of the fact that she was dressed up—an unusual state for her. They had seen her, of course, when she went out; she had not insisted that they come downstairs to greet Neal when he called for her, but she had said good night to them when she was ready to leave, and she had felt their solemn observation of her.

"You look nice, Mommy," Peaches had said. Peaches loved dressing up, and next best she loved seeing other people dressing up.

But the others had said nothing. They had not protested when she told them she was going out, but they had been unable to hide from her their—well, not their unhappiness, exactly, but their withholding of their full approval.

Now, safely home again, she wanted to explain to them that it was all right, that *she* was all right, that they need not worry that she would go away one day and not return. But of course she did not say these things; perhaps tomorrow she would say them if she felt that it was necessary, but not tonight.

It was necessary, however, for her to say something in the face of their silence. She felt so different—so transformed from the woman she had been when she had left them a few hours before—that she wondered if she looked different, too. Perhaps that was what was making them so solemn, so—no, not sullen, but oddly withdrawn, distant almost, as if she were a stranger. In a way, she felt like a stranger, she felt glowing—sparkling. She would not have been surprised to look in a mirror and see herself enveloped in a golden mist. Surely the children must see that something about her had changed?

"How's the movie?" she said.

"It's not a movie," said Lily. "It's a play."

It was, in fact, *Our Town;* Lily was correct. Margaret wondered how she knew.

Just then it ended. Without a word, attuned to the silent communication between themselves, Lily and David stood up, said good night, and went upstairs, leaving Margaret alone to confront the fact that her happy state, her golden glow, had ever so slightly dimmed.

16

❧❧❧

Aɴᴅ ꜱᴏ, ʜᴀᴠɪɴɢ ꜰᴀʟʟᴇɴ ɪɴ ʟᴏᴠᴇ, Mᴀʀɢᴀʀᴇᴛ
began to learn to live with her condition as a victim
stricken by disease learns to live with her affliction:
cautiously coming to terms with it, discovering its
quirks, its ups and downs, the strictures it imposed on
her as it took over her life.

She had been in love only once, and that had been
so long ago that the self she remembered—a college
girl—seemed like someone else. The person she was
now was very different, and therefore her condition
was different as well. It felt odd: like a dress that did
not fit.

And yet it felt oddly familiar; she had been in this
place before. She was like a traveler visiting a country
after many years away: the general terrain was recog-
nizable, but most of the details had changed, so that
she could not walk confidently, she needed always to
go with caution, to look for landmarks, to make sure
of her route so that she would not become hopelessly,
irretrievably lost.

Neal did not call for three days. When he did (remembering that she had gone to the concert on the
Esplanade), he invited her to go to hear a jazz group
at the Top Hat, the night after next. After she ac-

cepted she remembered that that night was open house at the children's school. She called him back, explained the conflict, and asked for a rain check for the following evening. Graciously, he gave it to her.

She called the same baby-sitter; the children overheard her making the arrangements. They said nothing after she hung up, and that alarmed her, for they always commented on whatever she did. But then she remembered that they had not talked about her evening at the Bay Tower Room, either, and so she understood that she needed to bring up the subject of Neal Donovan herself.

"I'll be going out on Wednesday night, all right?"

They regarded her with solemn eyes: her precious little quartet.

"With that man?" said Thomas at last.

"He isn't 'that man.' His name is Neal Donovan."

Silence.

"Well?" she said. "That's all right, isn't it?"

"I guess so," said David. But his face, his eyes, said *No*.

"I mean, it's just for a few hours. And it's in the evening when you're doing your homework and going to sleep—"

"How old is he?" said Peaches.

"I'm not sure. Thirty-seven or eight, I'd say."

"That's old."

"Not really. I'm thirty-two. And Grandma and Grandpa are—"

"He looks older."

"He was in the war. Maybe that's why."

They regarded her, their eyes still serious, still questioning: *Why are you deserting us?* She realized, and understood that they realized, that she was asking their permission to go out with Neal Donovan. Surely the child psychologists would agree that that was improper? She should not *ask* them; she should *tell* them. Gently, of course. They were like a team, the five of them. And, of course, they would go on as a team. It was just that—

It was just that some part of her that had been long dormant, left for dead, had suddenly come to life again. Like a plant in the garden once that she thought had not survived the winter; she had intended to dig it up in the spring and discard it, but through absentmindedness or sheer neglect she had not done so and one day she had looked at it, shovel in hand, intending to do away with it, and had seen small green shoots all around its base. And so she had trimmed back the dead stalks and fertilized it and watered it and it had bloomed and bloomed all summer.

When Neal came to call for her the children, again, were upstairs; and again she did not summon them to say hello. They had made no further comment about him, but she was aware of a slight, constant tension, an attitude of watchfulness on their part, and she understood that no matter how much she was attracted to this man, no matter how much she wanted to see him, she needed to go slowly as she introduced him into her life. And theirs.

At the Top Hat they listened appreciatively to the Mississippi Ramblers. Between sets she listened to Neal talk about this group, and about others, and she realized that he was quite knowledgeable about jazz and, more, that he had a kind of passion for it: its performers, its history, its fate. She liked that. He did not at first glance seem to be a man who was able to have a passion for anything, but if he did for one thing, then he could for another.

Afterward they went to a nearby bar to have a beer. It was a quiet place, not crowded; unlike the Top Hat, a place where they could talk. They sat at a small table near the back. When the waitress brought their drinks Neal lifted his glass and said, "To Bunny MacPherson."

Margaret laughed and, lifting her glass in return, said, "To Bunny MacPherson." And, after she had taken a sip: "Who is that?"

"The fellow who used to be the bassist in the Mississippi Ramblers."

"What happened to him?"

"Wine, women, and song. Not enough song, unfortunately. Last time I saw him—about six months ago —he was in tough shape. And not only from wine and women, either. He was on God knows what—cocaine, uppers, downers. Too bad. A terrific musician."

"Was he a good friend?"

"Good enough. People like that will pull you down with them if you let them. You try to help them straighten out. Then after a while you see that they're determined to wreck their lives, and you can't do anything to stop it."

"Yes." As she did so often, she thought of how fortunate she was in spite of everything. Her life and those of her children had been damaged somewhat, but not destroyed—not wrecked beyond repair the way so many lives were.

He watched her; then, as if he read her mind, he said, "Did he wreck your life?"

"Who?" But she knew whom he meant. She remembered the previous time that he had questioned her, bluntly, almost hostile; now he seemed very different—gentler, almost kind. She looked down; she looked away. She waited until she was sure that her voice would not break; then she said, "I thought so, for a while. But as it's turned out, no. He didn't."

"He left you?"

"Yes."

"Any particular reason?"

"He said he'd fallen in love with someone else."

"Did he marry her?"

"No."

"Would you have taken him back?"

It was a question that had occurred to her more than once. "No," she said.

"Why not?"

"Because at first I thought I couldn't survive—I thought *we* couldn't survive without him. I don't mean economically. But then when I realized that he was gone, and that he wouldn't be back, and that we *were* surviving, I thought, what's the point? The children had made the adjustment. It was hard on them, particularly the older ones, but they made it. And so then I thought, they've accepted it, so let it be."

"Did he ask you to take him back? What's his name, anyway?"

"Richard. No, he didn't. The surprising thing was—I thought for a while that he might. I suppose I hoped he would. And then, when he didn't, I realized that I felt relieved. I might have said yes, you see. For the wrong reason. For the children. But it wouldn't have worked."

"You couldn't have trusted him any more?"

"Something like that."

"Does he see the children?"

"From time to time. He moved to California. He comes East a couple of times a year."

He nodded, seeming suddenly to lose interest in the subject. She wondered—but did not have the courage to ask—about him: had he ever come close to marrying? He had said not—had said that he had never met a woman with whom he wanted to spend his life. Surely there must have been attachments, long-standing affairs? But she could not put the question, not yet; it was not shyness so much as it was her feeling that she was in danger of being overwhelmed by him. She could not absorb too much at once; she needed to take him in small doses.

Until she built up a tolerance for him?

Or until she became so addicted that no amount of him would be enough?

Driving home she remembered the question that hovered over getting-to-know-you dates in her high school years: will he or won't he? She shivered a little in her black velvet jacket.

As it turned out, he did. It was a quite satisfying kiss, sensuous but not intrusive, skilled but not over-bearing, promising but not demanding. She could not remember the last time she had kissed her former husband (although she could remember the first: it had been, like this, in a car, at the end of a date—their third).

She was aware that times had changed, and that many women nowadays were expected to offer, or at least to assent to, far more than a kiss on the first date, never mind the second. While Margaret would have defended the right of any woman to do as she pleased (*if* she pleased), such behavior was beyond her: it was another indication, perhaps, of how the world was passing her by. In this case, she did not mind.

She put her right hand at the back of his head as she kissed him (the exercise was, of course, more than a matter of simply letting him kiss her); she liked the feel of his hair, his jacket collar, his strong neck. She enjoyed the kiss very much—and a good thing, too, she thought, since she was already in love with him and a disappointing kiss (sloppy, or too long, or too short, or inexpert in any way) would have thrown her into a quandary with which she was not prepared to deal.

He did not, however, ask to see her again; and he did not call the next day, or the next. The children were of an age to have many telephone calls (although not so many, she knew, as they would have when they were teenagers); every time the phone rang she felt her heart jump a little, so that by the end of the second day she was worn out with reacting to the telephone's ring and she willed herself into a condition of refusal to answer it unless she was alone in the house.

Despite this display of willpower she began to grow so depressed at the thought that he would not call again that by Saturday, when he did, she was frightened at how relieved she was; her euphoria, which had begun to fade, returned more intensely than before, and she was happy to have it back.

17

A WEEK LATER THE CHILDREN HELD A WAR COUN-
cil in the backyard. Lily was in charge. The purpose of
a War Council was not necessarily to make war; they
used the term simply to describe discussions that were
more important than their ordinary give-and-take.
Today the topic was—of course—Neal Donovan.

"Well?" said Lily. "What should we do?"

"You say first," said Peaches.

"I think we should tell Grandma and Grandpa,"
said Lily.

"Why?"

"I don't know. But I think we should tell them."

"I think we should tell *Mom*," said David.

"Tell her what?"

"That we don't want her going out on dates."

"I don't care if she goes out on dates," said Lily. "I
just don't like her going out with *him*."

The others nodded: that was it, that was what the
trouble was.

"Maybe he's not so bad," said Peaches, always the
optimist. "I mean, maybe he's really nice. If he knows
you and everything."

"Aaaah," said David. "No way."

"Gail Stubbs' mom has a boyfriend, and *he's* really

nice. He takes Gail out in his boat and buys her a lot
of presents and helped her build a dollhouse and
everything."

They were silent for a moment, contemplating such
largesse, aware that Neal had offered nothing similar.
They were hardly even on speaking terms with him;
last evening, for the first time, Lily and David had exchanged a few words with him (his polite, rather cautious questions about how school was coming
along—the standard questions put by adults who had
little contact with children and did not know what were
the important things in children's lives; their polite,
rather cautious answers that school was fine, thank
you—the standard answers given by children who
understood that certain adults, no matter how intelligent they were, were not intelligent when they dealt
with children).

"I want to see Daddy," said Thomas abruptly.

At this, David and Lily, for reasons that they could
not have explained, felt suddenly angry and guilty and
sad all at once. It had been a long time, it seemed,
since they had seen their father. He lived all the way
across the country, where he worked with computers,
doing they knew not what, and where the distractions
and demands of his life were such that he found it difficult to get away to see them. When he had last been
East he had taken them to Maine for a few days and
they had had a good time, but then, inevitably, he had
gone away again. He had promised to return, just before school began, but then he had called and said that
he would not be able to come. They had been disappointed, of course, but not unduly surprised; he had
done so before. He had promised to come at
Christmas; they all hoped that he would, but the older
ones, at least, had learned not to hope too much, thus

protecting themselves from the pain of having those hopes dashed when he did not appear.

"Why?" said Peaches.

"I just want to."

"Daddy can't help," said Lily.

"Yes he can. He can make him go away." They understood who "him" was.

"No he can't."

"Gail Stubbs said her mom's boyfriend was going to be her new father," said Peaches. "But he isn't yet."

They thought about that: they allowed themselves to imagine, for a painful moment or two, Neal Donovan in that role. Then Thomas began to cry.

"I don't want a new father," he said, sniffling.

"He isn't going to be," said David; but they heard the lack of conviction in his voice.

"I want *our* father," said Thomas. "We already have a father. I want *him*."

"Mom wouldn't do that," said Lily. "She doesn't want to get married agian." She spoke sharply, angrily. As worried as she was about Neal Donovan, she was annoyed that Peaches had brought up Gail Stubbs, whose situation, as Peaches described it, was so different from their own.

"She might," said Peaches. She did not want to make Thomas unhappy, but she sensed the power that telling Gail Stubbs' story had given her—the power to frighten them with that cautionary tale—and she could not resist exercising it just a little more. "What if she does? What then?"

"Be quiet," said Lily. Thomas was crying hard now, heedless of embarrassment.

"I know what *I'll* do," Peaches went on. "I'll run away. Anybody can come with me who wants to. I'm not going to stay here. Not if he's going to be our father."

"You just said he might be nice," said David. "Now you're saying you're going to run away. How come you're going to run away if he's so nice?"

"Just because he might be nice doesn't mean I want him for a father. I wouldn't mind if he was nice, though. What if he had a boat? What if he took us out on it?"

As so often happened in their War Councils, the discussion had wandered from the intended issue. Now Lily brought them back to it: what should they do— and, indeed, what could they do—about Neal Donovan?

"Let's scare him away again like we did before," said David.

"We didn't scare him."

"Yes, we did. Remember how he went down?"

"We could just be mean to him when he comes," said Peaches. But she spoke without conviction; Margaret had brought them up to be polite to adults, and they were not yet old enough to disregard that training.

"We could keep a log on him," said David, "and write down what he does."

"Why?" said Peaches.

"Just to keep a record. We could write down every time he calls, every time he comes, what time, and how long they go out for. Stuff like that."

"That's right," said Lily. "Like a private detective or something. They always watch people. And then if we do want to tell somebody about him, we'll have everything right there."

She called for a vote. Because they did not know what else to do, they voted yes. David volunteered to buy a small notebook at the drugstore. He took up a collection and they all contributed; he got thirty-seven cents.

They realized that it was not a terribly effective plan, but it was the best they could do at the moment. If their mother was determined to allow the intruder into their lives, there was little they could do, finally, to prevent it.

They would consult together, and watch, and wait. Perhaps some better plan—some better opportunity to defend themselves—would come their way.

18

❧❧❧❧

THAT NIGHT MARGARET AND NEAL WENT TO A movie. It was a proper movie, with plenty of plot: both of them enjoyed it. Afterward they went to Chef Chang's for beef with black mushrooms (Neal) and sweet-and-sour shrimp (Margaret) and vegetable lo mein for both of them.

It was raining when they left the restaurant, a gentle, misting rain, a mild night. Neal turned on the windshield wipers. Their soft, hypnotic swishing provided just enough sound for Margaret to feel that she did not have to talk. She could watch the windshield wipers and the lights glimmering in the rain, and think about whether, tonight, she would invite him to stay for a while when he took her home, and about the meaning of that invitation, and about how he would interpret it.

A further complication was that if she invited him in, should she do so before he kissed her good night, or after? Assuming, of course, that he did kiss her; she saw no reason why, having done so before, he would not do so tonight as well.

These qualms about etiquette made her feel about sixteen again, as if she had been caught in a time warp; it seemed very odd to worry about such things, the things that high school girls worried about, when she was on the far side of thirty, with four children.

And really, she thought with a flash of irritation, really she was worrying too much, she was making too much—as she tended to do in general—out of what was something very simple: did she, or did she not, want to ask him in?

Before she was able to answer that question, she needed to know—or at least to surmise—what would happen if she did. Almost certainly he would see it as an invitation to more kissing, and possibly more than that.

In the old days, Margaret knew, "nice girls" did not want to be kissed—or, at least, did not seem to want to be. The old days, she supposed, were gone forever. She was not sure of the rules for these new days. Possibly, she thought, there were none.

When they reached her street and he turned into her driveway and stopped, he turned off the engine. Looking as she was for signs, hints, clues as to how to behave, she thought that that was significant: he expected an invitation. A further sign came when, turning toward her, he smiled a little; she could see his face in the light coming from the porch. He did not move to kiss her as he had done on other evenings. He was, she realized, waiting to be invited in; it was as if he was prompting her, not in any unpleasant or pushy way, but as if he was giving her a signal to do what (as she realized) she wanted to do in any case. Go ahead, he seemed to be saying; it's all right, it's the next step.

And so, hearing the slight nervousness in her voice, she said, "Will you come in for a while?"

"Sure," he said.

And so it was as easy as that: like many obstacles and difficulties in her life that turned out not to be obstacles at all.

The baby-sitter reported that all was well, the children were asleep, no phone calls. Since it was raining Margaret offered to take her home, but she declined. She was, Margaret reflected wryly, growing rich off this affair. No matter: she was a good, dependable girl, one who would not, Margaret thought, gossip too much through the neighborhood with the details of Margaret's gentleman friend.

After the sitter had gone Margaret went upstairs to check on the children. Each of them was asleep, as reported. She did not check too closely, did not stand by their beds and straighten their covers or kiss them; she did not want to wake them up. The inspection done, she returned to Neal, who was waiting for her in the living room. Gladly, her lingering doubts vanished, she walked into his arms.

A few moments after Margaret left his room, David caught himself on the brink of sleep. He had stayed awake until she came home by reading with a flashlight under the covers. But when he heard the sound of Neal's car in the driveway he had turned off the flashlight and shoved it and his book under the bed and feigned sleep; he knew that his mother would come upstairs to look at them all. The clock beside his bed said eleven thirty-five. He needed to remember the time she had come back so that he could write it in the notebook he had bought that afternoon. He had spent an hour in consultation with Lily reconstructing Neal's appearances until now, beginning with the day they had first seen him. Eleven thirty-five, he thought; he needed to stay awake until Neal left so that he could record that time as well. He was glad that his mother had not come all the way into his room; usually he could successfully pretend to be asleep, but sometimes she knew that he was pretending, and she would speak to him. Wanting to share the joke, he would begin to laugh as he struggled to keep quiet.

He lay in the dark, his eyes wide. The house was silent. He was listening for the sound of Neal driving away, but he heard nothing. Probably his mother was making coffee. He hoped that they would not take too long to drink it.

The door of his room opened; he could see Lily's bathrobed figure silhouetted against the hall night-light. She came in, shutting the door behind her, and approached him.

"Are you awake?" she said.

"Yes."

She perched on the edge of his bed. In the dim glow from the streetlight he could see her face but he could not read her expression.

"They're in the living room," she said. "Did you write down when they came in?"

"Not yet."

"Where's the notebook?"

"Under the mattress."

It was a relatively safe place: they were responsible for stripping their beds every week and making them up again after Margaret had washed the sheets.

"D'you want to see what they're doing?" said Lily.

"You mean spy on them?"

"Yes."

"All right."

They paused at the balustrade in the upper hall. They could tell that only one light was on in the living room, a small lamp with a leaded glass shade near the big bay window in the front. They crept down the stairs. Cautiously Lily put her head around the door and peered into the living room. It was a large room; the small lamp left much of it in darkness. For a moment she thought that she must have been mistaken:

they were not there, after all. But then she saw them.
They were on the sofa, which faced the fireplace. They
had lighted the fire, which blazed up bright and crack-
ling, giving off a ruddy light. The two adults were silhouetted against it. Her mother seemed to be sitting,
but she was slumped down so that Lily could see only
the back of her head. The intruder was sitting also, but
turned toward her mother and bending over her. He
was kissing her.

Lily made way then for David to see, too, but she
did not look at him and of course she could say nothing. She felt very odd: embarrassed.

Lily had seen adults kiss on television or at the
movies; she could not recall ever having seen them do
so in real life. Not like this. A casual smack on the
cheek, perhaps, but not anything like this. And this
was not some unknown actress in a movie; it was her
own mother. Lily knew that when adults—or even
teenagers, people hardly much older than herself—fell
in love, they kissed. It was difficult for her to believe
that her mother was in love with this man, but if she
was not, why was she kissing him?

It went on and on. Save for the snap and hiss of the
burning wood, there was no sound. Lily's feet were
cold and she was tired; like David she had not slept
but had pretended to be asleep when her mother
looked in.

And yet, embarrassed as she was, and cold and
tired, she could not look away. She had the sense of
witnessing some mysterious and powerful tribal rite
into which she had not yet been initiated. She knew
what it was, but she did not understand it. She would,
she knew, hardly be able to describe it to Peaches and
Thomas. It would be as embarrassing for them as it
was for her. And what would David write in his notebook? What if someone—their mother, for instance—

got hold of that notebook and read it? Comings and goings were one thing; this was very different.

And still it went on. Lily thought that it must be very boring for them; she wondered why her mother did not take him out into the kitchen and sit and talk with him over a cup of coffee, as she did with her other friends.

David touched her arm. She glanced at him. He looked angry; he looked as though he was about to cry. He motioned with his head, and she understood that he wanted her to go back upstairs with him.

She agreed. It was pointless, standing here, catching cold and feeling bored and embarrassed and excluded all at the same time. There were things about the adult world that frightened Lily (violence, for instance) and things that intrigued her (freedom, for instance), but some things (like this display in her living room, for instance) simply baffled her; they made no sense at all.

She followed David up the stairs. He went into his room and she went on to hers. She climbed into her bed and fell asleep at once. David decided that he would try to stay awake to see at what time Neal left, but he, too, was tired and he could not resist getting into bed while he waited.

And so neither of them knew when, shortly after two in the morning, Neal said good night to Margaret, got into his car, and drove home.

19

❧❦❧❦❧

"On the other hand," said Barbara Kimball, "I could just tell the bastard to go to hell."

"You could," agreed Margaret. She spoke tentatively, in what she hoped was a neutral tone; she understood that her role was that of sounding board rather than adviser, and she did not want to come down too heavily on one side or the other.

They were silent for a moment, each working out the ramifications, the possible consequences of such drastic action on Barbara's part. They sat, as usual, in Margaret's kitchen. It was the next day, a Sunday afternoon. When Barbara had called to ask if she might drop by, Margaret had jumped at the phone's ring because she thought it might be Neal. She was disappointed that it was not; on the other hand, she was happy to hear from Barbara. She had not seen or talked to her in some days, and the last time she had done so, on the telephone, she had thought that Barbara had sounded rather unhappy with her "Marlboro Man." The unhappiness did not surprise Margaret, for she had assumed that sooner or later it would appear, but its timing did: surely, even for Barbara, this was a sudden cooling off?

"But I don't *want* to tell him to go to hell," said

Barbara. "I really don't. I mean, why should I?" She stared at Margaret defiantly, as if challenging her to answer.

"Why should you?" said Margaret, agreeing with her.

"I mean, why should I deprive myself of him?" said Barbara. "Maybe that's what he wants me to do. Just break off. Well—I won't."

Margaret nodded.

"I'll just—oh, *I* don't know. I don't *know.*" Barbara sat slumped in her chair, her eyes unfocused. Margaret had never seen her so; she had no idea how to console her. Except, of course, to listen—to let her talk it out. The problem, it seemed, was that Craig McCarren was undependable: he made dates and broke them; he made dates and, not bothering to break them, neglected to appear; and now, it seemed, Barbara had caught him out. "He said he was called out of town. So to cheer myself up I went to hear James Galway at Symphony Hall, and who was sitting down front? With a blonde? You guessed it."

The obvious thing, Margaret thought, was to drop him, but that, apparently, was not so simple.

"I don't *want* to drop him," Barbara said. "I *adore* him. Don't ask me why. I can't explain it. I just do. He's wonderful. No—he really is. When he's with me, that is. When he's not, he's terrible. As you can see from the way I talk about him."

She was silent then, drinking her coffee, working it out. Then: "I'd like to marry him."

"Don't you think you ought to stop wanting to tell him to go to hell before you do that?"

Barbara laughed. "All right. Point well taken. Maybe I don't know *what* I'd like. I'm all—oh—just so terribly up-and-down. You're always so calm, so *sane*. I suppose it's the children. They keep you stable."

"Yes."

"You're lucky to have them. On the other hand, not everyone was meant to be a mother. I don't think I'd do well with children."

Margaret did not think so, either, but she said nothing.

"On the *other* hand, would *you* ever think of marrying again?" said Barbara. Momentarily leaving her own concerns she said, "Whatever happened to that man, anyway? The one you told me about?"

"I've seen him again."

"Really?" Barbara perked up, forgetting her own troubles. "It's working out, then?"

"It's—well, I've seen him again, that's all."

Barbara beamed. "You like him."

"Yes."

"There you are. You might be married before I am."

They both laughed, then, as if to acknowledge the ridiculousness of the remark.

Later, however, after Barbara had gone, Margaret allowed herself to recall it: she let it slip quickly into her mind before pushing it out again, rather as if she were trying on, in secret, a new dress that was too daring, too revealing, too showy, so that after only a glance at herself in the mirror she quickly turned away.

20

❦❦❦❦❦

"Margaret, this is Jason Goodrich. Jason, Margaret Merrill."

They smiled at each other, and when Jason offered his hand Margaret shook it. It was a busy night. The Rising of the Moon was very crowded, very noisy. Someone had just finished singing; in a few moments someone else would begin. They were at the bar. Margaret sat on the stool next to Jason's; Neal stood between them.

"Welcome!" shouted Jason. "Neal tells me you're fond of German movies."

She didn't understand for a moment; then, when she did, she smiled and said something that they couldn't catch. Neal thought that she seemed out of place here: she was too quiet, too gentle, for the rough-and-ready atmosphere. But he had wanted her to meet Jason; or, rather, he wanted Jason to meet her.

They did not stay long, but Neal knew that Jason would have formed an opinion of her one way or the other. Jason was never undecided about anything, and certainly not about women.

"Definitely not your type," said Jason the next evening when Neal walked into the bar, much quieter

now, and sat down next to him. "Very sweet, very nice
—she seems quite shy, actually—but I just don't think
she's got enough—uh—*spark.* I mean, you're not
looking for a doormat. And I don't mean that she's a
doormat, either, but she just seems a little—uh—
vague."

He was right. Margaret *was* a little vague. About
herself; about the world around her. That was one of
the things that Neal liked about her. He did not like
women who were too conscious of themselves, whose
minds always seemed to be clicking, computerlike, cal-
culating the effect they thought they were making.
Margaret was not like that at all. She seemed completely unaware of herself. He approved of that.

"Listen, Neal, she's very nice. Very nice. But how
about someone with more—uh—*snap?* Now I met a
girl the other night, her name is Linda. No. Not Linda.
Brenda. I think it's Brenda. Never mind. She's about
five feet six, black hair, blue eyes."

"Good night, Jason."

"No, listen to me. She's Italian but she's not preju-
diced. I think she'd go out with you if you were polite.
She's a beautiful girl. Beautiful body. Smart. Assertive
but not aggressive. Runs her own software company.
She might even be too much for you, but she'd be a
challenge, you know? A real challenge."

"Good night, Jason."

"She doesn't even want to get married, that's the
beauty of it. If I had a brother I would introduce him
to this girl. Listen. Here's her phone number. Just do
me a favor and call her. Say I sent you. She trusts me.
She trusts me. Why don't you?"

"Good *night,* Jason."

21

NEAL UNDERSTOOD VERY WELL WHAT WAS HAPPEN-
ing. Once or twice before, when it had begun to happen with other women, he had fought it, resisted it,
run away from it.

He did not want to do that now. He wanted to linger
awhile: he wanted to experience it, even only briefly.

He understood that she was falling in love with him.
He understood that one or both of them might get
hurt. People did get hurt: it was in the nature of the
experience.

Then, too, there was the matter of the children. He
had had little contact with children; he had none of his
own and no nieces or nephews. He understood that it
was important to try to make friends with Margaret's
four. Or at least to try to make their acquaintance.

He was not sure how to approach them. They were
foreigners; he did not speak their language. They were
a challenge to him. Their coolness added in a way to
Margaret's attractiveness: they were an obstacle that
he needed to overcome.

Understanding so little about them—about any
children—he knew enough, at least, not to come
bearing gifts. He was not in any case the kind of man
who bought gifts for no reason, but even if he had

been he would not have known what to bring to the Merrills. Their life was so different from what his own had been at their age—so much richer in every way— that he could not have imagined what to buy them. And he sensed that no matter what he bought it would have been received with suspicion, if not contempt. They were not fools, these children; and they had a further advantage over him in that they were four to his one. He remembered their first reaction to him, well before they had had any notion that he would come into their lives in a personal way: the four of them lined up, waiting for him, trying to—what? Threaten him? Frighten him? The fact that they had not expected him to be frightened was beside the point.

So he needed to proceed with a certain care.

One evening, calling for Margaret, he waited for her in the living room while she finished dressing. It was unlike her to be late; he wondered if there had been some trouble, some domestic crisis. The older boy, David, had answered the doorbell; he had been polite in a distant way, asking Neal to come in and sit down. The baby-sitter had not yet arrived. David hovered near the door, as if he could not decide whether to join Neal or retreat upstairs.

"Bad traffic," said Neal in a conversational way. "An accident tied things up. I should have come on the trolley. You have a stop near here, right?"

"Yes."

"Do you go on the trolley at all?"

"Sometimes."

"You could easily get to my place. Just change at Park Street and take the Red Line to Savin Hill. Six stops. Easy as anything. There's a little beach near where I live, right on Boston Harbor. You could come down on the trolley sometime and I'll show it to you."

David nodded but he made no reply; after a moment he muttered "s'cuse me," and ducked out.

Neal shrugged. Children were unfathomable—a strange, uncivilized people who might, someday, grow up and join the rest of the human race. He was not surprised that Margaret's did not take to him; he understood that in their eyes he was an unnecessary addition to their lives.

Nevertheless, he thought, he would stay with it—with her—for a while, at any rate. He was growing very fond of her. Her sweetness, her earnestness, her lack of pretense, touched him, threw him slightly off balance. It was a not unpleasant sensation.

Certainly he did not want a doormat. Jason had been right about that, at least.

And certainly Margaret was a little vague. Jason had been right about that, too. A little shy, a little unsure of herself.

Neal was intelligent enough to understand that self-confidence comes from feeling competent. Therefore, because he was fond of Margaret, because he wanted to be good to her, he undertook to give her that.

He began with basic home maintenance. First (on a Sunday afternoon not long afterward) he showed her fundamental emergency measures: how to turn off the main electrical switch; the pattern of the water pipes, and how to turn the water off where she wanted it off.

Then he moved on to specific jobs. He began with the leaking faucet that he had seen on his first meeting with her.

"You just loosen the packing nut," he said, showing her how to position the small wrench. "Then you remove the stem assembly. You remove this screw at the bottom of the stem assembly that holds the worn-out washer. You replace the washer, replace the screw, replace the stem assembly. Like that. All right?"

"Yes."

"Easy, isn't it?"

"Everything's easy once you know how."

The faucet was in the bathroom where the high, antique toilet tank was not working properly. Neal brought up a ladder from the cellar, climbed it, looked into the tank to make sure that the problem was what he thought it was, and then ordered Margaret to climb up to see for herself.

"You see the float—that baseball-sized thing? Pick up the rod attached to it."

She did. The running stopped.

"All right," he said. "We have to turn off the water for this one. Sometimes the turnoff is in the bathroom, but this one isn't so we have to go downstairs."

He accompanied her to the cellar to make sure that she got the right line. On the way they encountered Thomas.

"Hi, sweetie," said Margaret. "Want to help?"

"No." He watched them go down; he watched them come back up. Then he went to tell David.

It took about twenty minutes to fix the toilet. Margaret was very pleased.

"I always wanted to be handy," she said. "I meant to take a course when Richard left. I thought I should know how to do all these things. But it meant going out at night, and the children were still so little and I was always tired. And I just never did."

Neal was pleased also: it pleased him to give her competence and therefore confidence. He rumpled her hair affectionately. "Next week," he said, "auto repair."

22

❧❧❧❧

"THEY AREN'T EXACTLY *HOSTILE*," SAID MAR-
garet. "But I have the sense of being watched all the
time. There's a real feeling of—oh, I don't know—
discomfort in the air."

"Naturally," said Barbara. "Look at it from their
point of view. Their father went away, didn't he? Now
they're afraid that you will, too."

They were talking on the telephone. Barbara had
called to report that her romance was progressing
somewhat more happily. In answer to her routine
question, "How's everything?" she had heard the concern in Margaret's voice as she replied, "All right,"
and so the conversation had quickly shifted.

"You have to help them," said Barbara. "Once they
get to know him they won't feel so theatened." Like
many people without children, Barbara considered
herself an expert on child care. "At this point, he's
literally just someone who comes to take you away. Or
else he comes to see you and not them. Why not ask
him to dinner?"

"I've thought of that. But I didn't want to rush
things."

"You mean you didn't want him to feel pressured?"

"Yes."

"But you have to do something, or the children will be so alienated that it will be impossible to deal with them."

"I know."

"He does know that you have four children?"

"Of course."

"All right, then. He has to get to know them sooner or later. And it sounds to me as if sooner is better."

"I suppose so."

"You're afraid he'll be frightened away?"

"Something like that."

"So it's better to find out now. Besides—he won't be. Your kids are super. Some people's aren't— they're little monsters. But yours are real live human beings. He'll like them, you'll see."

But would they like him? Margaret wondered. However, she knew that Barbara was right: something needed to be done to bridge the gap that was widening, day by day, between her children and herself on the issue of Neal Donovan. If she knew him better— or, rather, if she were more sure of him—she could ask his help; she could put it to him as a problem that he could help her to solve. As it was, she would have to proceed on her own.

Accordingly, the next evening, she made her announcement. "Neal Donovan is coming to dinner on Friday evening," she said.

They made no reply. They watched her.

"All right? Isn't that nice? We're having company."

Still no reply.

"And I want you to be polite to him."

They resented that. They took pride in being polite; she did not need to caution them.

"I want you to make him feel at home. All right? I want you to be *very nice* to him."

Suddenly Thomas jumped up and pushed back his

chair—they were at supper in the kitchen—and ran into the hall and up the stairs.

"Thomas!" Margaret started after him, but Lily was ahead of her and Margaret let her go instead. She came back and sat down again with David and Peaches.

"You don't want him to come?" she said.

No answer. They would not look at her.

"Answer me. David?"

He shrugged. "I don't care."

"Yes, you do. You all do. What's the matter?"

Silence. Then Peaches said, "Does he have to come?"

"No. Of course not. But I thought it would be a good idea. Look—"

But how could she explain to them? That, suddenly, the four of them were not enough? That she needed— wanted—something more? How could they be expected to understand that?

"All right," she said. "I'll tell him not to come."

Wrong, she thought. Unfair to manipulate them into feeling guilty.

"That's rude," said Peaches. She looked worried. "You might hurt his feelings."

"I'd rather hurt his feelings than yours."

They struggled with it: whose feelings were more important?

David thought about his notebook. Having Neal come to dinner would give him at least a page and a half of information. "Sure," he said. "Let him come."

Peaches nodded. "Since you already asked him."

Lily reappeared. She glanced at her mother as she slipped into her seat, but she said nothing.

Feeling like an interloper herself, Margaret went upstairs to see Thomas. He was lying face down on his bed. She sat beside him and smoothed back his silky brown hair. His face was turned away from her, damp from crying although he did not seem to be crying now.

She thought that she should talk to him but she could think of nothing to say. Or, rather, nothing that would not be a long litany of explanation and regret: I'm sorry that you are unhappy, I'm sorry that your father went away, I'm sorry that you think that our lives are being disrupted, I'm sorry, I'm sorry, I'm sorry.

And so she said nothing, but simply bent and kissed his cheek and sat with him, half bent over him, her arm around his small, thin body. After a while he fell asleep, so that when the phone rang and it turned out to be Neal, she was able to leave Thomas and answer it without explaining to either of them why she had to attend to the other.

23

❧❧❧❧

"WOULD YOU LIKE TO MAKE DESSERT?" SAID MAR-
garet. It was Friday afternoon, the day of Neal's visit.
The children had just finished their after-school snack;
now all of them except Lily had gone their separate
ways. Lily had stayed behind—to talk? But she had
not initiated a conversation, and had replied in mono-
syllables to Margaret's attempts to start one.

"What is it?" said Lily, meaning dessert.

"Whatever. You could make the chocolate vinegar
cake if you want. I have whipped cream to go with it."
It was not only the best chocolate cake in the world, it
was the easiest; Lily had mastered it years ago, and
recently she had taught Peaches to make it, too. They
all loved it.

"No. I don't feel like it."

"There's brownie mix if you'd rather."

"No."

Lily's expression was not hostile, but it was not
friendly, either. It was nothing, Margaret thought—
blank. Unnerving, surely, in a child? Adults dissem-
bled; children showed what they felt.

What's wrong? Margaret wanted to say. Tell me
what you're thinking—what you're feeling.

But she did not. Perhaps, as she admitted to herself,

109

she was afraid that Lily would answer her truthfully—
that she would say, for instance, that she did not want
Neal to come to dinner that evening, that none of
them wanted him, and please would Margaret call him
and tell him to stay away.

"All right," she said after a moment. "We can have
ice cream. OK?"

"Sure."

Lily left then; Margaret heard her running up the
stairs to her room. She felt irritated, and vaguely
guilty: an opportunity had passed, she had let it pass,
and it would not come again.

During dinner the children were polite: no more.
They spoke when they were spoken to; they showed,
as they always did, good table manners. Margaret
found that after a while she was annoyed with them—
a feeling that she acknowledged was unfair. But they
were so reserved, so completely withdrawn, that they
might have been automatons. As Barbara had said,
her children were real human beings: they had personalities, and pleasant ones at that—appealing, even
winning personalities. Everyone liked them. Now they
sat like four little zombies, unwilling to come alive for
the unwanted guest. They were doing themselves a
disservice, she thought, and Neal, too: they were de-
priving him of the chance to get to know them, they
were presenting themselves as something they were
not. As she tried to keep some kind of conversation
going, she felt as though she was struggling with an
intolerable burden.

"Did you have clubs today?" she said to Peaches,
whose class had an activity period every Friday afternoon. This term, Peaches had chosen the art club.

"Yes."

"What did you do?"

"A painting."

"Did you bring it home?"

"No."

"Because—?"

"It had to dry."

"What did you paint?"

"A house."

"Our house?"

"No. Just a house."

Then it was David's turn, but he was no more willing than Peaches to relax and chatter; it was the same with Lily and Thomas. After a while Margaret turned to Neal, who had been silent for some time, and struck up a somewhat less one-sided conversation with him. The children seemed not to be listening; they sat with downcast eyes, they finished the food on their plates but they did not ask for more.

After dinner Margaret, determined to salvage something from the evening, determined not to let her attempt to draw them together fail completely, suggested that Peaches bring out some games. Thomas was amenable to playing a round of Chutes and Ladders with Peaches and Neal. Peaches won, which brought a momentary smile to her face before she remembered that this was not an evening for smiles and she went blank again. Then David and Neal played a game of checkers. Neal won quickly. Then Lily and Neal played checkers; this time Lily won, a little less quickly but even so, she thought, unfairly: Neal had let her win, he had deliberately passed up a triple jump. She was sure he had seen it. She was not grateful to him: on the contrary, she felt contempt for him. She glanced at David and saw that he had seen it, too. Lily understood that Neal was trying to make friends; it was too bad, she thought, that he was going about it in such a stupid way.

Margaret suggested a game of Monopoly, then, but

she was relieved (she admitted to herself) when the children declined. Yes, she said when they asked, they might be excused. When she went up shortly to tuck the little ones in, they were already asleep. Lily was reading; David was writing something in a notebook.

Neal said nothing about the children's behavior, and she, prompted by her sense of loyalty to them, said nothing either. It was possible, she thought, that he had not realized that they were unhappy at his presence—possible, but not likely, since he was not a stupid man. He knows, she thought.

And then she thought: love me, love my children.

And then she thought: who said anything about love?

24

THE NEXT DAY THE CHILDREN HELD ANOTHER WAR Council.

"I think we should ask her," said Peaches.

"Ask her what?" said Lily.

"You know—if she's going to get married."

Marriage was one of the things that adults did; divorce was another.

"No," said Lily. "That's not a good idea." Even mentioning such a thing, she thought, might make it happen.

"Well—what, then?"

"We have to make him go away," said David.

"How?" said Peaches.

"We could just say to him, Go away."

But they were too shy to do that, and they knew it. Older children—teenagers—might do such a thing; they were too young.

Lily nervously twisted the ring she wore on the third finger of her right hand. She had won it in a game of jacks at school; it was a "mood ring," a fad of a few years before, set with a translucent oval stone that supposedly changed color with the wearer's emotional state. At the moment, she saw, it was black.

"Hey," said Peaches, noticing it. "Let's make a wish on your ring."

"*That* won't help," said David.

"Maybe it will. It'd be better than that stupid notebook. That stupid notebook isn't doing any good at all."

True enough; nevertheless he did not like to hear her say it.

"So," Peaches went on relentlessly, "let's make a wish on the ring. Unless somebody has a better idea."

Since no one did, they hesitated for a moment more, and then, feeling slightly foolish, Lily thrust out her hand, palm down, and clasped Peaches'. Thomas put his hand on top of Lily's; David clasped Thomas'.

"Shut your eyes and wish," said Peaches.

They did, squeezing shut their eyes and holding tightly to one another: *stranger go away.* For a moment, in the silence, it seemed as if their concentrated thought was so powerful that it would have the effect they desired. Then they let go, opened their eyes, and stared at the ring. The stone was pale blue. Knowing better, nevertheless they allowed themselves to hope: maybe, just *maybe*—

But when they trooped back into the house they heard the telephone ringing. Their mother answered it, and they could tell from the way she spoke that she was talking to Neal.

25

✦✦✦✦

AT LAST, CASUALLY, ALMOST AS AN AFTERTHOUGHT, Margaret told her parents about Neal. "It's nothing to get excited about," she said. "I'm just seeing him, that's all."

They wanted to question her: who was he, exactly? From where? Doing what? But they restrained themselves; she was, after all, a grown-up woman and for the moment she would tell them as much as she wanted them to know. Later, if it seemed a serious affair, they would question her in detail—not because they wanted to pry but because they loved her. And because once they had allowed her to marry a man of whom they had not entirely approved, and they had blamed themselves in no small measure for her ensuing unhappiness.

Every other Sunday or so Margaret took the children to dinner at her parents' house. In the old-fashioned way, her parents had Sunday dinner in the early afternoon. On this day, therefore, Margaret announced afterward that she was going to take Thomas to buy him a pair of sneakers; there was a particularly good shoe store nearby, with a good selection and low prices and, right now, a half-price sale.

When they had left, her parents raised the question

of Neal with the other children. They did so in a very low-key, casual way, not openly probing, simply seeming to bring up the subject in passing. Although at one point Lily had wanted to tell them about Neal, now she did not. Telling them, now, seemed like an appeal for help. She did not want their help; not just now, in any case. And, moreover, telling them seemed in some way a betrayal of her mother: and because Lily had not settled for herself the question of whether Margaret was betraying them, she was not yet ready to do the same to Margaret.

"He's all right," said Peaches, meaning Neal. "He's just—"

"Shut up, Peaches," said David. Everyone including himself was startled by his rudeness; they did not speak that way to each other. But he agreed with Lily; this was their own family problem, and even people as close to them as their grandparents had no part in it. Not yet.

26

ONCE EVERY AUTUMN MARGARET TOOK THEM
apple picking. This year, the day before they planned
to go, she said, "I was thinking of asking Neal to come
along. He's never been. But it's up to you."

They thought about it. At last Margaret realized
that they wanted to withdraw to consult in private.

They went to Lily's room. None of them wanted
Neal; none of them wanted to hurt their mother's feelings.

"No," said Thomas.

"All right," said David. "We'll just tell her no."

"She wants him to come," said Peaches. "She won't
have a good time if he doesn't come."

"So?" said David. "We won't have a good time if he
does."

Either way, they understood, the day would be
spoiled, and so they voted, for their mother's sake, to
let Neal join them. They felt pressured: manipulated.

"Maybe it will rain and we won't have to go," said
Lily.

It did not rain. It was a mild, sunny day, a perfect
day to go to the country. The roads were crowded with
Sunday drivers. They went in Margaret's car, since it
had more room than Neal's, but Neal drove. Margaret

sat with him up front; the children sat in back. Anyone seeing them would have thought that they were an ordinary family. The children hated that.

The orchard was crowded, too, when they arrived, but they found a parking space and took their baskets and a ladder and made their way out to the trees. When other people glanced at them, Lily looked away. "He's not our father," she wanted to say. "He doesn't belong with us." But of course she did not.

Neal held the ladder for them, more firmly than their mother could, while they took turns picking. Thomas went first, then Peaches, then Lily, then David. Their mother did not pick; she stood talking to Neal. Now and then she called a cautionary word to them.

While Thomas was waiting for the others to finish, he thought of something that he wanted to tell his mother. He tugged at her hand. She was listening to Neal and so she removed her hand from his and patted him on the head. He understood: he was to wait a minute and not interrupt. While he waited he grew nervous; he was afraid that he would forget all the details of what he wanted to say. Neal went on and on; his mother replied, laughing a little; Neal continued. David was on the ladder; Lily and Peaches were sitting on the grass, waiting, their backs to him.

Suddenly Thomas no longer wanted to talk to his mother; he did not want to talk to anyone. He thought that it was boring, standing and waiting for David to finish; and besides, he did not like to watch his mother talking to Neal.

He took a step away from her. She did not seem to notice. He took another step, and then another. She went on listening to Neal. Thomas turned and ran down the path between the trees. The orchard was filled with people, as crowded as a big department store at Christmas. Thomas ran as fast as he could without bumping into anyone. He reached the entrance to the orchard, ran past the neatly tended rows of shrubs for sale, and ducked into the big open shed filled with apples and cider and vegetables from the adjacent farm. At one side of the shed was a small room, a kind of storeroom. He slipped in, ducked under the high counter at the back, and crouched against the wall. He could feel his heart pounding in his ears. While he had been running he had not been frightened; but now, hiding, he realized that no one knew where he was, and that frightened him very much.

It was David who noticed that Thomas was gone.

"Where's Thomas?" he said when he climbed down.

"He was right here," said Lily. She and Peaches scrambled to their feet.

Margaret froze. This was the eternal fear, this was what you read in the papers: the family on an expedition, every child accounted for, and then suddenly, in the twinkling of an eye, one child missing.

"Mother of Four Loses One..."

She looked around. There were a number of small boys in the orchard, but none of them was Thomas.

"Thomas!" she called. Several people glanced at her. Thomas did not appear.

"David—you and Lily go that way," she said, meaning along the path to the far end of the orchard; and, to Neal, "Will you stay here? Peaches can come with me. He's probably gone back to the car." For the children's sake she kept her voice light, assured, but she heard the fear in it and she thought that from the way they looked at her, they must hear it too.

Neal nodded and gave her a reassuring squeeze on the arm. He was content, in this domestic emergency, to let her take charge.

"Come back to check in here," Margaret called to David and Lily; they waved to show her that they understood. Years ago she had taught them the drill: you had to have a checkpoint, or everyone would wander around for hours missing one another.

Clutching Peaches' hand (more for her own reassurance than for Peaches') she hurried back toward the parking lot. They would probably spot him on the way, she thought. For one awful moment she could not remember what color shirt he had been wearing, and she was embarrassed to ask Peaches. Green, she thought; she was sure it was green.

They reached the lot; they reached their car. No Thomas. Margaret held tightly to Peaches' hand.

"Have You Seen This Child? . . ."

"Let's try in there," she said. They headed for the stalls of produce. People shuffled up and down the aisles. It was a family kind of place: there were many little boys about Thomas' size, and some of them had on green shirts. None of them was Thomas.

"Maybe we should go back to the orchard," said Peaches. "Probably he's back there with them."

"In a minute," said Margaret. She made her way along the aisles, peering underneath the broad selling tables, not caring how odd she looked.

"You lose your dog?" said a large, bluff, friendly looking man.

"Yes," she said. She could not admit to herself, never mind to a stranger, that she had lost her child.

No Thomas.

They left the shed and hurried back to the orchard. Margaret could feel the perspiration running down her face and body. She saw people looking at her. She supposed that she was beginning to look frantic. She did not care. Any minute now, she thought, she would begin to scream. Then, of course, everyone in the orchard would stare at her. She did not care. Neal would think she was not the kind of woman he wanted to be seen with. She did not care.

Neal waited for them alone: no Thomas. Lily and David were running down the path toward them, dodging people as they went. Thomas was not with them.

"Come on," said Neal. "He can't have gotten far. But maybe we'd better get help." He lifted the basket of apples and led the way back. Margaret and the children followed. Her way had failed; now she would let him direct them for a while. She could not speak to the children; she could hardly look at them.

They reached the shed. "Go on to the car," said Neal. "I'll pay for these" (meaning the apples). "And I'll speak to someone. What do you want to do? Do you want to call the police?"

"Yes," said Margaret. She did not, but she could think of nothing else to do. She walked to the parking lot with Peaches and Lily and David. No one said anything. Margaret, hating herself, began to cry. She knew that she should not cry—that her crying would only upset the children and make a bad situation worse. But she could not help it. As she felt the tears well up in her eyes and slip down her face she felt her self-control slip away as well. She saw, as if in a nightmarish film, herself making a scene in the middle of the parking lot: screaming, hysterical.

In the storeroom, Thomas sat under the counter with his back against the wall, his legs drawn up, his head down, forehead pressed against his knees. He did not know how long he had been there, but it seemed a long time. He wanted to leave, to find the others, but he was afraid. He was sure that his mother would be angry. He did not want her to be angry with him—certainly not in front of Neal. The intruder. Because of

Neal, he had run away; now, because of Neal, he was afraid to go back.

He was aware that someone had stepped into the storeroom. Peering out, he saw brown leather shoes and chino pant legs. Another pair of legs—sneakers, blue jeans—came behind. Neal's face appeared under the shelf.

"Hey. There you are."

Neal crouched, held out his hand. Thomas did not take it. Neal smiled; Thomas did not smile back.

"You found a good hiding place," said Neal; and, turning to the person behind him: "He's all right. Thanks very much."

The person to whom he spoke bent to see that Thomas was really there. "OK," he said. "Glad you found him." He straightened and left.

"All right?" said Neal, turning back to Thomas. "Your mom's waiting for you."

He stood up and moved back to give Thomas room to get out. Thomas briefly considered refusing, but he was beginning to be bored; further, he thought that the longer he stayed, the angrier his mother would be.

So he scrambled out, not looking at Neal, and made straight for the door. As he passed he saw that Neal had put out a hand as if to take his. Thomas would have liked very much to take an adult's hand at that moment, but not this particular adult's. He ignored it and hurried outside.

"Look!" said Lily. She pointed toward the shed.

For a moment Margaret was so blinded by her tears that she could not see; the glare of the sun on the row of parked cars shimmered and wavered, and she brushed the back of her hand across her eyes and blinked rapidly and peered where Lily had pointed.

She saw Neal coming toward them. Thomas was at his side.

She went weak with relief. She ran to give Thomas a big hug.

Lily and David and Peaches, following behind, were slightly embarrassed. They knew that their mother had been upset, but they thought that she had overreacted. If any of them ever got lost, it would not be in this way. Even Thomas had too much sense to get lost in a place like this.

They wished that it had not been Neal who found him.

27

PEACHES THOUGHT THAT IT HAD BEEN STUPID OF Thomas, while they were picking apples, to run off in that way, but she held her tongue. She understood, or thought she did, why he had done it: he had been unhappy. Undoubtedly about Neal. She remembered that she herself had threatened to run away, and, guiltily, she thought that perhaps it was she who had put the idea into Thomas' head.

He had been unable to explain why he did it, not to Margaret, not to any of them. He had not, he realized, intended to *run* away; he had merely wanted to *get* away, just for a while, from Neal.

The others would have liked to get away from Neal, too. He came by two or three times a week now, usually to take their mother out but sometimes to spend the evening with her after they had gone to bed; in between he called nearly every night. David's notebook was filling up. Lily's ring, they realized, was useless: their wish had not been granted. She threw it away.

They felt as though they were under siege. The intruder—the enemy—had breached the walls of their castle—their fortress—and had put himself squarely in their midst. Even when he was not with them they sensed his presence: in the sparkle in their mother's eyes, the lilt in her voice, the happiness in her smile. They had always known that they made her happy. Now someone else did.

Naturally they hated him.

When he came they made themselves scarce; the house was big enough to allow them to retreat. If they happened to see him they said as little as possible. They were not rude, exactly, but they were hardly polite.

Their behavior was not lost on their mother.

"Keep trying," advised Barbara Kimball when next she spoke to Margaret. "They'll warm up. It may take more time than you thought, but they'll come around. They're really terrific kids."

"Thomas was trying to send me a message," said Margaret. "I'm sure of it. He didn't get lost. He *hid*. On purpose."

"Probably you're right," said Barbara. "He probably wants to be reassured."

"I *have* reassured him."

"All right, then. That's all you can do. For Heaven's sake, Margaret. You deserve a life too, you know. More than just mothering, I mean. You just have to keep trying."

"There's nothing wrong with mothering."

"Don't get defensive. You know what I mean. Next year this time they'll adore him. By the way, has he done your insulation yet?"

"Not personally. But his crew is here today, as a matter of fact. And the storm windows are coming tomorrow."

"There you are. He's a dependable guy, he runs an efficient business. What are you going to do? Break up with him because of the children? It would be different if he didn't like them or if he was nasty to them. Then you could tell him to buzz off. But he's trying, isn't he?"

"Yes. In his way."

"Which is?"

"Well, he's not stupid. He understands that they haven't exactly welcomed him with open arms. So mostly he just speaks pleasantly to them when he sees them and doesn't try to force it. He let Lily win at checkers and she didn't like it at all. So he knows that the harder he tries the more they'll back off."

"All right, then. My advice is to wait them out. Hang in there. They can't stay mad forever."

But as the days passed, the children maintained their stance: watchful, wary, unyielding.

28

~~~~~~

Halloween came. Next to Christmas, it was their favorite holiday, and Peaches thought that she even preferred it to Christmas because on Halloween you got to dress up and when you went around trick-or-treating people would ooh and aah over how wonderful your costume was.

Peaches' imagination always outstripped the possibilities for costumes. Every year, beginning around Labor Day, she had fantasies of that year's getup: she would be an angel with gossamer wings and a golden halo which would somehow be fastened so as not to slip; she would be a gypsy with several layers of colorful skirts and bangle bracelets up her arm and a dark, flowing wig. One problem with trick-or-treating costumes, however, was that their mother always insisted that they wear their winter jackets over them; never in their memory had a Halloween night been mild enough to go out without being warmly dressed. Some costumes, of course, could be worn over a coat. David always went as a ghost: he simply threw on an old sheet (which he kept and used from year to year) and wore his heavy jacket underneath. But such a costume did not, in Peaches' opinion, fully exploit the possibilities that Halloween offered. And so, every year, she struggled with the problem of being gorgeous and authentic and warmly dressed all at once, and every year her fantasies disintegrated in the face of the reality of the weather.

This year she believed she had solved the problem. She would go, she announced, as the Queen of Hearts. She would wear three sweaters underneath her bright red ankle-length smock, over which she would suspend a sandwich board made of large pieces of poster board decorated (with Lily's help) to look like the playing card. Margaret, understanding Peaches' love of glamor, of dressing up, agreed that Peaches, so costumed, would probably be warm enough, but she reserved a veto until they learned what the weather was to be.

On Halloween they raced home from school to make ready. Lily would go as a tramp—an outfit which she had worn last year and whose appeal lay not only in its ease and comfort, but in its resemblance to some of the more avant-garde fashions which she had glimpsed from time to time on excursions into Boston or in photographs of popular singers. She clapped a battered fedora onto her head, holding up her long hair behind, and peered at herself in the mirror. She felt that perhaps she was getting too old to participate in trick-or-treating. It was a neighborhood custom for the teenagers to accompany the younger children on their rounds, more from friendliness than to relieve any parental fears; it was a safe neighborhood, as safe as any could be. Next year, when she was twelve and in junior high, Lily thought that she would not dress up; she would help with the little ones instead.

She looked in on Thomas. He had inherited a clown costume from the boy across the street, and now, for the first time, he was trying it on. It was too long; its full, floppy pantaloons fell over the tops of his sneakers and dragged on the floor.

"Hitch it up," said Lily.

"I did."

"More."

"I can't."

Lily studied the problem, but she could see no solution. "We'll have to ask Mom if she can fix it," she said. "Did you ask Peaches about the makeup?"

Peaches hated wearing masks. One appeal of her Queen of Hearts costume was that she could dispense with a mask and wear elaborate makeup, including a beauty patch that she had cut from black cloth tape.

"I don't want to wear makeup," said Thomas. "I have a mask—see?" He held a clown's mask up to his face.

"You won't be able to see," said Lily. "Or eat," she added.

"We aren't supposed to eat anything anyway until Mom checks it."

Safe as the neighborhood was, and even though they went only to houses whose inhabitants they knew, Margaret insisted on this precaution.

"You won't be able to breathe, even," said Lily. "I hate masks. Why don't you just draw on a clown face with some of Peaches' lipstick?"

But Thomas shook his head. He was afraid that the makeup would not come off and he would have to go to school with traces of it still showing; he was just beginning to be fully aware of what boys and girls did and did not do because of their sex. Wearing makeup was out of the question.

Margaret had planned an early supper so they could be dressed and on their way by six o'clock; now, before she served it, she hurriedly took a deep tuck around the middle of Thomas' costume. "There," she said, holding it up to him. "That's better. And plenty wide enough for you to wear your jacket underneath. What goes on your head? A clown hat?"

"There's a wig," said Thomas. It was orange, thick and floppy.

Peaches appeared in her red smock, dancing with excitement. "Can I put on my makeup now?" she said.

"Wait until you eat or you'll smear it," said Margaret.

"Then can we eat now? I want to get ready."

"It's only four-thirty," said David. "You'll wreck the cardboard if you put it on too soon. You'll have to stand up. You can't sit down in those cards."

"I don't care. I want to get ready."

At last they had their supper. Then they put on their costumes and waited for Peaches while she finished her makeup. Then they took their UNICEF containers and went to wait on the front porch until their contingent came to pick them up. Already the night was cold. From the darkness beyond the pool of light on the porch they could hear the excited cries and laughter of other hobgoblins making their rounds; now and then they could see little bands of costumed figures. One such group arrived to beg; the Merrills recognized all of them, and exchanged greetings amid much self-conscious laughter.

Finally their group arrived—two teenagers and half a dozen trick-or-treaters—and they were off. Margaret called good-bye, half wishing she could go with them (an unpardonable breach of etiquette), but then the full onslaught of mendicants began to appear and for the next half hour she was preoccupied with attending to them.

In the midst of the heaviest traffic, Neal arrived. She had not been expecting him. He had called earlier in the day; when she had reminded him that it was Halloween, he had said that he would see her the following evening. When he rang the doorbell she answered it with her bowl of candies in hand, and she laughed, surprised and delighted to see him.

"Trick or treat," he said.

"No treat unless you have on a costume," she said.

He grinned, glancing at her offering. "That's a lot of stuff there. You get that many kids?"

"Sometimes more. I always worry that I'll run out."

He watched her, a half-smile on his face, as she dealt with another flurry of callers. Each child, of course, had to be complimented on its costume; some of them wanted to be recognized and, indeed, called out their names, while others did not.

"I think you're enjoying this," he said, laughing, during a lull.

"Of course I am, if I don't think about it too closely. Teaching children to beg, allowing them to get that huge amount of candy, to wander around in the cold and the dark—it's terrible, really, but who am I to call a halt to it? The UNICEF collection is the only part that makes it a remotely acceptable exercise."

A few blocks away the Merrill children were making their rounds. They were part of a group of a dozen or so. Every now and then one of the teenagers would do a head count, but with no sense of concern: no child had ever been lost in this neighborhood on Halloween or at any other time, for that matter.

Peaches trembled with excitement; she skipped along as they went from house to house, feeling in the dark a freedom that she never felt traveling these familiar streets by day. She felt as though she had left her safe, ordered life and had embarked, if only for this one evening, on some otherworldly adventure; and while she enjoyed her life very much, and would not have wanted to change it, she was not sorry to have this brief moment of escape into a fantasy world

of night and costumed familiars and the lurking promise of magical surprise at every corner. Even if the
magical surprise was only a schoolmate got up in a silly
costume.

She was aware that David and Lily were not so
caught up in the evening as she was; it was because
they were older, she supposed. They went along happily enough, laughing and bantering like everyone else
—but that was it, they made a joke of it instead of
taking it seriously. Peaches always took dressing up
and make-believe very seriously indeed.

In the midst of her enjoyment, however, she noticed that Thomas was lagging behind. He was standing under a streetlight, holding open his pillowcase (all
of them used old pillowcases to collect their "treats"),
trying to count how many candy bars and apples and
packs of chewing gum he had collected.

"Come *on*, Thomas," she said, jolted for a moment
out of her delight. "Hurry up. We're almost at Mr.
Ballard's."

"Did you get a Mars Bar?" he said. His thin, anxious face peered out at her from under the orange wig;
he had abandoned the mask and put it in his pillowcase.

"No."

"Here. I have two."

She took it only to forestall argument; she hurried
him along, anxious not to be left behind but more than
that not wanting to break the spell that held them—
held her, at least—under its enchantment.

"Come on!" she cried. She ran through the night,
Thomas pounding after her. A cold wind thrashed
through the bare branches of the trees; the moon
shone through broken, scudding clouds.

They caught up with the others, who were going up
Mr. Ballard's front walk.

"What's wrong?" said David.

"Nothing," panted Peaches. "Thomas was just counting his stuff." She giggled. "I knew he wouldn't want to come here without you guys."

Their visit to Mr. Ballard's house was always the highlight of the evening. He was a man of about sixty-five whose children were grown and gone. Nevertheless he always entered fully into the spirit of the evening; the children knew that when they rang Mr. Ballard's bell they would not be greeted simply by an adult with a UNICEF donation and a handful of candy bars, but by something very different—by an adult who had their own enthusiasm for the occasion.

They went up the steps, crossed Mr. Ballard's spacious front porch, and rang his doorbell. The teenagers waited on the walk below. Although the porch light was on, the house was dark. They understood: Mr. Ballard's house was always dark on Halloween; it was part of his "treat." After a moment they heard a noise: a low, moaning sound that rapidly ascended to a shriek. Then they heard the rattling of chains, the heavy thump of footsteps. As the door swung slowly open, they heard an exaggerated screech of rusty hinges.

The wide reception hall was dark at first, but then a faint blue light appeared.

"Yeeeessss?" came a voice—a low, echoing voice that seemed to emanate from the ceiling. "You raaaaang?"

The children shuffled and giggled at the open door. They knew, more or less, what to expect at Mr. Ballard's; nevertheless it never failed to delight them.

"Perhaps you wanted something?" the voice went on. "Come in, come in!"

They obeyed; only the smallest among them, Thomas included, were nervous about doing so.

"Ah-*hah*!"

Some of the children shrieked in delight, others in real terror, as a glow-in-the-dark skeleton suddenly appeared; it floated over the balustrade and hovered above their heads. It was the size of an adult, marvelously supple, undulating in midair.

"Now you must all tell me your names," said the voice (which did not seem to come from the skeleton), "and then perhaps we can find a little refreshment." A booming, sepulchral laugh filled the cavernous hallway.

There were eleven children in the group; all of them managed to remember their names.

"Goooooood," said the voice. "Very good. Now you may take what you like from my beautiful bride."

This, the children knew, was Mrs. Ballard. She was always costumed the same way, as a witch complete with a hideous green mask and a pointed, wide-brimmed black hat. She appeared from the back of the hall, cackling convincingly, shuffling forward in her billowing black robes. They each took a candy bar from the bowl that she offered them; then they held out their UNICEF containers while she dropped a quarter into each one.

"Good night, children," she cackled, "and happy Halloween!"

Lily thought that it was very sporting of the Ballards to rig up this little show each year. She understood that probably they did it because they enjoyed it: probably they were lonely without their children. It was rather sad when you thought of it that way. Would their own mother be lonely, would she miss them when they, too, had grown up and left home?

They trooped down the Ballards' front steps and continued down the block to the end. Then at last they were done. It was over: time to go home, where, still in their costumes, they would sit with their mother in the kitchen and sort out what they had gotten and weigh their UNICEF boxes in their hands, trying to estimate how much money they had collected. Margaret would have made cocoa for them, and while they drank it they would relate to her the evening's adventures, particularly noting any new wrinkles, so to speak, in the Ballards' performance. Lily enjoyed this part of the evening as much as she enjoyed the trick-or-treating; more, even. Telling their mother what had happened made it seem more real, somehow.

They left their group at the foot of their driveway and ran toward the house. They were laughing, cold and tired though they were, still excited from their adventure, still playing their Halloween parts.

Neal's car was parked behind their mother's.

Although not a word was spoken between them, the children as if at a signal slowed to a walk and suddenly grew sober, their laughter forgotten. They were not, it seemed, even to have their accustomed post-Halloween celebration with their mother without the presence of the intruder.

They climbed the porch steps, their eagerness to see her vanished. She was not at the door to greet them; instead they found her in the kitchen drinking coffee with Neal.

"Well!" she said. "I was beginning to wonder if you'd ever come back!"

They did not believe her; they were sure that she had not given them a thought since they left.

They said hello more to the kitchen than to either of the adults; they did not make eye contact.

"Let's see the goodies," said Margaret. They thought that her voice was a shade too bright, a shade too cheerful.

One by one they allowed her to examine the contents of their pillowcases. As she always did, she made little exclamations of excitement and approval at what they brought back, asking now and again if she could sample something, commenting on this or that.

"What's *this*?" she said, reaching into Thomas' sack, holding up a chocolate cupcake iced with orange icing, covered with chocolate sprinkles, and wrapped in plastic wrap that would, surely, destroy the icing when it was removed.

Since it was obvious what it was, they did not answer that question but another that she did not ask: "Mrs. McIntyre gave them out. She had a whole big platter of them."

"That's odd." Indeed it was, and they understood why: homemade "treats" carried the possibility of poison or imbedded razor blades or ground glass—monstrous "tricks" that, every year, some adults inflicted on some children in other, less civilized communities. Mrs. McIntyre would not do such a thing, of course; but still, she was aware of the fact that prewrapped, store-bought treats were generally considered safer.

Neal took no part in the discussion; he remained to one side looking on. The children ignored him. They felt odd in their costumes—undignified, and somehow at a disadvantage. This was a family ritual; they did not want him included.

"Here's your cocoa," said Margaret, pouring it into the four mugs lined up on the table. They each took one; it was too hot to drink, and so they blew on it to cool it. They did not even want it. They were dispirited, their pleasure in the evening spoiled. Eventually they took a few sips, burning their mouths and throats, and then as soon as they could they said good night and went upstairs.

Lily helped Peaches remove her cardboards so that they would not be bent or torn.

"Shall I put them in the closet?" said Lily

"I don't care."

"Maybe the closet is too crowded. I'd better lean them against the wall. Tomorrow we can wrap brown paper over them and put them up in the attic."

"I don't care."

Lily heard the tears in Peaches' voice. "You can use them again, maybe," she said; but she knew that Peaches would take no consolation from that.

Halloween had been spoiled: for Peaches, for all of them.

"I don't care what you do with them!" Peaches cried. "I just don't care!"

29

THE NEXT AFTERNOON LILY BUNDLED UP HER tramp costume, such as it was, and announced to Margaret that she was going to present it to the boy across the street since none of her siblings would want it.

Margaret looked at her in surprise. "Are you sure? You might want to wear it again next year."

"No. I'm not going out next year—not dressed up, I mean. I'll take the little kids."

It was, as Margaret understood, a declaration of independence, of growing up. She looked at Lily— really looked at her, as opposed to simply making sure that she was tidy, that she did not look ill. She realized that Lily was suddenly beginning to look older—a natural enough thing, since she *was* older, but Margaret had not noticed. Now all at once her eldest daughter seemed a stranger—someone different from the child she had been.

It had occurred to Margaret from time to time that of course her children, like everyone else's, would one day be adults. But she was so accustomed to them as children that she did not seriously consider the prospect. It seemed too remote, too removed from their daily lives, their roles as one adult and four children instead of, inevitably, five adults.

Now she saw that, indeed, Lily's face was changing, losing the look of childhood; she was growing quite tall; she was putting on weight, growing out of the spindly legged child she had been, developing a little bosom. Her hair seemed darker; even her voice, Margaret thought, was darker—deeper and heavier than the childish voice it had been a year ago, or even six months.

Margaret never felt the panic about aging that she had seen in other women. At thirty-two, she felt as she had ten years ago; she was never ill, she had never had a weight problem, she saw no lines on her face, no shadows under her eyes. She had always felt as though her life was ahead of her; it was, she understood, an attitude of youth.

Now, seeing her daughter on the brink of adolescence, next door to adulthood, she felt a ripple of mortality; she felt as though her life had somehow slipped away without her noticing, and that now she was poised at the threshold of middle age, with children who would be grown and gone before she knew, and she herself left alone and feeling vaguely cheated.

Later, after Lily had gone, she thought about the issue some more. She understood that she was, on the whole, more fortunate than not. Her husband's wish to leave her—to leave them all—had been, of course, a crisis of the gravest kind; and yet, unlike most women whose husbands had behaved so, she was very well off. And not just financially well off, either, but emotionally as well. They had survived, she and the children, as a family unit on their own which the infrequent and erratic visits of the children's father had failed to disrupt. They were all healthy; the children did well in school; they had been able to keep their home.

And yet she knew that their lives were incomplete. A family without a husband and father was a lopsided arrangement, difficult for her, difficult in other ways for the children.

"Mother of Four Marries Again . . ."

30

ON A WEEKEND IN EARLY NOVEMBER WHEN THE weather forecast called for sunny and unseasonably warm, Margaret and Neal went to Cape Cod. They were able to go because Margaret's parents had asked, as they occasionally did, if they could take the children for the weekend to visit Margaret's uncle, her father's brother, who lived in Connecticut and bred horses and beagles. He and Margaret's aunt, lacking children, were always happy to see the Merrills; and they, like all children, were always overjoyed to pay a visit to a place that had more animals than people.

It was Saturday morning. The highway was relatively empty; in the summer, traffic sometimes backed up halfway to Boston, but now the road stretched clear and straight before them as if beckoning them to make haste.

Yes, thought Margaret, she wanted to make haste. He drove fast but competently; she would not have wanted him to slow down. She wanted to arrive: in Chatham, where they had reserved a room at an inn near the water. She wondered if they would have lunch first, or if they would immediately fall into bed.

For that, of course, was the purpose of the trip: to fall into bed. This weekend was another step along the way in the journey that they were making together. In every relationship there was a time when either you went forward, you took the next step—or you stopped. Maintaining a relationship was like climbing a series of plateaus; it was not good to get stranded too long on any one of them. You had to keep moving on. Even in marriage. Particularly in marriage. Margaret had no idea how far one could go: her own marriage, her only "relationship," had become stranded on one of those plateaus and had then withered and died.

So far, with Neal, the progression had been about right, she thought. He hadn't pressed her too hard— hadn't made too many demands too quickly on either her person or her time. There had been, in fact, moments when she thought he was going too slowly. But that was all right: better that than too fast. Because of the children, of course, but because of herself as well.

Because of the children they were going to Cape Cod. Because of the children they had been unable and unwilling to move their relationship along to the next stage in the places where they lived: her place or his. As much as she wanted to fall into bed with him— and she did, very much—she had hardly been able to do so in her own home, with the children sleeping (or not sleeping) in the next rooms. And she had been unable to go for that purpose to his place of an evening after a movie, say. A quick stop at his place, a quick tumble in his bed—no.

She had seen where he lived; had been glad, for his sake, that he owned the building. It showed that he had some sense about practical things like money and security; but of course she had known that already because of Energyworks.

She had not expected his apartment to be "decorated" in any way, but she had hardly expected it to be as dreary as it was. Its only redeeming feature was his collection of books: in addition to what they told her about him, they looked good, neatly stacked and arranged on their shelves. They were the "decoration"; certainly nothing else was.

He had asked her, bluntly as was his wont, if she wanted to see where he lived. Yes, she had said; and so one evening after they went out to dinner he had driven her to Dorchester. She had never been there. It was slummy, some of it, but some of it was quite attractive, big old Victorian houses very like the ones in her own neighborhood. When they arrived they were of course completely alone, no stray child to put his head around the door asking for her. And yet they had only kissed: no more. He had not pressed her for more, and she, wanting him, was grateful that he had not. She would probably have given in, and not even given in but quite willingly cooperated. But then she would have felt bad about it afterward, cheap, perhaps, and badly used.

"Cheap" was a word from another era. Nevertheless Margaret kept it in her vocabulary, for it expressed something that was important. One must not, even in this modern day and age, be "cheap." One must price oneself—how? Decently, she supposed. The price of a weekend on Cape Cod, she supposed; Neal was paying.

As casually, as bluntly as he had asked her if she wanted to see where he lived, he had asked her if she wanted to go to Chatham for the weekend. It had taken her only a few seconds to say yes. She understood what he left unsaid: that he, too, wanted to move them along to the next plateau; that he, too, wanted to avoid a quick, easy—too easy—physical intimacy that would lack the necessary time and solitude to give it meaning. Now here she was, here they were, and it was happening. So simple, she thought: so easy.

And yet he was not a simple, easy man. However much she had yet to learn about him, she knew that much already, had known it from the beginning. This weekend should help her to learn a good deal more— about him, and perhaps about herself as well.

She looked at him.

"What's wrong?" he said.

"Nothing."

"You're looking at me."

"I like to look at you."

It was the kind of thing she often said: something that left her vulnerable, something simple and frank, spoken the way a child spoke, without guile. He hated coy women, arch, flirtatious women. He glanced at her and smiled.

His face always had the same expression: stern, almost angry. Even when he laughed she saw the anger. She did not fear it. She understood that much of it came from his intelligence confronting the stupidities of the world. Many intelligent people, of course, were not angry: her father, for instance. But you could not compare the two; they were completely different.

If the weekend went well, she thought, introductions would have to be made. Her parents, particularly her mother, had wanted very much to question her about this trip, but they had refrained. She had briefly considered not telling them where she was going, but in the end, of course, she had had to give them the name of the inn and its telephone number. One did not, when one had children, simply disappear. She was grateful to her parents, both for taking the children and for not interrogating her. As a reward she would introduce Neal as soon as possible and satisfy their curiosity.

If all went well.

They arrived shortly before noon. They were given

a large room with a fireplace, tastefully fitted out with antique furniture that was probably reproduction, but no matter. One of the pieces was a large, four-poster bed. They fell into it.

He was a gentle lover, almost shy at first, and that surprised her. She had thought that he would make love the way he spoke: blunt, direct, occasionally brutal. But he kissed her softly, putting her at her ease; it was as if he understood her nervousness, her awkwardness, and he wanted to reassure her. She was grateful to him. She knew that in this liberated world, men and women both took pride in their sexual skills just as they did in their athletic ones—their tennis, their skiing, their fast, brutal games of squash. Skill was highly sought after, highly prized. But one could not achieve skill unless one practiced, and she, God knew, was badly out of practice in this particular skill. Moreover, even when she had been married, even when she had had more or less regular sexual contact, she had not been self-conscious about it, she had not evaluated her progress. Or, for that matter, her husband's. It had been a normal, natural thing, like breathing: their expression of their love for each other. That was, she supposed, a quaint and stupid attitude—what would once upon a time have been called square. She had never wondered if she had performed satisfactorily; she had never had, until the last, any hint that her husband was unhappy with that or any other aspect of their life together. Now, suddenly, she was aware of her lack of sophistication, in this as in so much else.

"Relax," he said.

"I am relaxed."

"No you're not. You're nervous as hell."

"Aren't you?"

"No. Why should I be? This isn't some kind of performance test."

"No, but—"

"But nothing. How's that? Is that good?"

"Yes."

"And that?"

"Yes."

"You see? Isn't that sweet? Like that?"

"Yes."

He was, she supposed, a skillful and considerate lover. She had so little basis for comparison that she did not want to judge him. For her part, she did not recognize in herself the transports of ecstasy, the animal lust so beloved by the chroniclers of popular fiction, but no matter. She recognized little else in those characters, either. Neal was right: relax and enjoy.

When they were done they lay at peace, content, in the pretty room with the soft white curtains billowing in the warm breeze, so strangely warm for that season, and they studied each other as if they were seeing each other for the first time. As, in a way, they were. He liked the way her mouth, even in repose, looked as if she were about to smile; he liked the width of her face, a little too wide for perfect beauty, perhaps, but it gave her an open look, a look of generous femininity, the cheekbones just prominent enough to give definition, a few freckles scattered across the nose. An open, vulnerable face whose look had nothing to do with weakness.

To her, his face looked not vulnerable but strong. His wide forehead, his deep-set eyes, his rather beakish nose combined to give an impression of someone who knew exactly who he was and what he could do in the world. She liked that; she took comfort in it. Having had to find strength for herself as well as for her children for what seemed a very long time, she thought that it would be wonderfully comforting to be able to turn to someone like Neal Donovan, to draw strength from him.

After a while, hungry, they dressed and went downstairs to have lunch. They were late; the dining room was just closing. So they asked instead for a package of sandwiches and a half bottle of white wine and they walked down to the beach.

The tide was out. They sat on a small dune and watched a few strollers meandering up and down. Several small children ran across the wide expanse of sand, gathering shells, pausing to inspect something— a tiny bubbling hole or a horseshoe crab or something slimy that they did not want to touch. Margaret had a moment of guilt—*I should have brought the children, they would have enjoyed it so*—but she shut her mind to it. Another time she would bring them: this weekend was hers. It had been a long time since she had had a weekend of her own.

When they finished their lunch they walked up the beach. It was a pleasant, Cape Cod beach—quite broad, marked by dunes covered with precious grass to stop erosion, a few low, gray, salt-weathered buildings beyond. It was a spare, almost stark landscape: sky, sea, and sand. In the summer the Cape was so overrun with people that sometimes she wondered that it did not sink into the sea. But now it was nearly deserted: a lover's place. They saw one or two brave souls bobbing in the gentle surf. Even on so warm a day, she thought, the water must be cold. She shuddered.

Neal turned to her and said, "Want to go for a swim?"

"I'll roll up my jeans and wade," she said.

"You didn't bring a bathing suit?"

"I don't own a bathing suit."

"You don't swim?"

"No."

Something in the way she answered pulled him up short. He looked at her questioningly; she looked away, out across the beach to the water. Her face—her wide open, vulnerable face—had suddenly grown tight and tense.

"You never learned?"

"I—I started to."

"And?"

"I had—there was an accident. I just never learned, that's all."

Neal was a practical man. He understood that there were certain things you needed to know—certain skills to get you through your life. Driving, for instance; cooking; the kind of basic household maintenance that he had begun to teach Margaret. Swimming was not the most important thing, but it had its place.

The fact that she did not know how was, he thought, significant. Poor children—children such as he had been—had no access to water. He had not learned to swim until he was in high school, when he had taken the opportunity for lessons at the Y. But children from more privileged backgrounds—children such as Margaret must have been—learned to swim as a matter of course. They had summer camp, summer houses at the beach or near a mountain lake, private schools with swim teams—even certain public schools in the more affluent districts had swimming pools.

"Can your children?" he said.

"Swim? Yes. They've had lessons, off and on."

"Because you think it's a good thing for them to know?"

"Yes."

"But you don't."

"No." She started to walk again. He saw that she did not want to discuss it, and he wanted to know why.

"Don't you think you should? I mean, just as a safety thing."

"I'm never around water much. I don't own a boat or anything."

"Want to learn?"

"To swim?"

He thought that she would not have been more astonished—more appalled—if he had suggested fornicating on the beach. In daylight.

"Sure. Why not? It's a lot simpler than plumbing. Or auto repair."

"Oh, no. No."

He saw that the suggestion frightened her—really frightened her; her reaction was more than aversion or alarm.

"Listen. No—wait, listen." They had stopped. He put his arms around her and felt her tenseness; she would not yield to him, would not embrace him in return. "Tell me about it," he said. "What happened?"

She put her arm through his and they began to walk again. "It was when I was eight years old. I fell into the water. And I couldn't swim. And—" her voice faded; she had never been able to talk about it without the fear coming back, the awful moments when she was still conscious, when she knew that she was about to die, and she was powerless to save herself. She kept going down. She knew that she must hold her breath, she must not inhale the water. "It was in Maine," she said. She heard the high, thin sound of terror in her voice. "We were visiting friends of my parents. There was a dock. And I leaned over too far and fell in. And they almost didn't get me out in time."

She shuddered again—a violent tremor this time. She turned her face away so that he would not see her tears. He put his arm around her shoulders and they walked on. When they reached the path leading back to the hotel he steered her toward it. She looked at him questioningly.

"Will you do something for me?" he said.

"What?"

"Let's walk to Main Street." It was a short distance, perhaps a ten-minute walk to the village center.

"Why?"

"I want to buy you a bathing suit."

"No."

"There's a pool at the hotel."

"No. No, I really don't—"

"Listen." He stopped and took her face between his hands and kissed her. "Let's just try, all right? Just in the shallow end. I'd really like to see you try."

"No." Not if he leaves me, she thought; not if I have to leave him this minute and hitchhike back home.

"Come on." He took her hand and led her along. As if she were going to the gallows she allowed him to do so.

The bathing suit was blue, one-size-fits-all. She did not bother to try it on. All the way back to the hotel she tried to think of some way to explain to him the impossibility of what he was trying to do. She could not learn to swim any more than she could learn to fly—not fly a plane but flap her arms and will herself into the air. But she could think of nothing to say; she had already said no and he had not listened to her.

Neal went to their room to get his trunks. She waited for him in the lobby. While she waited she thought of running away, but she was too frightened even to do that. When he returned she allowed him to lead her to the pool. They changed in the adjacent dressing rooms. *"Mother of Four Drowns in Hotel Pool . . ."* Margaret was trembling so that she had to sit down on a bench for a moment. What, she wondered, was she doing here? Why was she not at home with her children? A Saturday afternoon: Lily would have a friend over, perhaps, or go shopping for a new record. Or she would help David with his tree fort, which seemed to need almost as much maintenance as the house. Or the four of them would tackle some project. They got on well together, they enjoyed each other's company. She missed them very much. She had been wrong to come away from them, and now she was being punished. Now she had to walk out of this dressing room and get into a swimming pool and drown, and she would never see them again. No, she thought, I cannot do this. It is impossible. A woman coming in, dripping wet, looked at her oddly. Margaret got up and walked out to the pool. It was a huge room that reeked of chlorine, filled with echoing sounds, patterns of watery light reflected on the high, arching ceiling.

Neal was waiting for her. His hair was wet, plastered to his skull. He had swum a length while he waited. Now he stood at the waist-deep shallow end and held out his hands to her.

Her knees were so weak that she could hardly stand. She sat on the edge. It was all right: even if she fell in she could touch bottom and not drown.

"Mother of Four Drowns in Three Feet of Water . . ."

"Come on," he said. "Just jump in."

"What are we going to do?" she said. She realized that she did not know him well enough to know whether he would try some trick on her.

"Whatever feels comfortable. Come on."

She slipped in. The water was pleasantly warm. He smiled at her encouragingly. "The suit looks good."

He stood back a little so that she had to walk through the water to reach him. She understood that he had no idea how terrified she was. Her legs were very weak; it was difficult to walk in the water, hard to move them.

"OK." He took both her hands. "Now relax. Just relax." She was holding on very tight. "Now. We're just going to duck and get wet. Very fast." She went partway down but she did not get her face wet. He didn't insist. He kept hold of one hand and walked her to the tiled coping.

"Hold on the the edge—like this—and stretch out and float." He demonstrated; his body floated, face down; his fingers just brushed the tile. Then he straightened beside her. "Now you try. That's called the dead man's float, just to cheer you up."

She could not do it; she could not take her feet off the bottom. Any minute now, she thought, he is going to lose patience with me and walk out—now, today— and that will be that. No weekend, no more love affair.

"Mother of Four Abandoned in Chatham . . ."

He began to understand her terror. "All right," he said. "I'll hold you. I'll stretch my arms underneath your stomach. You'll feel them. I'll hold you up in the water. Just stretch out. And put your face in the water for a couple of seconds. Relax. It's all right. Just relax. I'm right here. I won't let go."

And so, gently encouraging her, he coaxed her along; and after a while, against her better judgment, she did it. He kept his promise: he did not take his arms away. Three times they did it, and each time she was able to keep her face in the water a little longer. The last time he told her that he was going to ease his arms away when she signaled to him: he would watch her hands gripping the tile, and when she raised her right index finger he would lower his arms an inch or two. But they would still be there to catch her if she began to sink.

She did it: she felt herself float. Then, panicked, she

stood up, shaking the water from her face. But it was all right. She had done it once; she could do it again. It was enough for the first lesson. They got out and showered and changed and went back to their room where again they made love.

Margaret understood that he was trying to be kind to her. The plumbing, the auto repair, the swimming —obviously he cared about her or he wouldn't bother. And of course he was right: these were things—survival things—that everyone should know. She did not mind learning them; she did not mind his taking her in hand, so to speak, and teaching them to her. She had fallen in love with a man who cared about her enough to bully her a little for her own good, and that was all right, it was far better than indifference. She realized that she felt safe with him. She could not imagine a problem that he could not solve.

Safe enough for a lifetime?

Yes, she thought: even that.

They slept a little; when they awoke it was nearly dark, only a last narrow pink-orange swath between sky and land at the horizon. They were not yet ready to dress and go out again, so Neal called room service and ordered a vodka martini and a Coke and a plate of Camembert and crackers. When the order came, Margaret went into the bathroom because she had forgotten to bring her bathrobe. She did not own a negligee.

They had their drinks in bed because now, with the darkness, it was growing chilly even with the window closed. They turned on a lamp; they smiled at each other, delighted with each other, their bodies for the moment content.

"Am I forgiven?" he said.

"For what?"

"For insisting that you learn to swim. Or at least try to learn."

She nodded. "Yes."

"Of course I was right, but I didn't have to insist. I could have let it go. But I'm not a procrastinator. I see something that needs doing, I do it."

"Yes."

He kissed her. "Like that. That needed doing. Why are you looking at me that way?"

"What way?"

"A little sad. You certainly don't look very cheerful for a woman who's just been royally—uh—pleasured. But maybe you weren't? Are you trying to tell me you're dissatisfied?"

She laughed, but there was sadness in her eyes and he saw it. "No," she said. "No, I'm certainly not dissatisfied."

"What are you thinking?"

"That this is very nice. Cozy. A nice change of pace."

"Not your ordinary weekend pastime."

"Hardly."

"Tell me—if you don't mind a little personal talk— am I the first man you've dated since your divorce?"

"Yes."

Her answer made him a little uneasy.

"Why?" he said.

"I haven't met anyone I like. I don't have much chance to meet men anyway. I lead a sheltered life."

There it was again: her openness, her willingness to be vulnerable—which was, he realized, a kind of strength. Most people, men and women both, barricaded themselves behind layers of defenses.

"You know—" He paused; he wanted to proceed with caution. "You want to be careful."

"What do you mean?"

"I mean, it's a big bad world out there. You want to take good care of yourself."

"But I do."

"No, you don't. Look—you went out with me, didn't you? I was a perfect stranger. You didn't know who the hell I was."

"I knew. I trust my instinct."

"Aaahhh—" He shook his head. Instinct!

"What are you trying to tell me?" she said.

"I'm trying to tell you to take care of yourself."

"Thank you. I do."

"I don't want anything to happen to you."

"You mean anything bad."

"Anything bad, right."

"Because you've happened to me, and I think you're good. A good thing, you are."

"Do you think so? You still don't know me."

"I know you well enough."

"You should get to know some other men."

She stared at him. "Well, isn't this romantic? I go away for a weekend with a man I happen to—with an attractive man, and he tells me to go out with someone else."

"That's not what I said."

"Yes it is. What are you trying to do? Let me know that you've lost interest?"

"No. Not at all. Just the opposite, in fact."

She watched him; she held his eyes with hers. He could not be pushed: she knew that much, at least. And so she decided to end on that small victory. She got up and dressed. They decided to walk to the wharf for dinner, some place less formal than the hotel dining room. They sat next to a window looking out over the dark water streaked with lights from the shore; they had tiny, delectable broiled scallops and good crisp french fries. Afterward they went to an ice-cream parlor for hot-fudge sundaes and then walked slowly, contentedly back to the hotel. It had become quite chilly; a full moon shone. She put her arm through his. It seemed the most natural thing in the world, the two of them: she could hardly remember a time without him.

And it seemed, further, that if he felt the same way, and if he said so, she would have no choice but to agree. Yes, she would say, yes, you are right, we get along very well, I'm so glad you noticed.

He spoke then, startling her.

"Have you ever thought of marrying again?"

She held her breath. "Yes," she said.

"It doesn't scare you? I mean, after your experience?"

"No."

"You'd do it if the right man came along?"

"Of course. Wouldn't you?"

"The right man?"

"You know what I mean."

"I suppose so. I'm all right the way I am."

She wanted to tell him about the surveys that showed that married men lived longer, but of course she did not.

"You see," he went on, "you have the advantage over me. You've been married. You know what it's like. For me, it would be a brand new experience. I mean, how would I know until I got married whether I liked it or not? And then it would be too late."

She understood what he was trying to say: "I am not a marrying man." He meant it, she knew, as a kindly warning: Don't get your hopes up.

Very well, she thought; I have been warned. Forewarned is forearmed.

She thought of the years she had survived on her own since Richard left her. But of course she had not been on her own; she had had the children. And if she had been their means to survive, they had been hers as well. Now they would simply go on, all of them together.

All the same she felt suddenly desolated.

She and Neal made love again that night, and she was interested to observe of herself that she took less pleasure in it than before. She thought of Barbara Kimball and her many affairs.

She realized that she, Margaret, was a very different kind of woman. She was not capable of having "affairs"; she needed a sense of permanence, she needed commitment.

And because she needed to believe it, she told herself that Neal's commitment surely would come.

The next morning she had another swimming lesson. She did the dead man's float for two minutes, well away from the edge of the pool but still in shallow water. It was enough: a good beginning. She promised him that she would enroll for swimming lessons at the Y.

He promised her nothing.

After lunch they drove to Nauset Beach and walked for a while next to the surf. As far as they could see, huge breakers rose and thundered onto the shore. A permanent mist hung in the air along the edge of the water, and the sound of the breaking waves was so loud that you had to shout to be heard. Despite the parking lot and the uniformed National Park Service attendants, Margaret felt that this was a wild place untouched by civilization. Here you were able to sense, as you could in few other places, the power and barely withheld fury of the Atlantic. Like nearly everyone else, Margaret lived apart from Nature; most of the time she neither noticed nor cared. Here at the edge of the sea, which even on a calm day like today thundered onto the shore in great endless breakers, she felt properly humbled, herself and her life properly put into perspective: what did her little existence matter, compared to this?

It was not, however, a perspective which lasted beyond the time she left the beach and the pounding surf and climbed back into Neal's car for the return trip.

She had no idea, when he dropped her off at her house early that evening, whether she would ever see him again.

31

⤞⤞⤞⤞

"Swim?" said Margaret's father. "Margaret?"

"That's quite an achievement, Mr. Donovan," said Margaret's mother. "Congratulations."

"It was just the first step," said Neal. "The instructor will do the rest."

"But she never would have taken that first step without you," said Margaret's father.

"Probably not."

Samuel Wilson Brigham and his wife gazed fondly at Margaret. Even though she had been grown up for so many years, they often still thought of her as a child, someone who needed help and encouragement. And guidance—certainly guidance. They were glad, at last, to meet the man who had come into her life, to be able to begin to assess him.

Margaret and Neal had gone to an early movie; when she suggested that they stop by her parents' house afterward he had readily assented. She was curious to see how they would react to him, and, more, he to them. So far, she thought, everyone seemed content.

Everyone who met Margaret's parents realized very quickly that they were an almost idyllically happy couple. Even after thirty-five years of marriage, they still adored each other. They gave a sense of inhabiting their own world, a special place where no one else—not even Margaret—was allowed to enter. There was nothing rude about them, no arrogance or condescension. But even after all those years they were enveloped in a cocoon of love for each other so strong that it was almost palpable. They gave no offense, but it was obvious to all who knew them that their lives revolved around each other, and that either, without the other, would be lost.

Neal sensed this at once; like most people he was not offended by it but rather almost charmed. As he sat with them this evening, however, and with Margaret, and chatted amiably of this and that the way people do when they first meet, he began to get a sense of something else that had bothered him before when Margaret had talked about it, and now bothered him again. Just as the Brighams' love for each other was evident, so was their love for Margaret—and hers, of course, for them. Inevitably Neal's own childhood, his relations with his own parents—harsh, bitter, distant—was thrown into unpleasant contrast.

They did not stay long; when they left, Margaret's parents invited him to dinner "sometime"—the kind of offer intended to show civility without going overboard.

In the car she said, "I told you they'd be pleased about the swimming. Daddy tried and tried, but he never could get me back into the water. I was the only one of all my friends who never went to camp."

There had been, of course, no camp for Neal.

"You had a deprived childhood," he said; she heard the sarcasm in his voice.

"Of course I didn't. I had a wonderful childhood. It was—I don't know—sunny. Whenever I think of that

time I see it with a kind of golden haze around it. I
don't mean to say that there weren't bad times, like
the time I fell off the dock. But it was generally pretty
happy. I didn't realize it until I got a little older, when I
was in high school, and my friends' parents started
having troubles. Or when I got to college and I met
people who'd had illness all their lives, or some terrible accident. Or rape, or—my God—*incest*. We didn't
talk about incest then but people talk about it now and
you know it must have been happening all along. Or
the girl who'd grown up with a father who beat her
mother all the time. All kinds of things."

"You were lucky."

"I know."

But she did not know: how could she? She did not
know about bitter fights and cold apartments and not
enough money, ever—not for shoes, not for food,
not even for the rent. She did not know about parents
who had forgotten that they ever loved each other,
whose emotions had become so frozen that they could
not even show their love for their child. He realized
that it was not her fault that she did not know these
things, and yet he resented her for it.

Moreover, he was more than a little bit in love with
her. He resented her for that, too. He had not meant
to fall in love with her; it had not been part of his plan.
He had simply wanted to explore her, as one explores
new terrain: interesting, but one wouldn't necessarily
want to live there.

Being in love, even a little way in love, opened to
him possibilities that existed for other men; he had not
thought that they existed for him. Possibilities of tenderness, of commitment, of an end to his isolation—
an end to his freedom. He treasured his freedom, or at
least he thought he did; he did not want to lose it, or at
least he thought he did not. He had come to the edge

of his shell and peered out; now, touched, terrified, he withdrew from what it was that had touched him, he sought his isolation once again.

After he said good night to Margaret, he stopped to see Jason Goodrich at The Rising of the Moon.

32

∽∾∾∾∾

"Would I steer you wrong?" said Jason. "Would I? Come on. I *know* you, Neal. I know you as well as I know myself. This girl is a dream. Brenda? Forget Brenda. This girl is better. She's been through EST. Her autonomy is intact. She's just a terrific date, that's all."

Neal wavered for a while and then he took the telephone number that Jason dangled so enticingly before him. He wavered for a while longer and then he dialed it. Jason had described him, had prepared his way; the young lady was delighted to hear from him.

On the following Saturday night he took her out. She was moderately amusing, flip and hard and confident—everything that Margaret was not. Her name was Karen. She was a marathon runner; she was in middle management at a major bank; she owned not only the condominium in which she lived but also two others which she had bought for appreciation and tax deductions. She had an American Express Gold Card and an investment portfolio.

Three nights later he took her out again. With her, he felt no tenderness, no commitment—no threat to his freedom.

He did not call Margaret for several days, and when several days more had passed, he did not call her because he did not want to have to explain why he had not called her.

And she did not call him.

33

~~~~~~

And so the children's wish came true: as abruptly as Neal Donovan had dropped into their lives, he dropped out again. He disappeared. He never came to visit; he never called. Thanksgiving came and went and still he did not call.

Once—just once—Margaret called him, but when she heard his answering tape she hung up without speaking.

It was inconceivable to her that he had simply abandoned her. To make sure that he had not been injured, that he was not ill, she called the Energyworks office and asked to speak to him. As the secretary was putting through the call Margaret hung up; she had discovered what she wanted to know. He was there, he was alive.

The worst of it was that she had so much that she wanted to tell him. Particularly about the swimming: she was still only in the beginners' class, of course, but she was doing it two mornings a week, she was making progress, however slow.

The children had been astonished when she told them she was taking swimming lessons. They had always understood that she, unlike most people they knew, did not swim. It was a personal eccentricity:

some people did not like airplanes, some did not like elevators or high places. Their mother did not like to swim. Now, all of a sudden, she did—or, at least, she was trying to. When they asked her why, she had said something about how she thought it was high time. They did not believe her. They knew that there must be more to it than that.

Margaret hated swimming, of course—hated every minute of it, the panic she still experienced, the coldness of the water, the exhaustion when she was done. But she was persevering, more for Neal than for herself: because she had promised him that she would, because she had too much pride to quit.

She had been afraid that he would no longer care for her if she quit; and now, it seemed, he no longer cared for her in any case.

As the days passed and she realized that he was probably not going to call again ever, she began to cry herself to sleep at night. Once Lily woke up and heard her. She did not recognize the sound at first; when she did, she was frightened by it—too frightened to get up and go to Margaret and ask her what was wrong. The children were alarmed, the next morning, at Margaret's appearance at breakfast. She came down red-eyed, pale, her pretty face looking years older. Her hair was stringy because she had not washed it in days; she had on a pair of old jeans and a paint-smeared shirt. Her nail polish was chipped, her nails ragged.

Lily would not have needed to get up in the night and ask her mother what was wrong. She knew; they all did. They saw Margaret's woebegone face, her false cheerfulness, her inattention. Lily told David, but not the younger two, about Margaret's crying. David agreed that there was nothing they could do, but he told her to wake him if she heard it again.

At Thanksgiving dinner, Margaret's parents offered

one tentative question (really more of a comment) about Neal, and then, understanding that they had made a mistake, that neither Margaret nor the children wanted to talk about him, they let it go.

David and Lily, in particular, tried not to reveal to their grandparents how worried they were about their mother. She seemed to have changed very much; she had withdrawn, somehow, and even though she was with them all the time, she was apart as well. She seemed wounded: fragile. As if she were in great pain. They wanted very much to help her, to comfort her, but they did not know how.

They understood, however, that Neal was responsible for her trouble—that he had hurt her in some way. He had no right to do that. Their mother was very dear to them, they loved her very much, and they deeply resented the fact that this man who had intruded on their lives, thereby hurting them, had now withdrawn, thereby hurting their mother. Before, they had been angry with him on their own account; now they were angry on hers. They would have been glad to see him again, would have been glad to offer their mother for an evening with him, if his presence would cheer her up.

Only Thomas felt differently: Thomas was glad that Neal was gone. Now, he thought, his mother had more time for him again.

Nevertheless he liked to hear the others plot revenge.

34

"WE COULD BLOW UP HIS APARTMENT," SAID Peaches.

"We don't even know where he lives," said David.

"He's in the phone book." And she got the book and showed them. "Remember he said you could get there on the Red Line?"

"We could send him a nasty letter," said Lily.

"*That* wouldn't help," said Peaches. "He probably wouldn't even read it."

"We could booby-trap his car."

"Or kidnap him."

"Or sneak in and poison his food."

"We could tie him to a stake and shoot arrows at him."

"Or throw him out of an airplane."

"Or just—*splat*! Run him down."

So they plotted. They understood that such things would never come to pass, but their fantasies gave them comfort: made them feel, marginally, less helpless.

"I hate him," said Lily. "I *hate* him." She felt better for saying it, but she said nothing more because she was afraid that she was going to cry.

Peaches nodded. She hated him, too. Her usual

good nature had vanished; she was angry much of the time now, and frightened as well. Like the others, she knew who was to blame for all their unhappiness.

It was inconceivable to them that they could do nothing to help their mother. They had always understood that they were helpless in the face of adult power, but never before, not even when Neal first appeared, had they wanted so desperately to have some power of their own.

One day, in the midst of a War Council, Peaches went to her room and told them not to disturb her; she would be back in a while, she said. Before she withdrew she went around collecting things: the straight-edged shears, and the sewing box, and several cotton balls from the bathroom, and a few items from the catchall drawer in the kitchen. Peaches was handy; she could make clothing for her dolls, and she could embroider and even knit a little. She was imaginative, too: with a few scraps of cloth, or just an old sock, and yarn and a little stuffing, she could make a quite presentable doll. In addition to the good, store-bought dolls that she received for Christmas and her birthday, and two that she had inherited from Margaret, she had a number of homemade dolls on a special shelf in her room, each with its own name and personality and history ("this one I made when I had the chicken pox; this one I made last summer when it rained for a week").

So it did not surprise them when eventually she emerged with a small doll. It was, however, different from all her others. They were either beautiful or homely, but all of them had attractive personalities.

This one did not. This one was undeniably an unpleasant doll. Its skeleton was an old-fashioned wooden clothespin on which Peaches had made a cloth body padded with cotton balls. She had added a Popsicle stick for arms, and those were padded, too. With a fine-tipped marking pen she had made an ugly, frowning face on the clothespin's wooden head, and she had glued on bits of black yarn for hair. The body was a bit plump, but Peaches had known what she was doing. She had outlined a small red heart over the doll's chest. Into a scrap of extra cloth she had stuck four round-headed pins.

"Here," she said, offering the pins and holding the doll for them to see. "Take a pin."

"What's that?" said Thomas.

"A voodoo doll. It's him. Wherever we stick a pin in, he'll hurt."

Thomas was intrigued; Lily and David were, at least, impressed by Peaches' ingenuity and clever workmanship.

"Come on," said Peaches. "Let's try." She took a pin; then Thomas did; then Lily and David. Peaches was a generous soul; she offered to let the others go first, but she hoped they would save the heart for her. On the other hand, she thought, two pins or even three or four, all stuck in the heart, might be more effective. Depending, of course, on what results they wanted. If all four of them struck the heart, she was sure that Neal would die.

Thomas hesitated. "What if I want to put it in the head? There's no place to stick it."

"You can't put it in the head, that's all," said Peaches. "Just the arms or the body."

Thomas screwed up his face, thinking hard. They held their pins, not talking, letting him concentrate. It seemed to them that in their silent little circle, in the intensity of their concentration, a kind of power was building: they held not a crude little doll but Neal himself, and they were determining his fate. They respected that power: they would not treat it lightly.

"There," said Thomas. He stabbed his pin into the stomach.

Peaches giggled nervously. "Your turn," she said to David.

David licked his lips; his hand was trembling a little as he took the doll but he got the pin in right the first time—a good hard jab into the upper arm. There. He felt better.

They stared at the ugly little creature. It seemed to have become a living thing, even though it lay so small and inert in their hands.

David handed it to Lily. She felt a little sick. What were they doing, she thought. This was a silly game, a waste of time, and there was something very wrong about it, too.

"Go on," said Peaches. She was impatient; she wanted her turn. She giggled again.

Lily thought about her mother: how oddly she had behaved all fall, how visibly unhappy she was now. None of that would have happened but for Neal. Lily remembered the day she had first seen him. She had been looking for the enemy and she had found him: he had walked right into their lives. And now, apparently, he had walked out again. Both times had meant trouble—all Neal's fault.

And perhaps, after all, this wasn't a game: perhaps it would indeed have some effect on him.

Suddenly she hoped so. Suddenly she wanted to hurt him as he had hurt their mother. Oh, yes—she hated him all right.

She pressed her lips tightly together in hard concentration; she held the pin firmly; she plunged it into the doll's heart. *There.*

And now at last it was Peaches' turn, and she, too, stabbed into the heart. Afterward she held the doll out on the flattened palm of her hand for them all to see: a thing of cloth and wood bristling with four pins; and it seemed to them that those wounds must surely hurt, must surely be felt, somewhere, somehow, by the subject for whom they were intended.

35

❧❧❧

"WE HAVE TO FIND OUT," SAID DAVID.

"We have to see him," said Lily. "How else will we know?"

"How can we do that?" said Peaches.

"We'll call him up," said David. He paused; he was making it up as he went along. "And we'll ask him—"

"How he feels," said Peaches.

"No. He wouldn't tell us the truth, anyway. We have to *see* him."

"We can't ask him to come here," said Lily in a warning tone; she did not think that David would suggest anything so stupid, but she wanted to be sure.

"I know. I wasn't going to."

"What, then?"

"We'll call him up, and we'll ask him—ah—to meet us somewhere."

"He won't."

"Yes he will. If we tell him—"

"If we tell him it's a secret and we want him to help us," said Peaches. "I bet he will."

"And then what?"

"Then—we'll see. We'll see if he's sick or something."

"And what if he isn't?"

"Then—we'll do something else to him. I know what, we'll meet him in a store or something, and we'll start screaming that he was trying to kidnap us. Or—or molest us." Peaches was not sure exactly what molesting was, but she had been cautioned against it at school and in a recent television program that she had happened to see. Molesting and abusing were both very bad things, she knew, and they were things that grown-ups did to children. Neal would not want to be accused of them.

Lily did not think that it was a very good plan, but she could think of nothing better, and so at last she agreed. She and David and Peaches drew lots to see who would make the call, it being obvious that Thomas would not do well on the telephone with Neal.

David drew the short slip.

"When d'you want to call him?" said Peaches.

"Right now, I guess."

It was a Sunday afternoon. Their mother was having a cup of coffee with a friend in the kitchen. David would use the upstairs phone, therefore, which was in Margaret's bedroom. Lily and Peaches would stand by to give him moral support, and Thomas would stand watch in the hall.

"Don't talk if you get the answering tape," cautioned Lily.

"I won't."

He looked up the number and dialed. To his surprise, Neal answered.

Neal was surprised, too. He had thought that he might hear from Margaret again, but he had not expected one of her children to call him.

When he heard what David wanted, he hesitated. He would not have minded seeing Margaret again if he thought that she bore him no ill will (which she probably did, he admitted), but he was not eager to see her children. But something in the boy's voice gave him pause. A certain urgency, as if there were more on his mind than he could say on the phone. In the end, Neal's curiosity got the better of him. He said that he would meet them at three the following Saturday afternoon, downtown at the corner of Washington and Summer streets, on the Jordan Marsh side.

David hung up and nodded to the others. "OK," he said. He told them when and where, and then Peaches said, "What'll we tell Mom?"

"We'll tell her—we'll just tell her we're going Christmas shopping," said Lily.

"She won't believe us."

"Yes, she will. We went last year."

"Not Thomas."

"He's old enough now."

Margaret was in fact quite happy to have them use the public transportation system, at least the Green Line, which ran a safe route from their pleasant, peaceful suburb into the city. Lily and David knew exactly where to get on and off, how to deal with subway tokens, how not to talk to strangers. They even knew the more difficult skill of not making eye contact. And so on Saturday when they announced to her that they were all going downtown together she agreed to it, simply adding the automatic warning that they were not to separate, that Thomas was not to be allowed to stray, and that they were to be home by five at the latest. She did have a brief moment of doubt: Thomas was too young for such an expedition, surely? She remembered the afternoon in the orchard, and for a moment she thought that she must say no. But they were set on going; there were so many more dangers for children nowadays, it seemed, than there had been when she was a child, and she wanted to encourage their independence in any way she could. Subway lines to other areas were not always safe, even for adults, but there was no danger on the Green Line in the daytime.

She suggested, idly, that she might accompany them; her own Christmas shopping was badly behind schedule. She would go with them on the trolley and then separate; they would meet again to go home.

But they said no. She thought that they were oddly vehement in their refusal of her company, but she took no offense; they wanted to go on their own and she sympathized with that desire, she understood it. Perhaps they were going to buy a present for her. She knew that they put a great deal of time and effort into selecting her presents, and she could hardly spoil their surprise. They were good, dependable children; they would be all right.

When the children had gone to make ready for their expedition, Margaret returned to her conversation with Barbara Kimball.

"What are you going to do?" she said. "Break off with him?"

Barbara's eyes widened in alarm. "I couldn't do that," she said. "Not now. Don't you see, Margaret? It's too soon. It hasn't resolved itself yet."

"You mean you want to suffer some more." Margaret thought of herself and of her own suffering. A clean break, a swift, almost surgical amputation: there had been a good deal of pain—more, she assumed, for herself than for Neal—but in many ways it seemed preferable to the tortuous, lingering agony of Barbara's affair with Craig McCarren. On again, off again —why couldn't Barbara simply be done with it?

"I mean I love him," said Barbara. "I don't think that's ever happened to me before. Never. Not in any situation, any relationship, that I've ever been in."

How did she know, wondered Margaret; but of

course that was a question that she could not ask. Trying to be tactful, she refrained from mentioning Barbara's two marriages: what had they been, if not love? Needing to say something, however, she said, "Does he know that?"

"Yes."

"And he's told you—"

"He's told me that he doesn't want commitment. He misjudged me, he says. He thought I was a—a pleasant interlude. He didn't understand that beneath this gorgeous exterior"—she laughed in a self-deprecating way—"there beats the heart of a simple, old-fashioned girl."

She shrugged; she gave a long, exasperated sigh. "So here I am. Hooked. Done for. Three men asked me out last week. I couldn't even think of going out with someone else. Ridiculous, isn't it?"

Yes, thought Margaret, it was; but she kept her opinion to herself.

"And what about you?" said Barbara after a moment. "What about—what was his name?"

"Neal Donovan," said Margaret. It sounded odd, like the name of a stranger, or someone she had known long ago.

"Are you still seeing him?"

"No. It was—well, it didn't amount to much." She was pleased that her voice was steady; she met Barbara's glance without flinching.

Barbara nodded sympathetically. "You're lucky," she said. "Sometimes I think they're not worth it. The bastards."

"Yes," said Margaret, "I am. Very lucky."

As she spoke she realized that what she said was true: she was lucky. She felt as though a weight had suddenly lifted from her heart; she felt as though she was on her way to being well again, recovering from a painful and mysterious illness that no doctor knew how to cure.

She smiled at her friend, wishing her well, wishing her, if not happiness, then tranquility at least; and then, hearing the children on the stairs, she went out to bid them good-bye, to caution them to be careful, to experience one more time the rush of love and pride and joy that seeing them always gave her.

Yes: she was nearly cured of her affliction. Christmas was coming, and the New Year: a fresh start. As she watched them troop down the driveway she felt happier than she had in weeks.

36

A LARGE, CHEERY SANTA CLAUS WAS RINGING A
bell for his collection at the corner of the Common,
and crowds of people hurried back and forth. Up the
slope toward Beacon Street was the Christmas display,
a large crèche and a few sheep in a pen. Lights were
strung on the leafless trees; when darkness came they
would blossom into webs of color, red and blue and
green and gold, but now, in the afternoon, the trees
and the Common as well looked bare and drab, not
Christmassy at all.

Lily did not mind; she was not in a holiday mood.
As they crossed Tremont Street and plunged into the
throng of shoppers she realized that she felt oddly out
of place. Ordinarily she loved to go Christmas shopping, even if she didn't buy anything: the crowds, the
displays in the stores, the sense of excitement—only
eight more days until Christmas! But now she felt estranged. Her presence downtown today had nothing to
do with Christmas, nothing to do with peace and joy
and goodwill, or buying presents for people she loved.
In an alleyway a man was selling bits of pine bough
tied with red ribbon, and small evergreen wreaths
were sprayed with white stuff. At this same place, last
year, her grandmother had bought her a little

Christmas corsage. Lily would not have wanted one now; she would have felt wrong, somehow, pinning it on. She felt uneasy; more than that, she felt angry and apprehensive and thoroughly out of sorts with the day. Christmas seemed foreign to her now; it was something for other people, not for her. Not for any of them. They were not bent on a Christmas errand.

"What if he's not there?" said Peaches.

"We'll wait," said David.

"I don't want to wait," said Thomas. "I'm hungry."

"You just had lunch."

"I want a pretzel."

Street vendors were selling big, soft pretzels and roasted chestnuts and hot dogs.

"No, Thomas. Come *on*."

These few downtown streets were barred to traffic, and so pedestrians walked at will, spilling over the curbs, filling all the available space. In the intersection two mounted policemen watched the crowds, chatting in a friendly way with people who came up to pat their horses. Lily wondered if it was against the law to make a voodoo doll. Or perhaps it was all right to make one, and you broke the law only when you stuck in the pins.

They reached the corner where they were to meet Neal. He was not there. The younger children wanted to walk up and down a bit to look at the store windows, which were filled with exquisite, nineteenth-century Christmas scenes: a Christmas tree hung with gingerbread men and tiny, antique toys; gorgeously costumed mannequins with moving heads and arms, their faces frozen into eerie smiles. One window was an outdoor scene, with a miniature train that went around and around, and snow that fell evenly, endlessly, untouched by a breath of wind. Christmas carols blared from loudspeakers; more Santas clanged their big brass bells; a Salvation Army lady looked as thought she might freeze to death.

They walked up and down, looking at the windows, keeping the corner in sight; Lily and David kept looking back to see if Neal had arrived. He had not. People hurried by, laden with packages and overflowing shopping bags. Lily was getting dizzy looking at so many faces. Not many people looked happy, she thought; mostly they looked worried. It was expensive to buy Christmas presents. If you had a lot of people to buy for, you didn't want to hurt anyone's feelings by buying something that seemed less expensive than what you bought other people. Margaret told them, every Christmas, that it was the thought that counted. Not many people seemed to believe that; spending money seemed to be the thing to do.

"I'm cold," said Peaches. She had on her bright red parka and a white hat with red pom-poms which Margaret had knitted for her. Margaret had knitted white mittens to match, but Peaches seldom wore them because she was afraid that she would lose them.

"Go inside, then," said Lily. "You can stand just inside the door, there, and when he comes you'll see him and you can come out."

Peaches felt that she would miss some of the excitement, the tense, shared anticipation if she went alone; the others did not want to go, so she stayed with them.

They waited. Hundreds—thousands—of people thronged the streets. Patiently they searched for Neal. Lily thought that one of the policemen was staring at them. Perhaps he thought they were lost; perhaps he would come over and ask them if they were all right. He would ask them their names, and where they lived; perhaps he would even call their mother. She turned her back on the policeman, willing him to ignore her.

Finally David said, "I guess he's not coming."

"What time is it?" said Peaches.

There was a big clock with roman numerals on a tall post across the street.

"Three-thirty," said David.

"Maybe he took the trolley and it broke down," said Lily. She had been stuck on the Green Line once for an hour and a half in the summertime. The car had been packed and it had gotten very hot. "Let's wait a little longer and see."

"Then what?" said Peaches.

"Then we'll just have to go home, I guess."

It occurred to her that somehow Neal knew what they were up to. It would be very embarrassing if he did; Lily would not want to see him if he knew.

David was disgusted, but he was not sure with whom. His initial anger with Neal, which had led them to make this appointment in the first place, had mushroomed into anger with all of them, including himself, for being so foolish as to think that this plan would work. And even if Neal came, which now seemed increasingly unlikely, David was not sure what they would do with—or to—him, beyond checking him out as best they could for signs of weakness or injury in his upper left arm, his stomach, or his heart. David imagined himself asking Neal, apropos of nothing at all, how his heart was these days; or if he had had a stomachache recently. Pretty dumb, thought David: Neal would suspect that they were up to something, for sure.

On the other hand, since they had gone this far with their plan, it seemed too bad not to get something from it. And it was odd, David thought, that Neal had not appeared. Even though David disliked him, he admitted that Neal did not seem to be the kind of person who forgot about appointments, or who said he would be there and then simply did not bother to show up.

"Maybe we should call him," he said at last.

"Why?" said Peaches.

"Just to see if he's there. And then if he isn't, we can wait a little longer because he might be on his way."

"What's his number?" said Peaches.

"I wrote it down," said David. He fished inside his jacket, in his shirt pocket, and produced a slip of paper.

There was a row of pay telephones along the street to the side of the store. With a last glance around in every direction to make sure that Neal was not approaching, they went to a telephone; David took a dime from his pants pocket and put it into the slot and dialed the number.

It rang for a long time: four, five, six times.

He would let it go to ten, he thought. Then he would hang up and they would go home in defeat.

Someone answered on the ninth ring.

David did not recognize the voice, which did not say hello but made a sound that was more like a combination of a yes and a groan.

"Is this Neal Donovan?" he said.

Again came that odd sound.

"This is David," he said. The others were watching him. There was no response from the person at the other end of the line.

"I was just calling to see—"

"What's wrong?" said Peaches. Lily shushed her.

"We were waiting for you—" said David into the receiver. He was getting a response; he bent in toward the phone and put his hand over his right ear to shut out the street noise and the sound of the blaring carols.

The others waited impatiently. They could not see his face, could not hear what he said. He spoke again, and then again.

"What's *wrong*?" said Thomas to Peaches and Lily, but they could not tell him; they could only wait until David had finished. After a moment more he hung up and came away from the telephone; other people were waiting to use it.

"What is it?" said Lily, seeing his face.

"Let's go inside for a minute and get warm," he said, and he would not tell them until they had obeyed. The warmth felt good; they were very cold.

"Did he forget?" said Peaches.

"No."

"What, then?"

David looked around at them before he answered. "He's sick."

"He's sick!" said Peaches. "That means it worked!" Her face shone briefly with triumph, but she lost that little glow as she realized that Lily and David were not pleased at all.

"Maybe," said David. "I don't know."

"Did he tell you he was sick?" said Lily.

"No. But I knew it because he could hardly talk."

"But did he say something like he had a pain in his stomach, or his arm hurt, or something?"

"Or his heart," said Peaches.

"No. He sounded weird. Like he didn't really know it was me. Like just—weird. He said something like 'Get the kid, get the kid.'"

"Maybe he's delirious," said Lily. She had been delirious once with a very high fever, but she didn't remember anything about it. Margaret had told her that she had talked gibberish, and that maybe Lily felt uncomfortable. It was one thing to talk nonsense when you knew you were; it was quite another to do it when you didn't.

"Anyway I think he's really sick," said David. He

could see that Lily was not happy with that news either.

As they thought about it, Peaches became slightly defensive. "Well—good," she said. "So it worked. So now we know."

"I think we should do something," said David.

"I want to go home," said Thomas.

"What should we do?" said Lily.

"That's right," said Peaches. "Let's go home. We can tell Mom."

"Oh, no," said David.

"Why not?"

"Because. If you tell her he's sick, she'll want to know how you know, and why, and everything."

"No she won't."

"Yes she will. And she'll be mad. Are you going to tell her about the doll, too?"

"No. I don't have to."

"What if she finds it? Did you hide it?"

"Yes."

"Where?"

"I'm not telling."

"She better not find it. She'll think—maybe she'll think it worked, too. And she'll think we made him get sick."

"Is he going to die?" said Thomas. He spoke too loud because he was getting anxious, and a woman passing by stopped to look at them. They turned their backs on her and made a little circle around Thomas. After a moment the woman went on, but Lily saw that she paused to turn and look at them again before she went out onto the street.

Lily felt sick to her stomach. She wanted very much to go home—just walk up to the Common and get on the D train and go home and have a good dinner and read her book or maybe watch TV and forget the whole thing, forget Neal and the stupid doll and the pins and everything. She was sure, now, that Neal was going to die. Lily was not familiar with the fine points of the law, but she was sure that if you wanted to hurt someone, and maybe even kill someone, and if you tried to do it, and if you succeeded, even if you didn't expect to, then you were guilty.

So if Neal died now, they were all guilty of murdering him.

"I think we have to go there," said David.

"Where?" said Peaches.

"To his house."

No one said anything. None of them wanted to do that.

"Well, I'm going home," said Peaches. "You can go to his house if you want to, but I'm going home. Come on, Thomas."

David grabbed her arm. "You can't. Mom said to stay together."

"Then come on," said Peaches.

"We can't," said David. "We can't just leave him. What if he dies? And we knew he was sick and we didn't say anything?"

Lily reminded herself of how she hated Neal—hated him because he had made so much trouble for them all. He was making trouble still. But you couldn't just let someone die, even if you hated that person.

And if he was dying, if he really was dying, then someone needed to help him. It was strange to think of an adult needing help, strange to think of an adult so vulnerable that something she did might determine whether he lived or died.

She was the eldest: and in moments of extreme crisis their attempts at democracy vanished and they looked to her to direct them. A decision had to be made, and quickly.

She understood that they were confronted, now, with reality and not make-believe. You could do anything you wanted in make-believe—that was the beauty of it—but reality was more difficult, you had fewer choices. Moreover, make-believe seldom involved right and wrong; real life almost always did.

"All right," she said. "It's the Red Line to Savin Hill. Come on."

At least, she thought, if he did die, the police would take into account the fact that they tried to save him.

37

THE RED LINE WAS VERY DIFFERENT FROM THE Green Line. You went down one more level to reach it, for instance—deep into the bowels of the subway station. The cars were old and dirty, not new and sleek and silent like the Green Line cars, and the people who rode them looked different, too: poorer looking, many of them, and black- and brown-skinned. Lily heard some of them speaking to each other in a language that was not English. One boy had a large portable radio that was playing music that Lily had not heard before—a catchy beat, very loud.

They consulted the subway map on the station wall. It was easy to read: it showed all the different-colored routes, green and blue and red and orange, each stop clearly marked.

"Here," said David, running his finger down the Red Line from where they were, at Park Street, to Savin Hill. The train came thundering in. The doors slid open. The cars were crowded. A lot of people got off, but a lot stayed on, too. They held hands to keep together and allowed themselves to be carried in with the throng. They were so tightly packed that they did not need to hold on, but in any case there was nothing to hold on to.

The doors slammed shut; the train roared into motion. There was a small version of the subway map posted by the door. David counted: six stops, the one after Columbia. As he turned away from the map he caught Lily's eye. He hoped that he looked more confident than he felt. Peaches and Thomas stared around—and up—at the unfamiliar faces surrounding them: unfamiliar not only because they were the faces of strangers but because they were the faces of a different kind of stranger. People like this did not live in their town.

The train pulled into a stop; disgorged a few; took on a few; started up again. It accelerated rapidly, hurtling through the tunnel, carrying them farther and farther away from home, from their familiar world—the world where they were children and where other people, grown-up people, made decisions for them and where, to survive and flourish, they had only to obey.

After a while David became aware that halfway down the car a group of teenagers had become interested in him—in all of them. The teenagers were black. They did not look friendly. David looked away. He was aware of a small commotion in the aisle. The teenagers were shoving through to get closer.

The train pulled into another stop. Several people got off; only one got on. The crowded aisle was becoming a little less crowded.

The teenagers were right beside David now. They were trying to surround him, to cut him off from the others. David moved away, pushing the others along.

"Stop pushing," said Peaches.

"Go on," he said. "Move down."

The teenagers followed. They were grinning, but not in a friendly way. David looked around. Every seat was filled. No one would make eye contact with him, although some people were looking at Lily and the lit-

tle ones. David decided to hold his ground, but he also
held on to Thomas' arm so that they could not be separated. The real danger would come, he knew, when
they got off. If the teenagers followed them, they
might be in real trouble.

"Hey, honky."

David did not answer. The teenager pushed him but
he kept his balance.

"What you got, honky?"

David kept his hold on Thomas and turned his back
on the menacing foursome. Thomas peered around
him to see what was wrong. Then he looked questioningly up at David but said nothing.

One of the teenagers pushed David again so that he
nearly fell onto Thomas, and Thomas staggered back,
bumping into Lily and Peaches.

"Cut it out," said Peaches to Thomas.

"He's pushing," said Thomas.

Lily looked around the car for someone who might
help them. She saw a middle-aged man, a white man,
dressed in a worn woolen jacket and knitted cap. He
was looking at the teenagers; she could not tell from
the expression on his face whether he understood what
they were doing.

The train stopped. A few people went in and out. It
started up again. David bent down and said something
into Thomas' ear; Thomas repeated it to Peaches;
Peaches repeated it to Lily: "Hold on and follow
David."

The train slowed. They were approaching the next
station. Suddenly, gripping Thomas' hand, David
pushed toward the door. Just as the train halted and
the door slid open he darted out, the others behind
him.

"Hey—" said Peaches, but there was no time to explain.

"Come *on*," he called over his shoulder. Pulling them behind him, he ran down the platform beside the waiting train and into the open door of the next car. It slid shut. They were safe; the teenagers had not followed. David was trembling a little, but he felt good, too.

The train rumbled on. Another stop, and then another. They were aware that the train had left the tunnel; they were aboveground. It was dark now, lights flashing by. The next stop was theirs.

The train pulled in. They got out. The teenagers stayed on. They saw that they were on a high platform. A sign marked "Exit" led them to a flight of dirty, dimly lit concrete stairs. They went up. They passed through a turnstile in a tiny, dingy station and came out onto a wide, busy street. It was full dark now, and very cold; a strong wind blew, snatching their breath, making their eyes and noses water. To their right was a bridge over a big highway.

"I think it's that way," said David, meaning left. They trotted along. In a couple of blocks they came to a traffic light and a busy street. They turned left again and went along the nearly deserted sidewalk. There were a few poor-looking stores, a few seedy-looking bars. Some of the buildings were boarded up—apartment buildings of ugly yellow brick, or wood frame. There were no trees along the street, not even any little garden plots in front of the buildings. There were no people about, either: the sidewalk was empty of pedestrians, although there was a good amount of traffic. A car passing on their side slowed and the occupants stared at them, but after a moment it speeded up again.

They came to a corner. There was a tall metal post to hold a street sign, but the sign itself was missing. A young man in a leather jacket was approaching.

"Excuse me," said David. "Do you know where Grampian Way is?"

The young man did not pause. "Nope."

"Let's go in there and ask," said Lily, meaning a small, dingy grocery store. Its windows were obscured by a heavy metal grille, so that whatever might have been displayed could not be seen. They followed her in. An elderly man stood behind the counter.

"Do you know where Grampian Way is?" said Lily.

The man looked them over. "One block to the next light," he said at last, pointing in the direction in which they had come. "Then turn right and up over the bridge. Second left after that."

"Thank you," said Lily. They marched out again and started walking back. Lily realized that she expected at any moment to hear the little ones begin to complain, but they said nothing. They trudged along, heads bowed against the wind, and Lily thought that they must be so exhausted, so apprehensive, that they had not even the energy to protest. Lily herself would have liked to protest, but there was no one to protest to: it was at her insistence that they had come.

They turned at the light and passed the entrance to the Red Line and went on over the bridge. The wind battered them; below, in an endless stream of light, traffic flowed along the highway. They were going uphill now; the landscape had suddenly changed. They were in a neighborhood of big, old wooden houses separated by patches of lawn; there were trees and shrubbery. It was not exactly like their own neighborhood, but near enough to reassure them somewhat. Neal did not live in a slum, he lived somewhere that was like where they lived.

They came to the second left, where there was a street sign. "Grampian Way," said David, peering up at it. "This is it."

The street led up a steep hill. Some of the houses had numbers; some did not. Once or twice they had to go up the front walk to see. Neal's was number seventeen; when they came to it at last they were glad to see that it was clearly marked, large black numbers on a column on the front porch which they could read by the illumination of a street lamp. Neal's car was parked in the narrow driveway.

The house itself was dark: no porch light, no light in any window. They walked up the steps and tried the front door. It opened. Inside the little lobby were two mail boxes and two bells. They pressed the lower one. There was no answer. Then they tried the upper one, but there was no answer to that, either.

After a moment David tried the inside door. It opened. From the darkened entry way they could see a flight of stairs illuminated by a dim light from above.

"Come on," said David. They went up single file. At the top was a narrow hall and at the far end, a door. David knocked. No answer. He knocked again. "Neal?" he called. No answer.

He tried the door. It opened. They were in what seemed to be a living room; they saw a sofa, an upholstered chair, a rocking chair, a low table.

"Where is he?" said Peaches. Her voice seemed very loud in the silent room. Lily shushed her. They huddled just inside the entrance. Now they could see that an open door to their left led into a short hall.

The frightening thing was that they knew that Neal was there. David had talked to him, had called him at this place and he had answered. He had sounded sick. It seemed unlikely that he would have gotten up and gone out since David's call.

"I think we should go home," said Peaches, more quietly. "I don't think—"

"Listen!" said David. They stood in the dark,

straining to hear. It came again: a faint, labored sound like someone trying very hard to breathe through lungs that were hurting badly.

It was the most frightening sound Lily had ever heard. She felt her knees tremble so that she thought she was going to collapse. She leaned against the wall and concentrated on not collapsing. She realized that someone was holding her hand very tightly. It was Thomas. She hoped that he would not start to cry. She felt her tears well up and she clenched her teeth and fought them back.

David, at last, had the presence of mind to hunt for a light switch. He flipped it, and they stood blinking in the glare from the room's ceiling fixture. The light made them less afraid, so that when they heard the sound again they realized that it must have come from Neal, wherever he was.

"Come on," said David. He stepped into the little hall and Lily followed him; Peaches and Thomas stayed where they were.

At the end of the hall they could see what looked like a kitchen. Halfway down was a closed door. David knocked. "Neal? It's David."

No answer.

He turned the knob and cautiously pushed. In the light from the open door he could see a man lying in a rumpled bed. The room was stuffy; it had a sour smell.

"Neal?"

The voice that answered him sounded only faintly like Neal's.

"Get them on the right. On the right. Don't eat them. Don't eat them. He's all right now. Put a flower on him."

"Neal?"

"Put a flower on him. Now he's going to fly. Let him go. Let him go."

David stepped into the room and Lily followed him. They approached the bed. David switched on the lamp on the night table.

Neal lay in the rumpled bedclothing. His face was flushed and sweating, his eyes open and darting back and forth. The light hurt them; he winced and turned away.

"Neal?"

He did not respond.

"He's really sick," said Lily. She stood beside David, staring down at him. "What should we do?"

"See if someone's home downstairs," said David.

"There isn't. There weren't any lights."

"Just go and see."

They came out of the bedroom together.

"I have to go to the bathroom," said Thomas.

And so while Lily went downstairs to knock on the door of the first-floor apartment, David went into the kitchen and turned on the light and found the bathroom, which was off the kitchen.

"What are you going to do?" said Peaches.

"I don't know," said David.

"You should call a doctor."

"Or an ambulance."

"And we should call Mom." There was a large, round wood-framed clock on the kitchen wall; it said five twenty-five. "We're supposed to be home now."

They thought of going out again into the cold and the dark, and finding their way back to the subway station, and waiting for the train, and getting on it again with who knew what menacing teenagers, and getting off at Park Street to change to their own familiar Green Line. It seemed to them that they had been away from home a very long time, much longer than this afternoon; and it seemed to Peaches, at least, that she might never be home again. She was afraid of the journey back; she was afraid to stay where they were.

Lily came back. "Nobody's there," she said.

"All right." David thought hard. "I think we should call Mom and tell her," he said after a moment. "And then maybe she should call the ambulance. I don't think they'll come if we call them."

Lily had once tried to call a cab—a genuine call, not a prank—and the cab never came. They had been sure that it was because the person taking the call had known from Lily's voice that she was not an adult.

"Mom will be mad," said Peaches.

They expected that. They had stumbled step by step into something that was far more serious than they had anticipated, and now they knew that their mother would have to hear the whole story—the doll, the pins, the assignation, the journey to Neal's place—and that, inevitably, she would be angry.

"I know," said David.

They could not even think about what their punishment might be, could not sort out for which of their actions they would be held culpable. The important thing now was to get help. The situation was beyond them, and if in the process of extricating themselves they needed to reveal their secrets, then they would simply have to do so and take whatever punishment their mother chose to inflict.

The telephone was beside Neal's bed. David and Lily went back to him; Peaches and Thomas sat at the kitchen table. Thomas, who had been hungry all afternoon, would not have dreamed, now, of looking for food: his appetite had fled, for one thing, and he would not have wanted to eat anything in this place, for another.

"I'm calling Mom, OK?" said David.

Lily nodded. She looked at Neal. He lay quiet now,

his eyes closed. He had tossed off the covers so that he had only his pajamas to ward off the chill. But there was no chill; the room was very warm. Lily made no move to cover him again, not because she hated him (the man she had hated seemed to be someone else) but because she simply did not want to touch him or even his bedclothes.

David picked up the receiver and dialed.

38

AFTERWARD—LATER THAT NIGHT, THE NEXT DAY, the day after that—it occurred to Margaret that perhaps Neal would think that in an effort to win him back she had put the children up to arranging a rendezvous with him.

At the time, however, she thought only of the fear that she heard in David's voice, the urgent need not only to get an ambulance for Neal but to get them all home safe again.

"Just stay there," she said. "Don't leave. And don't stay in his room, either. Sit in the living room. I'm coming. And, David—" She tried to think, she tried not to let him hear that she, too, was afraid. "Listen. I'm going to call the police. So don't be afraid if they come, if they get there before I do. Just let them in, and tell them what happened, and tell them I'm coming. They'll get an ambulance."

They were unutterably relieved to take direction from her, to have her give orders—calm, sane orders that they could easily follow.

She dared not drive too fast, particularly not in the treacherous Boston traffic, and so by the time she arrived at Neal's the ambulance had already taken him away—to Boston City Hospital, said the kindly-

looking policeman who waited with the children in
Neal's living room.

She realized at once that their relief at seeing her
was overlayed by their fear of what she would say,
what she would do. She said nothing, could think of
nothing to say, but simply embraced the little ones,
and thanked the policeman, and got the children
downstairs and into the car as quickly as she could.

They were silent on the drive home, silent as they
ate the supper she hastily prepared. As curious as she
was to know about their adventure, she refrained from
questioning them. The story would come out in time,
she knew. Meanwhile the important thing was that
they were home safe.

Anxiously she looked for signs of the ill effects of
their adventure, but she saw none. They were tired, of
course, but aside from that they seemed all right. She
had no idea what Neal's illness was, or whether it was
contagious: if it was, it might be a day or two before
the children showed any symptoms.

For their part, the children were alternately relieved
to be home again and fearful of what she would do.
But mostly they were relieved. And after the first moments of their reunion with her, when they saw that
she was not terribly angry, that her concern for them
far outweighed any anger she might have felt, they
wanted very much to tell her everything, to unburden
themselves. And so after they had eaten, when at last
she asked them to tell her what had happened, they
were glad to do so. How, for instance, had they turned
up at his apartment?

"On the subway," said Peaches.

"But—how did you know? And *why*?"

And so they told her about the waiting, and the
phone call when he did not come.

"But why did you arrange to meet him?" she said.

As they told her about the doll, and their desire to see what effects it had had, and their desire to make some further mischief for him, her face went blank with disbelief. She did not know whether to laugh or cry, whether to praise them or scold them.

"But *why* did you want to hurt him?" she said.

They stared at her.

"Because you thought he hurt me?" she said.

Slowly, hesitantly, they nodded.

She was appalled: she had had no idea that they knew so much, had seen so much of her pain.

And then in the next moment she was overcome by a rush of love for them as she understood what they had done: they had come to her defense, they had wanted to avenge her.

"A voodoo doll?" she said.

They nodded again.

"But—where did you get it?"

Silence. Then: "I made it," Peaches said in a small voice.

"Let me see it."

They waited while Peaches went to fetch it. When she returned, holding it gingerly between two fingers as if it were a small, loathsome reptile, Margaret took it from her and studied it in amazement. It seemed to hold within its ugliness a concentrated hatred—her children's hatred, an emotion that seemed far beyond the power of any child to summon up.

No one spoke. The children looked both shame-faced and defiant. She was aware that they expected her to scold them, but she lacked the heart to do that. But at the very least, she thought, she must make it clear that nonsense such as voodoo dolls was strictly forbidden; on the other hand, should she not make it clear as well that they were to be congratulated for their coolheadedness, their very real courage in a situation that might have defeated even an adult?

And that, she thought, was the crucial part of the story: their decision to go to him when they suspected that he might be ill. Many children—many adults as well—might simply have shrugged their shoulders at that point, might not have wanted to become further involved.

And so, in the end, she had nothing but praise for them; she was very proud of them, and she told them so. "And I'm going to throw this little fellow away, all right?"

They nodded, but it seemed to her that they were not entirely in agreement. Then she realized what was wrong: putting the doll into the wastebasket was hardly the proper way to dispose of it. It could live on in the wastebasket; trash was collected on Wednesdays, and who knew what mischief it might cause between now and then? They followed her into the living room and watched as she stirred up the fire; when it was blazing well she dropped the doll into the flames. It burned quickly; in no more than a minute it was a lump of charred cotton and wood. Then it was gone.

And Neal, too.

39

ᘓᘓᘓᘓ

ON MONDAY SHE WENT TO THE HOSPITAL TO SEE
Neal. She went reluctantly, fearing that her composure
would vanish, that she would say to him all the harsh
and angry words that she had kept to herself over the
past weeks.

But it was important for him to know what had happened, and, more, to understand it. Even, she
thought, the part about the doll: it was not a bad thing
for him to know that the children had come to her
defense, even in such a bizarre way.

He was sitting up in his bed when she arrived. He
was weak, and in some discomfort, but he was lucid.
He was also surprised to see her; she realized that he
had no idea why she had come, or how she knew that
he was here. But he was not, she thought, unhappy at
her presence. A stubble of beard covered his face, and
there were shadows under his eyes.

"Feeling better?" she said. She stood by the bed;
there was a chair handy but she did not want to sit in it
because the chair was low and the bed was high.

"A little tired. But better, yes."

"The children—" But she could not tell him lies,
could not deliver good wishes to him that the children

had not sent. The children were in school; they did not even know that she had come to see him.

"Do you remember anything?" she said.

"About how I got here? No."

"They didn't tell you?"

"The hospital? No. They just said an ambulance came." He looked at her sharply. "Did you—"

"It was the children. They had an appointment to meet you." She was amused to see the beginnings of understanding in his eyes. "And when you didn't show up, they called you."

He shook his head. "Don't remember that. I must have been pretty far gone by then."

"Yes. David said you weren't making sense. That's why they went to your apartment."

"Really?" His face lighted up with interest, and he smiled a little.

"Really. They thought—well, they understood that something was very wrong."

"Plucky kids." He rested his head on the pillow, thinking about it: about them. "You mean they got on the subway all by themselves and went down to Dorchester?"

"Yes."

"And you didn't know?"

"I didn't know anything. I had no idea they'd arranged to meet you. If I'd known, I'd have forbidden them. To meet you, I mean—and certainly to go to your place, to go on the subway." She thought of David's description of the menacing teenagers, and she shuddered. "No offense. But a phone call could have done the job."

"But why—?" He paused, wrestling with it. "I don't understand why they wanted to see me in the first place. I remember that David called me, and we agreed to meet downtown. Then in the middle of the week I got sick. Really bad flu. And I never called him to tell him I couldn't come. Never thought of it. Why d'you think they wanted to meet me?"

She hesitated; she met his eyes and quickly looked away. Then she told him: about the children's concern for her, their anger at him, their attempt at revenge, the little doll stuck with pins. She could see, as she talked, that he was astonished at what she said.

She felt that she was burning her bridges behind her: he would never come back to her after this recitation. She did not care. His coming back was not important; his understanding was. She tried very hard to show him that if her children had acted unwisely, they had acted in desperation as well and that what they had done was perhaps her fault, too.

"I didn't talk to them enough," she said. "I didn't let them know that I was all right."

He put out his hand to her. "Are you?"

She did not take it. "Yes."

He wanted to explain to her, then, why he had not called her, why he had broken off with her. But he was suddenly very tired; he had no strength to go on talking to her, or even to listen. He would have been happy simply to lie quiet in his bed, holding her hand, looking at her, but apparently that was not to be. He realized that she was gathering herself to leave.

He understood that it was very awkward for her to be here. Awkward for him, too: he had not thought to see her again, but if he did, he thought that it would be on his terms, at a time and place of his choosing. This was very near to embarrassing. Only his condition—and, he admitted, her reserve, her studied, impersonal cheerfulness—kept it from being a well-nigh intolerable meeting.

But she had come only to make a business call, as it were; and, having made it, she left. They made no promise to see each other again; she did not ask when he would be released.

She was not sure she cared. She had thought that her visit would be painful, but to her relief it hardly hurt at all. She had come away, she thought grimly, with her dignity intact. She could not have asked for more.

Seeing him had been like lancing a boil: it had cleansed the wound. Now she would heal.

40

❧❧❧❧

AND SO, SHE THOUGHT, IT WAS OVER; SHE WAS DONE
with him and he with her. Considering everything, she
felt remarkably well.

She told the children that Neal would be all right.

"How do you know?" said Lily.

"Because I went to see him."

They were surprised at that—and, she could see,
alarmed.

"Why?" said Peaches.

"I just thought I should. They say that once you
save a person, you're responsible for him."

Lily thought that it should be the other way around,
but she let it pass.

"You didn't save him," said Thomas. "We did."

"I know that. But they wouldn't have let you in at
the hospital, so I went instead. Don't worry"—for she
saw the expression on their faces—"I'm not going to
start going out with him again. I just wanted to make
sure that he'd be all right. And I also thought that he
should know what happened. How he got there, I
mean."

"Did you tell him?" said David.

She hesitated for only a second, but they caught it.
"I told him as much as I thought he needed to know."

"That we went to his house?"

"Yes. And why you went—because he didn't meet you when he said he would."

"Did you tell him about the doll?" said Lily. Peaches looked angry, as if she expected to have to ward off their criticism.

"No," said Margaret. There were times when a lie was better than the truth, and this was one of them.

In the days that followed she made the last-minute preparations for Christmas: wrapped the presents; filled the stockings; baked and decorated, with the children's help, three kinds of cookies.

One evening the children's father called from California. He would be there shortly after the New Year, he said: the first week in January. Or perhaps the second, he wasn't sure. His voice sounded odd—too loud, the words carefully enunciated. It was not the first time he had sounded that way.

Margaret reminded him that the children would be back in school by then. It would be better, she said—more convenient for them, and more enjoyable—if he could manage to visit with them during their vacation.

He resented her suggestion; he told her, unpleasantly, more loudly, the words slightly slurred, to mind her own business and let him handle his. He was not free, he said, to travel at will; he needed to arrange his visits to his children around his business trips, and those were not always scheduled to his convenience. Or to theirs.

Margaret had suggested, once, that he use some of his vacation time to see the children, and had listened to some minutes of recrimination in return. Now she heard him out; she said nothing more about his plans. He would come when he pleased; for the children's sake she was glad that he came at all.

The day before Christmas it snowed; not enough to

cause disruption but enough to make a Christmas landscape. As they drove to her parents' house on
Christmas Day, Margaret felt happy—really happy for
the first time in weeks. In seven days, she thought, it
will be the New Year. She looked forward to it: she
was sure that one way or another it would be a good
one.

A slight shadow fell over her optimism, however, as
she watched her father through the day: the gift-
giving, the Christmas dinner, the friends coming to call
late in the afternoon. He looked tired, she thought.
She watched him anxiously; and then, when she saw
her mother watching her, she looked away. She said
nothing to her mother, nothing to cast a pall of worry
or alarm over the pleasant day; but the next evening
she called her mother to chat for a while and she
dropped the question in: how is Daddy, I thought he
looked tired.

Yes, a little, her mother said; just the usual end-of-
term tiredness, he has a month's vacation now and he
can rest.

And so Margaret hung up feeling reassured, and
safe again. It would be all right: her father was well,
her children were well. They would all have a good
new year.

On New Year's Eve, lacking a baby-sitter, she
stopped in early and briefly at the Olsens' party and
fell into conversation with a woman who was house
hunting. Or, rather, condominium hunting, since
houses had become so exorbitantly expensive. When
she heard that Margaret lived alone (which meant un-
attached to a man) in a house that was larger even
than the Olsens', she offered a suggestion: had Margaret ever thought of dividing her house, making it
into two condominiums?

Margaret had not. When she returned home, however, she did. It was not a bad idea, on the face of it. Since Carl Olsen was an architect, she resolved to ask his advice; it would be her project for the New Year, or, at least, for the first part of the New Year.

The next day—New Year's Day—the children's father called to say that he would see them a week from Saturday. He would call from his hotel on Friday night when he arrived; he expected her to have the children dressed and ready for him on Saturday morning. He was not sure yet whether he would want to keep them Saturday night.

She started to ask him a question; remembering her previous objections to his plan, he thought that her question was a protest, and he interrupted her: "Don't argue with me. I have a right to see my children." He sounded hostile, not open even to a question, and so she simply agreed to what he said and hung up.

On the third evening of the New Year Neal paid them a visit.

41

PEACHES CAME TO REPORT THE NEWS TO DAVID AND
Lily. It was after dinner; they were playing Scrabble in
David's room. Thomas was watching his fish; they had
given him two new ones for Christmas.

"I don't want to talk to him," said Peaches.

"Neither do I," said Lily.

"We don't have to," said David.

"Did you see him?" said Lily. "Is he all right?"

"I looked over the banister and I saw Mom letting
him in," said Peaches. "I didn't say hello or anything.
He looked OK."

She sat on David's bed and observed the game. If
their mother came to summon her, she did not want to
be alone.

Downstairs, Margaret sat with Neal in the living
room. She understood why he had come—or at least
she thought she did—but she wished he had not. He
was the past, he was over and done with; she wanted
only the future now, and he was not it.

She did not offer him a cup of coffee or a drink. She
did not offer to take his coat and so he put it beside
him on the sofa. Her attitude was cool, if not down-
right chilly. He had the feeling that at any moment she

would announce that she had a previous appointment and show him out.

He remembered her visit to him in the hospital, and so while he was disappointed, he was not entirely surprised. He had thought that perhaps he remembered incorrectly, that perhaps she had been warmer, friendlier, and he had simply missed it because he was still so sick. But now he saw that he had not been mistaken. She was polite to him: no more.

"What is it?" she said. "Why have you come?"

"I wanted to see the kids," he said.

She made no move to call them.

"I probably threw a good scare into them," he said.

"Yes."

"Obviously it was beyond my control."

She shrugged. "Don't worry about it. It's over. You've survived. They've survived. That's all that counts."

He was beginning to be mildly irritated. She looked very pretty, he thought, and her prettiness added to his irritation. She had on a soft pink sweater and gray wool slacks. She looked good in slacks—good in a sweater, too, for that matter—and so it was all the more irritating that unlike most women he met she seemed uninterested in making herself attractive to him.

He reminded himself that it had been he who broke off. He had been, he recalled, reluctant to become committed to her. He acknowledged that she had accepted his rejection with remarkably good grace. She had not pestered him, she had not flung his callousness at him, she had not made scenes.

Now, looking at her, he wondered why he had behaved so. It seemed to him that he had made a mistake. He would not mind starting up with her again. Her attitude, however, told him that he would probably not succeed. Perversely, this knowledge made him angry. He thought it unfair that he might approach her again and be rejected. He had been good for her; he could be good for her again. Apparently she was not going to give him that chance.

In fact, apparently she was not even going to let him see the children, and this irritated him even more. His visit had not been solely an excuse to see her; he had genuinely wanted to speak to them, to thank them for what they'd done. Although he remembered none of it (which made him feel a little awkward), he understood the effort they had made to help him. He was sincerely grateful to them, and he would have liked to tell them so.

"I'd like to thank them," he said.

She hesitated. Then: "I don't think they want thanks."

"Are you saying you don't want me to see them?"

"It's complicated."

"How?"

"It just is. You see, They didn't— Well. They were pretty frightened."

"I'm sure. All the more reason for me to thank them."

"I think it's best that you don't."

His pride kept him from arguing with her further, and so, defeated, he rose to leave. As he went out into the wide entrance hall, he glanced up.

The children were there, lined up behind the balustrade from tallest to shortest the way they always did. They said nothing; they did not acknowledge his presence by the slightest movement. They simply stared at him.

As much as they shied from speaking to him, they were curious nevertheless to see him. In some way that they did not fully understand, he was theirs. They had saved him. Now they wanted to see for themselves that he was well. They did not necessarily want him to come back into their lives, but they did not begrudge him his own life. For a moment, as his eyes met theirs, they felt a little ripple of pride, of satisfaction at having saved him. They had forged a kind of bond with him, even if they never saw him again.

Before he turned away he nodded at them; it was as if he understood what they were thinking. He put on his coat and said good night to Margaret.

If she had given him the slightest encouragement he would have asked to see her again. But she did not, and so by the time he reached his car he was more irritated with himself than ever—for having come, for having wanted to renew their relationship.

To prove to himself that he did not, when he got home he dialed the number of a pretty nurse he had met in the hospital. She said that she would love to go to the movies with him.

So much, he thought, for Margaret Merrill.

42

※※※

THE CALL CAME AT ELEVEN O'CLOCK ON A SATUR-day morning, and so when the telephone rang Margaret had no apprehension of bad news as she would have had from a ring, say, at midnight. It was her mother. The moment she spoke Margaret realized that phone calls at mid-morning can bring disaster as easily as those in the middle of the night.

"Margaret."

"Yes. Mother?"

"It's your father."

"What's wrong? You sound—"

"I'm at the hospital. It's— He had a heart attack. He went out early to shovel." There had been six inches or so of heavy, wet snow during the night. The children were outside now making a snowman. Margaret watched them through the window as she spoke. Her mother's voice resumed, shrill with fear: "He's in the emergency room." And then it broke: "Oh, Margaret. I can't—he's very bad, I think. He was unconscious."

"Where are you?" said Margaret. "What hospital?"

"Mount Auburn."

"I'll be right there."

After she hung up she stood quiet for a moment,

her hand still on the receiver, watching the children, adjusting her mind to the news, gathering up her strength. She would have to tell them, of course: would have to ask Ellen Lafferty to take them for a few hours while she went to the hospital.

She had never imagined that either of her parents might die. She knew that inevitably they would, of course, but she had never imagined it. Nor could she imagine either of them without the other: she did not know which would be more devastated by the other's death, but that devastation would occur she had no doubt.

She picked up the receiver again and dialed Ellen's number.

"Ellen? It's Margaret. Are you going to be home for a while?"

"Sure. What's up?"

"I've just had a call. It's my father. He's had a heart attack and I have to go to the hospital. I don't know how long I'll be. I'll call you from there when I find out what's happening. The kids are making a snowman so they'll be all right for a while, but they'll need lunch and a chance to warm up."

"Are you plowed?"

"No. But I have the snow blower."

"That'll take forever in this mess. Don has the truck. I'll ask him to do you right away."

"All right. Thanks."

"Margaret?"

"Yes."

"I'm sorry."

"Yes."

"If there's anything else I can do—the kids can stay over if you like."

"I'll call you."

And still, after hanging up, she stood watching the

children. It was as if she had suddenly been cast into a trance and she could not break out of it. Did not want to, in fact, for the moment she broke it she would be at a new place in her life, a further move down the road. And it would be lonely there, for her father would not be with her. It would be much worse, of course, for her mother.

It did not occur to Margaret that her father might live; she had instantly assumed that his heart attack would be fatal. She had seen its shadow on Christmas Day.

She heard the rumble of the truck plowing the driveway. She went to find her boots and her parka and went out to the back garden to tell the children. She briefly considered lying to them: telling them that she had a sudden emergency errand to run, or that Grandma did not feel well and she was going to see her. But she decided against it; she did not think that she would be able to carry it off.

As she approached them and saw the expectant look on their faces, she remembered: she had told them that they would spend this day with their father. But he had not called the previous evening, as he had said he would; she had no idea if he had arrived or not. Possibly the snowstorm had delayed his flight.

Now, as she gave them her news, she saw their mingled disappointment and concern. She tried to reassure them. The important thing, she said, was not to worry. They stared up at her, their pleasure in their task suddenly vanished, their faces reddened from the cold, their snowman nearly complete. They would use charcoal briquettes for eyes, coal being in short supply, and a carrot stub for a nose, and perhaps an old knitted cap. The sky was beginning to show patches of blue, the sun coming out, but it was cold enough so that the snowman would not melt.

She had planned to take pictures later, with the children grinning in triumph on either side of him. She was an intermittently avid snapshot taker; she let months pass without lifting the camera, and then in a spurt of guilt, or simple awareness of weeks and months going by, the children growing and changing unrecorded, she would buy half a dozen rolls of film and follow them around, snapping. The pictures that came of these efforts were mostly unremarkable, but once in a while she got a good one. These she separated from the rest and kept them in an album. From time to time she would look at them and be struck all over again by the swiftness of time's passing.

She kissed the little ones and told them all to go to Mrs. Lafferty's when they had finished the snowman. Then she returned to the house, picked up her purse, and went out the front door to her car in the freshly plowed driveway.

If Richard called and there was no answer, he would be angry; he would think that she had taken the children away for the day, perhaps, simply to spite him.

No matter: it could not be helped. She would simply have to explain to him when he called. If he called.

43

❧❧❧❧

Margaret's father died later that day without regaining consciousness.

She did not at first acknowledge his death. She pushed it away to the back of her mind and concentrated instead on persuading her mother to come home with her. "You don't want to go back to the house alone," she said. "And I can't come with you. I have to see to the children. So come with me."

To her relief her mother, too, seemed preoccupied with what must be done, without remembering why. She spoke of various family members who must be notified, and a number of friends; she insisted upon calling the funeral home herself. Margaret, standing by, heard her mother's voice calm and strong as she made the necessary arrangements.

And so together they returned to Margaret's house, and together they told the children. Even then neither of them cried: their grief was still too new. Margaret wondered about this: she wondered when she would adjust to the fact of his death, when she would understand that he was gone for good, she would not see him again.

The children, on the other hand, seized upon the news at once and had no thought for anything else.

Peaches and Thomas cried; Lily and David did not, but only because they fought their tears. Margaret wondered at this, too: did they think that they were too old to cry? Or that they must set an example for the little ones? An example of what, she wondered. Surely it was all right, even within the arcane strictures of preadolescent behavior, to cry if your grandfather died?

Later, as she took on the job of making the necessary calls, her grief came to her at last, and she was relieved to feel it. As she spoke to this person and that she heard her voice break, she felt her tears sting her eyes. She called her mother's sister in Northampton, and her father's brother in Connecticut. She called three close friends of her parents; she dealt with the obituary writer from the newspaper; she called the dean of her father's college.

With some misgiving she had sent her mother to bed: misgiving because she did not know whether her mother was better off alone or with the rest of them. But she had looked so tired, so suddenly bewildered, as if the realization of what had happened had only just struck her, that Margaret had thought it wise to urge her to rest.

Now, having made what calls she could, and having seen the children to bed, she sat for a while alone in the kitchen trying to come to terms with her loss. She turned off the lights, she was not sure why; it seemed to her a better way to let her mind run free. She could imagine better in the dark; the darkness was comforting, slightly mysterious, and it removed from her attention the distractions of the room, the furniture, the appliances, the plants and copper pots, the magazines and newspapers scattered about. Sitting in the dark, looking out the window at the snowman standing in the moonlight, she could drift a bit. Before she ac-

knowledged her father's death she wanted to remember him for a while: his face, his voice, the way he
had taken her on his lap to read to her when she was
small, the way he had helped her to learn to ride her
bicycle, his expression of sorrow and pride when he
saw her dressed for her high school prom, as if suddenly he realized that she was nearly grown up. She
had not understood his feeling then, but now, having
children of her own, she did.

Then, having conjured him up, she was ready at last
to confront his death; it was, she supposed, her way of
saying good-bye. She was glad that they had loved
each other so openly. She knew people who had become estranged from their parents, and when the parents died those people felt terrible—guilty, and
resentful, and doubly bereaved because they had lost
the parent not only at the moment of death but in the
years before as well.

After a while she went upstairs to look in on her
mother. She was awake, still dressed, lying on top of
the quilt with only an afghan thrown over her for
warmth. The light streaming into the darkened room
from the hall showed that her eyes were open; traces
of tears were on her cheeks.

"Do you want the light?" said Margaret.

"No."

"Can I bring you anything? You haven't eaten."

"No. I'm not hungry. I'll come down in a while and
pour myself a good stiff drink."

Margaret sat beside her mother on the bed and held
her hand. There was a brief silence. Then: "We had a
good time," her mother said.

"Yes."

"He was always *there*. I don't know how to explain
it, but he was with me, even when he was at work. Do
you know how some people can be in the same room

with you and yet they're not there? Well, he was *with* me, even when he wasn't." She paused again. Her voice, Margaret thought, was controlled: slightly choked from crying, but low and reassuringly steady. "I remember the first time I saw him," she went on. "He came rushing in late to the classroom. We were all sitting there waiting for him, a roomful of girls. He was very red and embarrassed because he'd gotten lost. It was his first semester on campus. I was annoyed because the course I'd wanted to take was filled. I was a senior and I thought I should have preference, but I didn't. So I had to take a course that was being taught by your father. He was a new man. No one knew him. It was like a pig in a poke, you know. And the course wasn't one I was terribly interested in, either, but I needed the credit to complete the major. It was seventeenth-century poetry. The metaphysicals. Of course it turned out to be a wonderful experience in every way. I loved the poetry, and I loved him."

They had married, Margaret knew, immediately after her mother's graduation: a student-teacher romance. Her mother had never seemed to escape that role: she had always been his student, his acolyte, deferring to him—and yet with no sense of abasement, for he had cared for her, too.

"Oh, Margaret." Then at last her voice broke and she cried, and Margaret cried with her, and they held each other and wept together in the dark.

44

THE FUNERAL WAS HELD ON THE FOLLOWING TUES-
day. After the ceremony, and the interment, and the
luncheon held at the home of Margaret's mother's clos-
est friend, the guests took their leave. Margaret
wanted to stay with her mother, but she also wanted to
take the children away; it had been a long day, a difficult day, and they had behaved very well. She wanted
to reward them for that behavior by freeing them, taking them home so that they could change from their
good clothing and settle back into their lives again, call
friends to check on assignments that they had missed,
take comfort from their familiar surroundings.

She wanted her mother to come with them, but
Mrs. Brigham said no, she would stay with her friend
for a while and then, with her sister, she would go back
to her own home. She would be all right; Margaret was
not to worry about her. It was she, in fact, who worried about Margaret: surely she should not be allowed
to go off alone with the children?

But no, Margaret said, she had to go and she, too,
would be all right. They would be in touch on the
phone that evening.

In the car, on the way home, she heard Peaches
sniffling. She thought at first that it came from crying,

and she glanced at Peaches, who sat next to her. The others were in the back. But Peaches was not crying.

"You catching cold?" Margaret said.

"I don't know."

"Is your throat sore?"

"A little."

And so when they arrived Margaret insisted that Peaches get into bed, even though she had no sign of fever. She took her two best dolls and a puzzle book and *Charlotte's Webb* and settled herself comfortably; after a while, when Margaret looked in on her, she saw that Peaches had fallen asleep.

Toward five o'clock, when Margaret had gone into the kitchen to see about dinner, the phone rang. Thinking that it was her mother, she answered it at once. It was the children's father. She had forgotten about his visit, she had not thought about him since Saturday.

"I'll come by in a while to pick them up," he said.

"Peaches has a cold. And anyway they can't go out on a school night. You know that."

"I won't keep them late."

"Come by tomorrow instead."

"I have a meeting."

"I just don't want them out tonight. Anyway they're upset. They don't want to go out. Daddy had a heart attack. He died—" her voice caught on the word. "He died on Saturday. We had the funeral today."

"That's too bad. I'm sorry."

She did not reply. She doubted that he was sorry: they had never gotten on, he and her father.

"Margaret?"

"Yes."

"I'll be by about seven."

"Look—I don't want to be difficult, but tomorrow would be better. This is just a bad night."

"I told you, I can't do it tomorrow. I'm tied up all afternoon and probably into the evening. Now am I going to see my children or not?"

The issue was not whether he would see the children. It was where and how he would insist on seeing them. Peaches in any case could not go out; and the others should not—not after their difficult and tiring day, not with homework to do, and school in the morning.

"I thought you were going to see them on Saturday," she said. "Or over Christmas vacation. That would have been the best time. They have schedules to keep, too. Keep that in mind, if you can."

Her stomach had begun to ache. He did not say anything for a moment, and she realized that he must be surprised at her tone—her attitude.

"All right, Margaret." His voice had suddenly turned ugly; she heard its menace, its threat, as clearly as if he had been in the room with her. "Now you listen to me. I already explained to you that I couldn't come at Christmas. The flights on Friday were canceled, and then something came up and I couldn't get away before this morning. I don't have to account to you for my actions. And I don't have to put up with this crap from you. I have a right to see my children, and I'm going to see them."

Before she could reply, he hung up. The harsh buzz of the dial tone echoed in her ear as she replaced the receiver. She had no idea what to do. Call for help? Who would she call? Or lock the door and refuse to let him in? She did not know if he still had his key; she supposed he did. There was a chain lock on both the front and back doors. Presumably, if he was angry enough, he could break in. And what would the children think if they saw her locking the door so early? Against what? She would have to tell them. It was one thing to chain lock the door when they all went to bed; it was quite another to do it at seven o'clock in the evening. Surely they would notice; they noticed everything. Not much got past them.

She realized that not only was she frightened; she was angry as well. He assumed that he could cancel a scheduled visit and show up any time and they would adjust to it. She remembered that her father was dead and for a moment she felt desolated all over again. Then she pushed the realization of his death from her mind. She had no time to think of that now. She took a package of thawed hamburger and began to shape patties.

She said nothing to the children about their father's call. She thought that she should warn them, but she did not want to worry them for no reason. Despite what he had said, she thought that perhaps he would not come after all. She carried a tray to Peaches and then returned to the kitchen where she ate with the rest of them. They were subdued, which was understandable in the circumstances, but otherwise they seemed all right.

Seven o'clock came and went. She did not chain lock the door; she did not switch on the outside light. Richard did not come. She called her mother; she resolved to say nothing about Richard. Her aunt said that her mother was asleep. "All right," said Margaret. "She can call me later if she wants."

At eight o'clock Thomas went to bed. Margaret took Peaches' temperature, which was normal. She tucked her in and turned out her light. When she looked in a short while later she saw that Peaches was sound asleep.

At eight-thirty the telephone rang, frightening Margaret badly. It was one of Lily's classmates. At a quarter to nine David announced that he was going to bed. Not long afterward Lily finished her phone call and she, too, went upstairs. Margaret was too jumpy to read. She went into the den, flipped on the television, and turned the dial. She had no idea what she was looking for. She found what seemed to be a movie and lay on the sofa to watch. After a while she fell asleep. She dreamed of her father; he and she were attending a funeral together and as they stood in the cemetery and watched the casket being lowered into the ground she realized that it was his casket, and that he had somehow miraculously escaped it and was whole and well again, standing beside her, very pleased with himself, or so it seemed to her, at having cheated death.

She was awakened, very late, by the sound of the front door closing. At first, struggling to come out of her dream, she thought it was her father come to find her.

She jumped up, still dazed with sleep. Without bothering to turn off the television, which was now showing another movie, she went into the front hall. Richard was in the living room, looking around in a curiously intent way, as if his sight was somehow impaired and he was trying hard to see.

She tried to come fully awake: to understand what day it was—or what night—and what time; to understand why this man was standing in her living room. She had not seen him in six months. He had put on weight, and his face had a high, unhealthy-looking color. His necktie was loosened, his trench coat unbuttoned.

After a moment, as he swung heavily around to look at her, she realized that he was drunk.

"All right," he said. "Here I am."

She could think of no reply that seemed adequate, so she said nothing.

"I said, I'm here." She could see that he was trying hard to enunciate clearly. He locked his eyes onto hers with the peculiar fixity of one whose head is swimming. "Well? Where are they?"

"Richard, it's very late. It's—" She glanced at the clock on the mantel. "It's nearly midnight."

"So what?" He swayed a little. She had a vision of him crashing down. She would not be able to move him; he was a big man, well over six feet. The children would see him in the morning. She thought that that sight would be worse than the sight of their grandfather in his casket. Fragments of her dream floated back to her but she brushed them aside.

"Go get them," he said.

"They're asleep."

"Then wake them up."

"It's very late. And besides, they have school—"

"I want to see them."

"Richard, not now. Not tonight. And anyway Peaches is sick."

He lowered at her, breathing heavily. She had no idea what to do. Even if the children were awake, she thought, she would not have wanted them to see him drunk.

He took a step toward her and even though she was beyond his reach she backed away. She was beginning to be afraid of him. "If you don't get those kids down here in one minute," he said, "I'll go up to get them myself." His face seemed numb; he had difficulty moving his lips.

She stood in the doorway. It was wide enough to allow him to pass without touching her, but she thought that at least she must try to prevent his going upstairs. She felt the onset of panic. She knew that if he was intent on going up she could not stop him. Still, she must try.

"No, you won't," she said. She saw that he understood what she said, and that he was surprised by it: confused, perhaps. Never before today had she seriously opposed him. Even when he had told her that he was leaving, that he loved someone else, she had not opposed him. She had assented; she had seen the pointlessness of opposing him and so she had saved her strength for more important things. The children, for instance.

She thought of how to get help. If she ran to the kitchen, to the telephone, it was just possible that she would be able to complete a call before he realized what was happening. But who would she call?

Suddenly he lurched toward her. Instinctively she stepped back, but then, recovering herself, she tried again to bar his way. She was very frightened, more frightened than she had ever been, even when she first tried to swim.

But she had done that: as she had learned to swim, she had overcome her fear.

If she could do that she could do anything.

"Richard, you have no right," she said. "Now get out."

That simple statement seemed to anger him more than anything she had said before. He seized her arm, pushed her out of the way, and then let go of her so that she was able to recover herself and step in front of him again.

He hit her then, slapped her face with his big open hand. Drunk as he was, he was able to hit hard. The blow stunned her for a moment, but she was still on her feet and she was able to recover herself. She stepped in front of him again and caught his arm. He was across the hall now, at the foot of the stairs. He tried to shrug her off, but she clung to him, holding him back.

Her persistence frustrated him. He turned on her and hit her again. She hung on. She was crying now, sobbing more in anger than fear. "No," she said. "No. You can't. Get out."

He hit her again. He was like a bull infuriated by a buzzing wasp. She clung to his arm. She had forgotten why she did it; she knew only that she must hold on, it was important not to let him go. He hit her again and again. She tasted blood. Her ears were ringing; she heard a high, unnatural whine inside her head. She held on. He grunted with the effort of trying to get free of her, with the effort of striking her. She was collapsing now, her knees giving way, and still she would not let go of him, she would not free him to awaken the children.

The last thing she remembered was his face: an ugly face, showing his ugly anger.

Some time in the night Lily thought she had a dream in which her father stood beside her bed, watching her. He did not speak to her, but she heard his breath come loud and harsh. She could not see his face in the dim light from the hall, but she knew that he was her father and not some stranger come to rob them.

Some time later she came fully, instantly awake. She remembered her dream and wondered if it had indeed been a dream. But now she knew that she was awake; she knew as well that she needed to get up out of her warm bed and discover why.

The clock by her bed said three forty-five. She put on her bathrobe and slippers. When she opened the door of her room she saw that lights were on downstairs. She went down. She heard the sound of the television. Her mother must have fallen asleep with it on, she thought—something that to Lily's knowledge

Margaret never did. She noticed that the front door was not chain locked.

When she looked into the den she saw Margaret lying on the sofa. She was on her side, her arm flung over her head. She seemed to be asleep.

Lily switched off the television set. She thought that perhaps she should let Margaret sleep undisturbed; nevertheless she thought that she should cover her with the afghan, since the house was so cold. It lay folded over the sofa's arm. Carefully she lifted it, unfolded it, and spread it over Margaret's still form.

It was not until she was tucking in the afghan around Margaret's shoulders that she saw, underneath the protecting arm, the bruised and battered face, swollen, disfigured—her mother's face, and yet the terrifying face of a stranger.

45

WHEN NEAL'S TELEPHONE RANG HE CAME OUT OF sleep at once and answered it before it finished its second ring.

He did not recognize the voice, and even after it identified itself he needed to think for a moment before he knew who it was: Lily Merrill. She sounded frightened; she wanted to know if he could come.

"Now? What's wrong?"

She told him—not everything, for she did not know everything, but that Margaret was badly injured.

"I can't wake her up," she said. He heard her voice break. For a moment he wondered if this might be another plot. But he didn't think that even a child as clever as Lily could act so skillfully. The fear he heard was genuine.

"All right," he said. "I'm coming. Don't try to move her."

When he arrived, Lily opened the door for him as he came up the steps. She held a blanket around her shoulders. She seemed smaller than he remembered, her eyes haunted with worry and fear.

"She's in the den."

"Still hasn't waked up?"

"No."

"Have you tried to wake her since you spoke to me?"

"I talked to her again but she still didn't answer."

As soon as he stepped into the room he knew that Margaret was alive: he had seen enough death in the war to recognize it instantly.

He paused. For a moment he was gripped by a kind of paralysis, unable to go nearer, unable to touch her. He shuddered—a violent tremor; then he took a deep breath and steadied himself. This was not the war. However bad it was, it was not as bad as that.

He bent over the figure on the sofa. Her breathing was shallow but regular; her muscle tone was good. He moved her arm slightly so that he could see her face. It was livid—shiny bright purple, badly swollen. No fluid at her nose or mouth. He did not think of it as the face of a woman he had once begun to love. It was a stranger's face. That was a better way, he realized, to confront it, to do what had to be done.

Gently he raised one of her eyelids. The pupil contracted. He ran his fingers lightly over her skull. There was a large swelling at the back. The jaw was out of line, badly bruised, probably broken. He pulled back the afghan and looked for a possible bullet hole in the body. He did not expect to find one: this was a beating, not a shooting.

"Lily—do you know what happened?"

Lily stood behind him, afraid to come too close. "No."

"Do you—was anyone here tonight?" Some new boyfriend, he thought; and he remembered how Margaret had trusted him, how she had accepted his invitation without knowing him.

"I didn't hear anyone."

"You didn't hear her—ah—making a date with anyone on the phone?"

"No. She wouldn't have, anyway."

"Why not?"

"My grandfather died. We went to the funeral yesterday."

And that, perhaps, was why Lily had called him and not her grandmother. But why him, and not a neighbor? "I'm sorry," he said. A good man, Margaret's father: too bad that he, Neal, had forfeited the chance to know him better.

Who, then, had done this?

Lily understood his question even though he did not say it. She remembered her vision of her father. She said nothing, however, but merely watched him as he bent over Margaret and gently touched her and softly spoke to her.

"Margaret?"

No response.

"Margaret, can you hear me? It's Neal."

Lily hardly dared breathe. She felt her heart beating very hard, pounding in her chest as though it would break through. She was sure that if anyone could help her mother, it was Neal. Not long ago they had helped him; they had probably saved his life. Now it was his turn. It seemed entirely right and proper and fully just that he would help them, that he had been given this chance to do so.

He turned away from her mother; he went into the kitchen. She followed him—a silent, fearful little presence. She had left the light on when she called him. Now she hovered by the doorway as he picked up the phone.

46

WHEN THE AMBULANCE HAD COME AND GONE, Neal thought briefly of calling Margaret's mother. It was after five—not yet light. Wait until seven, he thought. She's been through her husband's funeral, she probably took a sleeping pill.

He asked Lily if she wanted to sit with him, but she said no, she would go back to bed. She looked frozen, he thought; when he asked her about turning on the heat, she said that it was set to come on automatically at six-thirty.

"All right," he said. "Go on up, and I'll be here for breakfast." It did not occur to him to leave. He would stay, and see them off to school, and talk to Margaret's mother, and deal with the police—certainly the police would have to be dealt with. He would leave to Margaret's mother the decision of whether to call any of the neighbors; Margaret was good friends with some of them, he recalled.

"Lily—" He followed her out into the hall; she had already started up the stairs. "I don't think—perhaps we should just say to the others that your mother got sick in the middle of the night. I don't want to upset them, especially the little ones. Eventually they'll have to know what happened, of course, but for now perhaps we shouldn't tell them. And perhaps I should be the one to tell them why I'm here. What do you think?"

She thought about it for a moment: thought about trying to explain to them why their mother was not here and why Neal was. She had no idea what she would say. She had been very worried that one of the younger ones would wake up when the ambulance men came in. She realized that it would be a great relief to her if she let Neal do the explaining.

"You mean, just say I woke up and found her—"

"Yes. Just as you did. I'm talking about what happened to her. I think you should talk to your grandmother about it first, and then perhaps let her talk to them. It isn't that I don't want to tell them the truth, it's just that it's a kind of family thing where—ah—outsiders perhaps shouldn't interfere."

He was still the outsider; they both understood that. Even though she had called him, even though she had turned to him in her need, her desperation, he was still what he had always been: the intruder. He understood both her feelings and the reason she had called him. Despite the fact that he had been invited back, so to speak, he did not want to assume too much.

"Yes," she said. "That would be good. Just to say she got sick." She nodded at him and went on up.

Neal did not sleep. He found a book to read, a paperback of a novel popular some years before, and, keeping on his parka against the cold, stretched out on the sofa in the living room. But the story did not hold his attention; after a while he put it aside and spent the time until the children awoke, until he could call Margaret's mother, turning his thoughts over and over. Mostly they were of Margaret.

Before seven, when it was beginning to be light, he called Margaret's mother. He needed to speak to her alone, before the children came down. He told her what he knew, which was not much. She needed a moment to comprehend who he was, what he was saying. Then, when she did, she came through strong and clear, not confused or weeping as he had feared. She would be there directly, she said—probably before the children left for school. She agreed that the younger ones should not be told the truth at once; she agreed that they should all go to school, since there was nothing for them to do if they stayed home except sit around and worry. Before she hung up she said, "Mr. Donovan? I don't know how to say this, I don't know *what* to say. I don't know you very well—don't know you at all, in fact—but I want to say thank you. It sounds as though you've had a bad time."

Shortly afterward the children trooped downstairs. Lily had given the younger ones a sketchy description of the night's events. She could not tell which piece of news alarmed them more: that their mother had been taken to the hospital, or that Neal was downstairs waiting for them.

He sat at the kitchen table drinking a cup of coffee.

"Morning," he said to them.

They did not respond. He caught Lily's eye. "I told them Mom was sick," she said. They both understood that it was his cue. He started to explain: how Lily had called him, how he was glad that she had done so, how the ambulance had come—

"Where is she?" said David.

Neal told him.

"Can we see her?"

"Yes. I'm sure you can, after school. I'll take you."

"I want to see her now," said Peaches.

"She's—ah—probably getting some medicine now," said Neal, "and so we'll have to wait. I don't think the hospital has visiting hours in the morning anyway. It would upset their routine, because that's when the doctors go around to see all the patients."

Thomas said nothing. He looked very frightened.

"The important thing," said Neal, "is that she's going to be all right." He hoped his voice sounded more sincere to them than it did to him. None of them, not even Lily, looked as though they believed him.

"How long will she be in the hospital?" said David.

"I don't know. Probably for a few days. Maybe as long as a week."

They thought about it. He had the uneasy sense that despite the fact that Lily had called him, and had told them that she had, they held him responsible for their mother's absence.

"Now," he said, to break the uncomfortable silence. "What do you want for breakfast?"

Lily and David took care of that: orange juice and oatmeal. Neal had wondered briefly about his ability to get the four of them fed and off to school in an organized way, but they had been well brought up, they knew their routine and they followed it.

They were getting on their boots when their grandmother arrived. They were very glad to see her; as Neal watched her greet them and assure them that everything would be all right, as she saw them out the door, he thought admiringly that she, like Lily—like Margaret, for that matter—was, as they say, a real trouper. All of them—all three generations of them—looked more fragile, more helpless than they were; underneath they were very strong.

"All right," she said when she came back to the kitchen. He saw that there were dark circles under her eyes; her hair looked as though it had been hurriedly brushed, as it probably had. She wore no makeup. "Let's have some coffee before we call the police and you can tell it to me again."

47

≈≈≈

"Feeling better?" said Neal. He was unutterably relieved to see that she was conscious; he had feared that she might not be.

"Yes." She did not smile because smiling hurt. She hoped he understood.

He put down his parcels: a dozen red roses wrapped in cellophane and tissue and heavy paper, a box of soft-centered chocolates. The candy was superfluous, he saw, because her jaw had been wired shut. On the tray beside her bed were a glass of milk and a glass of orange juice, each with a bending plastic straw.

"I spoke to your mother," he said. "She's been here?"

"Yes."

"And I told her that I'd pick up the kids at the house after school and bring them along. Just for a few minutes, so that they can see you're all right. Your mother spoke to the doctor, and he agreed that they should come."

She lowered her eyes to indicate her assent, her gratitude. He realized that probably she should not speak, not move her mouth. Her face was swollen, the left eye nearly shut, an ugly purple bruise around it spreading across the cheekbone, another bruise along her jaw.

He wanted very much to question her: who did this? How? Why? Later, he thought. All of it later, when she had recovered. As he looked at her lying small and wounded in the starched white hospital bed he wanted to gather her up in his arms and heal her through the sheer force of his will.

That was, he supposed, a kind of love. He acknowledged it: he bowed to its demands. He wanted to tell her that. He had wanted to tell her on the night he came to see her, shortly after the New Year. He had allowed himself to be silenced by her pride—a pride, a self-assurance which he had helped her to acquire. The irony of his situation did not escape him, but he did not dwell on it. He was not interested in irony; he was interested in Margaret. And in loving her.

He put his hand on the headboard to balance himself and kissed, very lightly, the top of her head. She watched him through her right eye. She did not smile; he preferred to think that it was because she could not.

"Anything else you want?" he said. He heard his voice, a little hoarse, a little rough with his emotion.

"No."

"All right. I'll be back with the kids."

He hesitated. It was hard for him to break away. He wanted to stay with her, as if he was afraid that if he left her again—if he allowed himself to be pushed away, shut out as she had shut him out the night he went to see her, harm would come to her again. If he had not gone away, if he had stayed with her, she would not have been alone, she would not have been vulnerable to attack.

Her eyes were closed. She seemed to be going to sleep. Still he lingered; and then, suddenly, her right eye opened and she looked at him. Her battered face subtly changed into the faintest hint of a smile.

He could live on that, he thought, until she was well.

48

LILY'S FAITH IN THE STABILITY OF THEIR WORLD HAD been shattered forever the night she found her mother beaten and unconscious. Anything seemed possible now.

The others asked her, over and over again, to tell them what had happened: how she had awakened knowing something was wrong, how she had gone downstairs to find her mother, how she had called Neal.

"I don't think you should have called him," said David. He was annoyed that Lily had not awakened him, that he had missed all the excitement.

Peaches was annoyed for the same reason. "How come you didn't call Grandma?" she said. "Or—or Mrs. Lafferty?"

"I didn't call Grandma because she was upset already," said Lily. "And I don't know why I didn't call Mrs. Lafferty. I never thought of calling anyone else. Only him."

"Because we helped him," said David skeptically. "So he should help us."

"Yes. Sort of. I mean, it was the middle of the night and everything. I didn't want to wake Mrs. Lafferty up. But I didn't mind waking him."

It had been, they understood, a kind of challenge to him: would he play fair? He did; they could not deny it. They still resented him, they still disliked him, but they granted him that much: however unreliable he had been in the past, he had, in this emergency, behaved splendidly.

Lily worried that by calling Neal she had ruptured her solidarity with the others. Perhaps they were right; perhaps she should at least have awakened them, consulted with them, before she asked him for help. At the time it had not seemed so. But she felt the breach, ever so slight; her stance toward Neal had shifted, if only by a fraction, while theirs had not.

She had felt guilty, too, about not telling the truth right away about her mother's condition. Their grandmother had explained, that first day, before they visited Margaret in the hospital: their mother had fallen asleep in the den and had awakened to find an intruder in the house. She was not just "sick," she was badly injured.

Shortly after Margaret returned from the hospital she gathered them around her and told them that now, because someone had broken into the house, the very next day she was having an alarm system installed.

"It will connect us to the police," she said. She spoke slowly, with difficulty, but she made the effort because it was important to let them know that what had happened to her would not happen again. "If anyone tries to break in, an alarm will sound. Either he will be frightened away or the police will come and catch him."

As she spoke her glance met Lily's. For only a second or two, Margaret saw a spark of memory, of recognition, of understanding in her daughter's eyes. Each of them veered off that glance and looked away.

What did Lily know? Had she seen her father that

night? I will have to find out, thought Margaret. But not now. Lily doesn't want to talk about it now, she doesn't want to talk about it in front of the others. She will accept what I say, for now at least, because that is all she is capable of accepting. She cannot bear to acknowledge any other version of what happened. Later, perhaps, she will tell me what she knows. Or what she thinks she knows.

The children nodded; they understood about the alarm. Their mother had acted, as she always did, to keep them safe. They had been badly frightened by what happened to her, but they need be frightened no longer. She would be all right; she would recover.

Only Lily seemed unconvinced, but she said nothing.

49

"MARRY ME."

She smiled at him. She was healing nicely; she could smile easily now, and she was talking better every day. She was not mocking him, or even refusing him, and he understood that. Her eyes held something that he thought must be very like love—that, and a kind of compassion, something like pity, that he did not understand.

They sat in her living room on an evening two weeks later. The children were asleep—or in bed, at least—as was Margaret's mother, who was staying with them. Neal had eaten dinner with them, had played several games of checkers with David (Neal, four; David, two), had read a story to Thomas, had listened to Peaches describe a rehearsal for a school play. He was not yet entirely comfortable with them, nor they with him, but the sense of strain that had marked their earlier encounters had nearly disappeared. If he was not yet an accepted member of the family, neither was he the hated intruder. He wondered what Lily had told them about calling him for help. That would account for their change in attitude, he thought.

Now he sat with Margaret before a warming fire

and tried to find the words to explain himself, to convey his feelings to her, to make her understand. It was extraordinarily difficult; he was alarmed to see that he was trembling—with fear, with a longing such as he had never known, with joy at being able, at last, to say to her the things that were in his heart.

"Marry me," he said again. He fumbled in his jacket pocket and took out a small jeweler's box. He put it into her hand and folded her fingers around it. It was black velvet, a round-topped cube with a hinged lid.

She looked away, then—and then at what he had given her. She knew what it was. She shook her head. Without even attempting to open it she gave it back to him, putting it into his hand as he had put it into hers.

Her lack of curiosity alarmed him. "Aren't you even going to look at it?" he said. "How do you know what it is?"

"I know."

"Well, then. Don't you want to check the size, or—"

"It's not the right time now," she said.

"Why not?

"It just isn't. Three months ago it was. Or at least I thought it was. Perhaps in three months it will be again."

She did not want to offend him—did not want to throw his offering back in his face. But she felt that even to look at the ring he had brought would indicate a kind of acceptance—a willingness to consider his offer—that she was not prepared to make. Not yet: perhaps not ever.

Despite the fact that she had been so gravely injured, despite the fact that she was still recuperating, he felt her strength—a strength that she had not had before. He understood that she had taken it, at least in part, from him. He was the needy one now, trying to find a way to express his need to the woman he had, in a sense, created. Understanding these things as he did, he was nevertheless shocked that she did not even want to see the ring that he had bought for her. Vainly he cast about for a vestige of his former pride.

"I'll take it back to the jeweler's, then," he said.

"No. Don't do that. Hang on to it for a while."

"Margaret—" He was afraid to touch her. He wanted to put his arms around her and hold her close, he wanted to kiss her as once he had done on this very sofa, in this very room, weeks ago. But she had not mended yet, and so he could only seize her hand and put her small warm palm against his cheek and try to tell her that he loved her.

He felt as though he had been locked into himself all his life. She had found the key, had turned it, had brought him out—and now she was leaving him abandoned, exposed for all the world to see. He had no idea how he would live the rest of his life without her. His fear that he might suffer that fate left him without shame, without pride. To his horror he felt tears come to his eyes. He blinked them away. He searched for some hope—something to cling to so as not to give way to despair.

"I love you," he said; he heard the urgency in his voice and prayed that she heard it too.

She nodded. "I know." She was suddenly very grave, as if she understood that to be loved by him was a serious thing, a responsibility that she did not take lightly.

He took what comfort he could from her response; he took a little courage from it. "I think I always loved you," he said.

She did not believe that, and she let him see her disbelief.

"I know," he said. "I behaved badly. I was stupid. But don't you see, I was afraid. I'd never loved anyone before. It scared the hell out of me."

She couldn't help smiling. "Big brave man," she said.

"And now—perhaps I don't have the right to say this, but now I want you back. I had you once, I know that, and I just couldn't deal with it. It was too new. It happened too fast."

"Yes. It was very fast, wasn't it?"

"And so I said to myself, pull back a little, you don't want to make any mistakes. All I could think of was my parents, how miserable they were. And then when I met your parents I was even more put off. I saw that they lived in a different world. It wasn't a world I ever thought I'd live in. I just couldn't accept the possibility that I'd ever be happy in that way. With another person, I mean. I was perfectly happy in myself—*with* myself—but I didn't trust myself to be happy with anyone else. It just all seemed too risky."

He could think of nothing else to say—he did not know how else to plead his case—and so he fell silent.

She did not reply at once; she seemed to be turning his words over and over in her mind. Then: "I need to be alone for a while," she said. "Not—no, not *alone*. I want you, and the children, and mother all with me. But I can't think about *us*, just now. I need some time."

"Yes," he said.

"I'm not telling you to go away. You understand?"

"Yes.

"But I just need time. Space. I need to sort things out."

"Yes."

"Wait," she said, and she smiled at him again. "Just wait for me. Who knows what will happen?"

He understood that she was not being coy; he understood that she was being honest and prudent and as kind as possible—more kind than he had been to her. It had been he, after all, who had given her the strength that he saw in her now. He had encouraged her to be competent, confident, independent—he had even, in a burst of what now seemed to be incomprehensible folly, suggested that she go out with other men.

And she was right, after all: after everything that had happened, life being as strange as it was, anything at all might happen next.

She had given him that, at least—that hope. She had not turned him away completely.

He leaned in, carefully balancing himself, and kissed her lips gently, barely touching. "Who knows?" he said.

He was glad that he was able to smile at her.

50

❦❦❦

"Y<small>OUR SHARE WILL COME TO YOU DIRECTLY, OF</small> course," said Margaret's mother. "The rest will come through me, after I go." She peered at Margaret over her reading glasses. They were finishing breakfast, reading the paper, relaxing a bit after having seen the children off to school. The kitchen was filled with light: bright sun reflecting off new snow. But it was a February sun, brilliant with the promise of spring, the end of winter: a sparkling day, a day to plan the future.

"That makes you a good catch," she added, smiling. And then, seeing the warning look that Margaret gave her: "Only joking, sweetie. Only joking. Neal loves you enough just as you are. I don't imagine the fact that you are an heiress will make any difference."

Margaret laughed, then. She was still so newly healed that she delighted in laughing, in being able to eat, to move her jaw freely. A hundred thousand dollars was a lot of money, but "heiress" was too archaic a term to take seriously.

"You never give up, do you, Mother?"

"I just want to see you happy. I'm not pushing, I just want—"

"Don't, dear." Margaret leaned over and put her

hand over her mother's. They were suddenly both close to tears.

"I'll never have a marriage like yours," Margaret went on. "But it's all right, you know. I have other things. I'm fine, really I am. And very lucky."

Mrs. Brigham nodded. "I know. I know." She wiped her eyes and blew her nose and smiled. "Sorry."

Margaret understood that her mother's hurt was deeper than her own, and would take longer to heal. Moments like this would probably often recur. Henceforth her mother would always be bereft—incomplete, wounded, stranded in that twilight life inhabited by widows and widowers who cannot begin anew, who cannot adjust to being alone after decades of being half of a pair. In the weeks since her father's death Margaret had occasionally seen a frightening look on her mother's face—a look of utter loss, a bewildered look, as if she were disoriented, as of course she was, and could not find her bearings. Possibly, Margaret thought, she never would.

Now, casting about for something to distract her mother, she said, "I've decided to do over the third floor. We're two-family zoning here. I can make a condominium—Carl Olsen will do the plans for me—and I can sell it for more than enough money to pay back the loan I'll need to do it and to pay off the mortgage as well."

It worked: she saw a glimmer of interest in her mother's face.

"That's a very good idea. How clever you are. I never would have thought of it. But of course it makes sense, doesn't it, now that—well. Now that you aren't sure of your income."

A practiced diplomat could not have put it more delicately, thought Margaret. Her "income"—the child

support that she had received from her former husband—had not appeared since before his trip East.
What was more, he himself had vanished. The police
had put out a warrant for his arrest on a charge of
assault and battery, but he was nowhere to be found.
Margaret had sworn out a complaint against him. She
had called his company in California, but they had not
seen him since he left. People did that, she knew:
dropped out of sight, changed identities.

The fact that he had vanished meant that he knew
what he had done. Drunk as he was, he had been able
to remember. It had occurred to her that he might return to attack her again. That was one reason she had
been glad to have her mother stay with her. She supposed that eventually she should move. Then he would
be unable to find her. The support money would undoubtedly not resume. She would have to find a way to
survive; this renovation was the first step. Carl Olsen
had talked to her briefly not only about it but about
others as well. If she had a little money left over, he
said, she could buy houses and fix them up and sell
them. If she did it right she'd make a profit on each
one. She had never thought of houses as other than
someplace you lived. Carl's ideas had sounded vaguely
exploitive. "You make me feel like a capitalist swine,"
she said, laughing to take the nasty edge off her words.

Carl shrugged. "It's better than being on welfare."

Which was true enough.

When she'd told Neal about the idea, he had looked
doubtful. "It takes a lot of know-how," he said. "I'm
living proof that you don't know the first thing about
houses, or fixing them up. Why not just go out and get
a job?"

She did not want to go out and get a job. She was
not trained to do anything; there was nothing she

wanted to do. The more she thought about it, the more she liked the idea of buying and selling houses. She liked it particularly because Neal thought she wouldn't be able to do it.

The following week she began swimming again. She was in the advanced intermediates now.

51

~~~~~

In the weeks that followed her mother's return from the hospital, Lily saw that what Margaret had said about feeling responsible for the person you saved seemed to be true for Neal. He had started to visit them again, and to call every day. It was odd, but she did not mind him now the way she had before; none of them did. It was almost as if he was an old friend who had gone away and now had come back again. They had a shared past, a history that bound them. He and their grandmother, in fact, had become very friendly; often they talked and joked together, and they carried on running debates over silly things— say, the best way to put a pig into a poke.

On the other hand, Lily was not yet ready to welcome him fully into their lives; she was not ready to accept him, for instance, as their stepfather. Nor were the others. She discovered this one day when they held a War Council in her room (a drizzly March day, too unpleasant to gather outside).

"I don't care," said Peaches. "I don't want him to be our father, but I like him better than I did. He said he'd help us build a go-cart in the spring." Gail Stubbs' dollhouse was nothing compared to a go-cart.

Thomas looked at her warily, considering it. "A real one?" he said.

"Of course a real one."

David shook his head. "Listen," he said. "What if they get married?"

"Mom wouldn't do that," said Lily. But she spoke without conviction; the certainty that she had had on the matter the previous autumn had vanished.

"But what *if?*" David persisted.

"*If*," said Peaches, responding to David's question, "*if*—" She caught Thomas' eye. "Oh, *I* don't know. I'll worry about it later. Wouldn't a go-cart be neat, though?"

It seemed to David and Lily that Peaches, even after everything that had happened, did not comprehend the seriousness of David's question. You could not compare a go-cart to a stepfather. On the other hand, a go-cart was not to be sneezed at; and they were, in truth, tired of worrying. They had been worrying for weeks—months. It was time to stop.

Shortly afterward, when they adjourned, David went to his room and retrieved his notebook from under his mattress. He opened it to the first entries. He felt as though he was reading a chronicle of events that had happened ages ago instead of last fall. He felt that the person who had written down all that information was someone he did not know—someone he might have known perhaps, but not any longer. That person had disappeared. The person whose comings and goings were noted in such detail had disappeared also. The Neal Donovan who came to visit now was not a threatening stranger, an enemy; he was a familiar and not unwelcome presence in their lives.

Not entirely welcome—not yet—but not unwelcome either. Certainly not someone whose comings and goings needed to be written down in a dossier.

David thought for a moment and then, carrying the notebook, stepped out into the hall. He could smell the familiar, pungent odor of wood smoke from the fireplace in the living room. He went downstairs. Lily was sitting by the fire reading. She was alone. She looked up when he came in; then she saw the notebook.

He stood in front of the fire.

"What are you going to do with that?" she said. She had seen it from time to time; he had let her read it when he felt he had made a particularly good entry. Often she had supplied details that he had overlooked.

"I'm going to burn it."

She understood: it had served its purpose. They no longer needed it. More than that: it had become an embarrassment, a relic of their former, younger selves that they needed to dispose of. It was as if they could not move on to their future until the notebook and what it represented—their fear, their anger, their powerlessness—was safely, thoroughly destroyed.

"Go on," she said. "Throw it in."

He did. At first the fire did not catch it, but then it did, and it blazed up fiercely, briefly, the edges of the cardboard cover blackening and blistering before they exploded into flames. In a moment only thin black sheets remained, more fragile than moth wing. David took the poker and shattered them, stirring them to dust which sifted down onto the brick hearth. Cautiously he fished out the notebook's blackened metal spiral; moving aside the fire screen he scooted it out to cool at his feet. It looked like a skeleton of a prehistoric creature dug out of a bed of coal formed at the beginning of time; as he picked it up and held it for Lily to see, he was, briefly, a paleontologist.

"David—"

"What?"

He was struck by her expression, which was suddenly intent, as if she was concentrating very hard on something she wanted to say, as if she was trying to find just the right words to say it.

"What?" he said again. "What's wrong?"

Suddenly her face went blank. "Nothing." She shook her head.

He knew that it was not so. There had been something that she wanted to tell him, but she had decided not to. He knew better than to persist. She would tell him when she was ready to tell him, and not before.

"Throw it in the kitchen trash and she'll never find it," Lily said. He understood who "she" was.

But he did not do that. He carried it instead up to his room, where he deposited it at the back of the top drawer of his bureau—his cache of miscellaneous treasures, curiosities worth saving for one reason or another. This, too, was worth saving—not the pages it had held together, but this. No one except Lily would ever know what it was—what it signified—unless he explained. That was the beauty of it: it was a mysterious, unforthcoming, inexplicable artifact, a relic of what had been. It would mean nothing to anyone else; but to him, whenever he looked at it, it would resonate with the emotions of that autumn and winter when, desperate to protect them against the intruder, the enemy, he had stored up information in the pages of a cheap little notebook.

He shut the drawer; he pulled shut the door of his room as he went out; he ran downstairs to get his lunch.

52

LILY COULDN'T STAND IT ANY MORE: SHE HAD TO know. She had lain in bed in the dark, listening to the rain, since nine-thirty; now it was past eleven. The thing that had sunk into the back of her mind that cold January night had refused to stay submerged; every day she thought of it, and now, tonight, it tormented her worse than ever, she did not know why. Perhaps because they had done reports on California at school that day.

She got up, put on her bathrobe and slippers, and padded down the hall. Her mother's door was ajar, the light on. She pushed the door open a bit.

"Mom?"

Margaret was reading in bed. She looked up, mildly surprised, and smiled at Lily. "Hi, sweetie. Come on in. Can't sleep?"

"No."

Lily perched on the edge of the bed. She had thought of what she was going to say, but now she couldn't remember the right words.

"What?" said Margaret. "I hope you're not worried about tomorrow?"

Tomorrow was the class play. Lily knew her lines;

she wasn't nervous, at least not in any serious way. "No," she said. "It'll be OK."

"Of course it will. It always is."

"Mom—" Lily still did not know exactly how her questions should be phrased, but she needed to get them out, she was weary of carrying around their terrible burden.

"Mom, do you remember the night that man came and hit you—beat you up?"

Here it comes, thought Margaret. She had not forgotten the flash of—what? memory?—that she had seen in Lily's eyes the day she told the children about the intruder and the installation of the alarm system. Careful, she thought: proceed with extreme caution.

"Yes," she said. "Of course I do."

"Well—did you see him?"

"I saw—someone. I'm not sure—"

"I mean, was he anybody you know?"

Margaret hesitated. She heard the rain pounding on the porch roof outside her window; it seemed very loud.

"It all happened so quickly," she said at last. "I had been asleep, and when I woke up he was—he was right there. I didn't exactly have a chance to study him."

Lily made no reply. Then abruptly, she said: "When is Daddy coming?"

Margaret shook her head. "I don't know, sweetheart."

"Why didn't he come when he was supposed to, that time last winter?"

"I don't know that, either."

"Well—can't we call him?"

"As a matter of fact—"

"Right now," said Lily. "Let's call him right now. It's funny that he hasn't called us, isn't it?"

She had not intended to suggest such a thing, but now that she had, she thought it was a good idea.

"All right," said Margaret after a moment. "Here. You dial." She had never been able to remember the number; she looked it up now in the little address book beside the phone. She showed it to Lily, and Lily dialed it. Margaret knew, of course, the response she would get.

After a moment Lily put down the receiver. "The operator—or is it a machine?—said that number has been disconnected." She spoke in a defeated way, Margaret thought.

"Lily—sweetheart—I don't know what to say to you." And that, at least, was the truth. "Do you understand me? I just—"

"I saw him," said Lily.

"What?"

"I saw him that night. Daddy. He came into my room. I thought it might have been a dream. But then when he never called to tell us why he didn't come—when he never called at *all*—I figured maybe something had happened to him. Or, I thought, maybe he had done something wrong and he needed to run away."

Lily thought that her mother was going to cry, then, but she did not.

"Mom?"

"What, love?"

"Was it him? Who hit you, I mean."

Margaret could not speak. She put out her arms and Lily came to her and they held each other very tight. Then Margaret said: "You know, he wasn't himself."

"What do you mean?"

"I mean—he'd been drinking. You know what happens when people drink too much."

"They get drunk."

"Yes. And then sometimes they do things—terrible things that they wouldn't do ordinarily. And he was—well, he was angry with me, he wanted to wake you all up, and it was late, and it was the night of Grandpa's funeral, and Peaches was sick. And I said, no, he couldn't. And he got very angry."

Lily thought about it.

"Lily?"

"What?"

"I'm sorry."

"For what?"

"For—I don't know. For having to tell you this."

"It's not your fault."

"No. It isn't. But I'm sorry all the same."

"I don't think we should tell, do you?"

"You mean David and Peaches and Thomas?"

"Yes."

"No. I don't think we should."

Lily thought about it. Maybe David, she thought. But certainly not the little ones.

Another silence. Then: "What will happen to him?" Lily said.

"To your father?"

"Yes."

"I don't know."

"Won't they arrest him?"

"They have a warrant out. But he's disappeared. They have to find him before they can arrest him."

"So we won't see him again?"

"Probably not for a long time." *If ever*, she thought.

Lily nodded; she accepted it. She had known it all along; only now did she realize that she had known it. She could not think what to say. She sat up straight; she glanced around her mother's room. Everything seemed the same: the double bed, the photographs of herself and the others on the bureau, the easy chair by the big bay window. A long time ago her father used to sleep there. Then he went away. Somehow over the years—and Lily was struck by this thought now for the first time—he had stopped being her father. Each time she saw him on one of his visits he was her father a little less. Now, it seemed, he was not her father at all.

Once upon a time she would not have been able to bear that thought. Now she felt it like a dull pain in her heart, but it was bearable, it was a tolerable pain. She could live with it. Oddly, she felt that she should somehow comfort her mother. Her mother, just now, looked very bleak.

"Lily."

"What?"

"Come here."

She did. Margaret hugged her tight for a long moment. Then she pulled back and stared hard.

"You OK?"

"Yes."

"You sure? This is a lot to digest."

"I'm all right."

"You can talk to Dr. Bluestein if you want." Ann Bluestein was their doctor. They all liked her very much. There was nothing that you could not say to her.

"No."

"You sure?"

"Yes. I—maybe I will. In the summer. But I don't want to now."

She needs time, Margaret thought: time to come to terms with it. She knows that we are here if she needs to talk. She's a sensible child. She will be all right. This was what she needed—to talk to me, to find out what she wanted to know.

Suddenly Lily felt very tired. She did not want to talk any longer; she wanted to go to sleep. She kissed Margaret's cheek, still remembering to be very gentle even though Margaret's face had healed, and then she said good night.

53

"DARLING," WHISPERED BARBARA KIMBALL. "I'M so happy." Her eyes were brimming, her cheeks a shade too pink. She was wearing a chiffon dress, draped layers of sheer mocha-colored fabric that would have looked impossibly drab on anyone else; on Barbara it looked stunning. She reached to embrace Margaret; as they hugged each other Margaret realized that her friend was trembling. She took it to mean not that Barbara was afraid but that she was deeply moved, her emotions keyed up to meet the solemnity, the significance of the occasion.

Recklessly, improvidently, Barbara had chosen to marry out of doors in May—a treacherous month that might produce snow as easily as warm and benevolent sun. Barbara had won her gamble: the day was mild and bright, the garden where they gathered adorned with flowering dogwood and crab apple trees, azaleas and tulips and hyacinths.

Margaret had been, if not appalled, then at least moderately surprised when Barbara had announced that she and Craig McCarren were going to be married. Given the agonizing tales that Barbara had produced over the winter, Margaret realized that in the course of her own troubles, her injury, and recovery, she had missed certain crucial developments in Barbara's story. By March, when she had gotten fully caught up with news of Barbara's affair, events had taken a happy turn. "He's proposed," Barbara had said, beaming. Margaret had wondered why Barbara wanted to marry a man who had been so—well, so unreliable. Naturally she had kept that question to herself; one did not, in the face of happiness as radiant as Barbara's, bring up unpleasant details.

Margaret stood with her arm loosely linked in Neal's, watching the happy couple mingle with the hundred or so guests. Happy and handsome, she thought. Craig McCarren was as good-looking as Barbara; together they were almost too much. A photographer dogged them, a nimble little fellow in jeans and designer jersey; Margaret thought that he could probably sell a portrait of Barbara and Craig to one of the glossy, expensive magazines that catered not to the upwardly mobile but to those who had already risen as far "up" as possible.

"Dream Couple Marries; Friends Envious . . ."

"Think it'll last?" said Neal, smiling at her.

She shook her head. "I don't know. I hope so."

"You like him?"

There had been, two weeks before, a small getting-to-know-you dinner at which Barbara had introduced her man to her friends. When Margaret had asked if she might bring Neal, Barbara had been delighted; like all happy people she wanted to share her happiness, she wanted her friends to be as happy as she was. Or almost.

"Of course!" she had said. "How marvelous! Is he the one you went out with last fall? And you've started up with him again? Oh, Margaret! I'll say a little prayer for you! It can't hurt, and who knows how it may help?"

The dinner had gone well, the guests in a jolly, celebratory mood. Craig had been charming. Barbara had been slightly flustered—a condition in which Margaret had never seen her, and which she had taken to mean that Barbara was madly in love. Margaret wondered if being madly in love, for Barbara, meant the same thing that presumably it meant for other people: commitment, not leaving at the first sign of boredom, tolerance of the loved one's inevitable failings. She wondered, too, if being madly in love was the best condition in which to marry.

Now, considering Neal's question, she watched Craig as he charmed his guests.

"I suppose so," she said. "I mean, it's hard to tell, isn't it? Who knows what's behind that beautiful face?"

She glanced at Neal as she spoke. He was squinting a little in the bright sunlight; she thought he looked uncomfortable in his summer-weight suit. He was not handsome at all, she thought. Strong-looking, intelligent-looking—but not handsome. He was all rough edges, none of the Madison Avenue, rugged charm that Craig McCarren possessed. And yet he had his own charm, his own kind of attractiveness. She would not have wanted to trade with Barbara.

She was, she thought, beginning to love him again. There were certain kinds of love in the world, she thought: parental love, of course, and filial love; and the painful, frantic infatuation that she had suffered for Neal the previous autumn. What she felt now was different, because now she was different. What she felt now was calm: a serenity and certainty that was, she realized, something new in her life.

She gave his arm a little squeeze, and she was touched to see his quick, affectionate smile in response.

"Whatever happens to them," she said, "I'm not worried about Barbara. She can take care of herself."

He watched her. "Just like you," he said. She thought she heard a note of proprietary pride in his voice; she did not begrudge him it.

"Yes." It was true: she *could* take care of herself—if necessary, for the rest of her life.

And only because of that, she thought, she was ready to welcome—what? A partner? A helpmeet? Whatever: someone who would stand beside her, just as Neal stood now. Not someone on whom she would lean, not someone she would need to cling to, a pretty, trailing vine twined around a strong support, collapsing if that support were removed.

Yes, she thought: just like me.

54

AT THE BEGINNING OF JUNE MARGARET AND NEAL
went to Martha's Vineyard for a weekend. Margaret's
mother had taken the children to Connecticut: there
was a new foal to see, and a litter of seven puppies.

Margaret and Neal stayed at an inn in Edgartown
which had once been the home of a whaling captain. It
was large and white and comfortable; the furnishings
were said to be genuine antiques, and, indeed, they
had a certain worn look that showed, at least, that they
were not new.

There was no swimming pool.

As he shut the door to their room and locked it, she
recalled for a moment their previous weekend together. It had not gone well. This time would be better. She was a different woman now. He was different
too, she thought. Easier; gentler. His attitude had
changed. He knew her now as he had not known her
before. And, she thought, there was more of her to
know. She had changed—in large part because of him
—and to his credit he had been able to accept her new
self. More: to love her, to admit that love.

She came into his arms as if she had, after long absence, come back at last to where she belonged. He

enfolded her as if, after a lifetime, he had found not only her, but himself as well.

No regrets, she thought: no second-guessing, no "what if?"

Later, over dinner, she announced to him that she had received a permit from the municipal authorities to convert her house into two condominiums. Carl Olsen had put her in touch with a reliable contractor; work would begin in a week or so.

They were both well aware of the implications of her news: she had made her decision, she was following through on it. Some weeks ago she had told him what she planned to do, but she had not thought it necessary to consult him—to ask his advice.

She sipped her wine; she smiled at him. "I'm going to do the bathroom in gray and white," she said. "And the kitchen like mine—red, and natural wood."

He knew enough, now, not to caution her about getting in over her head—a turn of phrase which had as much to do with any endeavor in life as it had with swimming. He realized that it no longer applied to Margaret in anything she did. He nodded, therefore, and smiled at her in return. "Good," he said. "Do they know how long it will take to finish?"

"A couple of months, they said. Certainly by the end of the summer, but probably sooner."

She was, he realized, slightly abstracted: she was with him, of course, but some part of her mind was concentrating on something else. She was as gentle, as sweet as she had always been, as she had been when he first met her; but now, he thought, there was more going on behind her pretty face. He liked that—liked it very much. He would not have wanted one of Jason Goodrich's hard, assertive young women, but he was pleased that Margaret had come along as far as she had, that her confidence, nurtured with his help (as she would have been the first to admit), had blossomed to this degree. Even if that blossoming left him feeling somewhat left out. As it did.

She sensed what was wrong. "I think that if we—ah—well, if there were going to be any major change in my situation, I'd probably want to move."

"To a single family house again."

"Yes."

"How do the kids feel about this conversion?"

"I explained it to them. They think it makes good sense."

"And how do you think they'd feel about—ah—any major change in your situation?"

She watched him. "It hasn't been easy for them, you know."

"If anyone should know that, I should."

"Right."

"But they seem OK. I mean, they aren't showing any ill effects."

"No."

"What I mean is—" He was the supplicant again; they both understood that. "What I mean is, they seem to like me now."

"Oh, yes, I think they do."

"Even Thomas."

"Even Thomas, yes."

"I think the go-cart will help a lot."

"You're really going to do that?"

"Of course. I promised. I told them I'd bring over the wood the first weekend after school is out."

She reached across the table and put her hand on his. She smiled; she was, he thought, even laughing at him a little. "Good," she said. "After you've worked up a sweat on that, we can all go swimming."

55

~~~~~~

"WELL?" SAID MARGARET. "WHAT IF I MARRIED him?"

The children stared at her, caught off guard. They were appalled. There it was, the thing that they had feared so long, coming at them now all of a sudden.

It was a warm evening in the middle of June: a long, sweet twilight, impossible to shoo them off to bed even though school would not be done for another week. They sat on the front porch eating chocolate covereds, watching fireflies; Thomas, as he always did at the beginning of every summer, had spent a half hour or so catching them, but then had become bored with running about and was now content, as they all were, just to watch.

Peaches was the first to recover enough to ask the pertinent question. "Did he ask you?" she said.

Margaret felt the intensity of their interest in her answer. She suppressed a smile.

"No," she said. "He hasn't. Not yet—or, at least, not recently. He did, last winter. After—after I was in the hospital."

They were too shocked to say anything. They had never dreamed such a thing. *He had already asked her!* And—obviously—she had said no! Just as Lily had promised. "But I think he might again," Margaret went on. "And I wanted to talk it over with you."

"You mean—" David hesitated; he wanted to get it right. "You mean, if we say we don't want you to get married to him, you won't?"

"Not—well, not exactly. I mean, I don't think that children should have that kind of veto power. Not even children as sensible as you. But certainly I want to talk it over with you. I don't think it would be fair just to go ahead and do it without giving you a chance to tell me how you feel about it."

They were not sure—not absolutely sure—that she wanted to hear the truth. They were not sure what the truth was. They were not sure how well they could articulate whatever truth they came up with. Or whether, in the end, they would find it more prudent to lie.

They did not want to lie. They wanted to tell the truth, and—just as important—to hear the truth from her.

Depending, of course, on what it was.

"Well?" She watched them.

After what seemed a very long time, Peaches spoke first. "I guess he's all right," she said.

"He's going to build us a go-cart," said Thomas.

"I know," said Margaret.

"Gail Stubbs' mom is getting married next week," said Peaches.

"Oh?" said Margaret. This was the first time she had heard about Gail Stubbs. "Is that someone in your class?"

"Yes."

"And what does she say about it? Is she happy?"

Peaches shrugged. "I guess so. He's always bringing her presents."

"Are you saying you wish that Neal would bring presents to you?"

"No." Peaches spoke in a not very convincing way. "I'm just saying—"

"But he's going to build us the go-cart," said Thomas, "and that's better than anything."

Margaret was acutely aware that David and Lily were not participating in the discussion. "David?" she said.

He was thinking of his notebook, glad he had burned it. If he had not, he might be tempted now to take it out and read it, conjuring up the hostility, the anger and fear that Neal had aroused in them all last fall and winter. David was content to let those feelings lie buried. It had been an unhappy time; he did not want to relive it.

"I think you should, if you want to," he said.

"If I want to, I probably will. But I don't want to force him on you."

"You're not *forcing* him on us. I mean, if we all just said no, and really meant it—"

"But we wouldn't," said Lily.

"Why not?" Margaret thought she knew the answer, but she wanted to hear Lily say it.

"Because—" Lily couldn't find the words. She knew what she wanted to say, but she didn't know how.

"Because—" David struggled with it too. "Because you wouldn't do anything that would hurt us."

"Not intentionally, no."

"But more than that. You would always be very careful. Wouldn't you?"

"Of course. But people make mistakes."

"I know, but—"

"But you wouldn't make a mistake on purpose," said Peaches. She spoke with an air of triumph: she had sorted it out. "So you'd be careful, and we know you'd be careful—"

They were all remembering a time when Margaret had, they thought, made a very bad mistake indeed, when she had not been very careful at all. But in the end it had turned out all right; they could not deny it.

"How does anybody know anything is the right thing to do?" said Lily. "I mean, you do what you do because you think it's right. Right?"

"And we know that—" said David.

"And so we trust you," said Lily. She glanced around. It was nearly dark now, but she could still see their faces. She saw that she had hit on the vital point: they trusted their mother. It was, she thought, all that they could do—all that they wanted to do. Their mother would do the right thing: they could trust her for that. And if she did not—

Marriage was one of the things that adults did; divorce was another.

"If you got married again," said Peaches, "would you get divorced again?"

"I certainly wouldn't get married with the idea that it was a kind of trial period. Like a thirty-day trial period for those record clubs you see advertised. 'If you are not completely satisfied, return the records to us—'"

"'—and don't pay anything,'" said Peaches.

They all giggled, imagining themselves putting Neal into a package and sending him back to wherever he'd come from.

"Look," said Margaret, when they had stopped laughing, "I'm not saying it's going to happen. I'm saying it *might*. And I'm also saying—I suppose—that everything you do in life is a risk. A chance. So this would be a risk too. But not a very big one. It's not as if he's a stranger."

"Grandma said everybody's a stranger till you get to know them," said David.

It was the kind of thing her mother would say, thought Margaret: a kind of sunny, optimistic thing that her mother would think a suitable axiom for children. The point was: most strangers remained strangers, and that was just as well.

It was full dark now, the mosquitos out in force. They went inside; the children went to bed. They were glad—relieved—that their mother had talked to them about Neal. Each of them, going to sleep, tried to imagine him joining their family, living with them, being with them all the time.

The little ones didn't imagine much; they fell asleep right away. David and Lily stayed with it longer. They were not exactly comforted by what they imagined, but they were not upset by it, either—nor as they had been before.

It would be all right, they thought. They were older now: almost a whole year older. That made everything seem different.

56

※〜〜※

"CAROL," SAID JASON GOODRICH. "HER NAME IS Carol. Where've you been, anyway? I was going to call you if you didn't show up by Saturday."

"Busy," said Neal. "It's the start of the busy season." He saw that Jason did not quite believe him.

"Anyway," Jason went on, "she's just gotten tenure in the math department. Believe me, my friend—"

"No," said Neal. He spoke in a way that allowed no argument. Nevertheless Jason pressed on.

"Listen, old buddy, I know that I haven't always been a hundred percent right when it comes to—ah— introducing you. But believe me, this time I'm on target. Bull's-eye."

"You're wasting your time," said Neal. "I'm not in the market."

"You're never in the market. I know you. But all I'm saying is, just take a look at her. You don't even have to call her. You can come with me tomorrow night, there's a party and she said she'd be there. Just meet her. Talk to her. *Look* at her, for Pete's sake. An opportunity like this does not come along every day, my friend."

Neal did not reply. He looked away, to the stage,

where a red-haired young man was singing a lament, slightly off-key.

"What is it?" said Jason.

"Nothing. I'm really not in the market, that's all."

"Is is that one you brought in here that time?"

"I think it is."

"You *think*—! Neal, listen to me. I wish you all the best, you know that. But—"

"Sorry." Neal noted with mild interest that Jason seemed genuinely perturbed. Where did friendship end, he wondered, and meddling begin?

"She has kids, right?" said Jason

"Four."

"*Four!* My God." Jason rolled his eyes toward the ceiling. "You really must be bit."

Neal shrugged. "Guess so."

"Is it definite? I mean, are you setting the date?"

"Not yet. We're not sure yet about the kids."

"What do you mean?"

"I mean, they need time to adjust."

"To you?"

"Yes."

"My God. If you give them that kind of power, you'll never have a minute's peace."

Neal shook his head. "It's not like that. Not *power*. But they need time, that's all."

"Good," said Jason. "At least you're not rushing into anything. I mean, she's a very sweet girl and all that, but—" He caught Neal's eye; he smiled in a shamefaced way. "Hey. All the best, all right? All the best. She's the one who understood *Maria Braun*, right? Terrific. Even if she didn't like it. She's got some smarts. That's good."

The young man finished his song. Neal got up to leave. "I'll invite you to the wedding," he said. "If there is a wedding."

But there would be, he thought. He was almost certain that there would be.

57

〜〜〜

IT WAS SUMMER VACATION: A SATURDAY AFTER-
noon in late June, a warming sun, the air sweet with
new bloom.

The children were running free. They swarmed up
the hill behind the house, hot on the trail of the
enemy—Indians, this time, and the children were
the beleaguered settlers fighting their way across the
plains. Lily scrambled up the lookout tree. They
waited for her bulletin: was the enemy in sight?

She peered out. She saw nothing; she imagined
nothing. Now that she was here, she no longer wanted
to play. She would not have minded resting at the top
of the tree for a while, feeling the pleasant breeze on
her perspiring skin, thinking about the swimming party
to which she had been invited that afternoon. It was an
end-of-school party at the home of a classmate. Everyone in her room would be there. Especially Brian
Lansing. Lily felt a twinge of excitement when she
thought of Brian Lansing. All the girls in her class had
long since identified the cutest boy in their room. It
was not Brian. He was, in fact, rather homely. Nevertheless a certain something had sprung up between
them during the school play, in which they had both

had parts. Lily looked forward to this afternoon, when she would see Brian in a new setting.

Lily knew that she was far too young to begin to think seriously about boys. Once she had asked her mother when she could begin dating.

"Sixteen," said Margaret.

"Lorrie Simmons started going out when she was only fourteen." Lily did not care—fourteen and sixteen seemed almost equally far away—but she felt obliged to test the issue.

"Good for Lorrie," said Margaret.

"So why can't I?"

"Because I say so. Fourteen is way too young."

"Why?"

"Because—" Margaret had shaken her head in exasperation; Lily was not one to argue, not one to pester. "It's too young, that's all. For dating? That's what we're talking about, right? Dating? The boy comes by to pick you up, you go to the movies, whatever? He may even have a car, God forbid? Is that what we're talking about?"

"Yes."

"Sixteen," said Margaret; she glared at Lily in mock annoyance.

And that, Lily understood, was that.

Now, perched at the top of the tree, she tried to imagine what Brian Lansing would be like when he was sixteen. It was difficult; she could not even think what she herself would be like then.

"Lily?"

It was Peaches, getting restless, calling from below.

"What?"

"Don't you see them?"

"No," said Lily, not looking. She was examining her fingernails. They were reasonably clean. Perhaps, she thought, she would borrow some nail polish from

Peaches (who inherited all of Margaret's) and paint
her nails before she went to the party. But not bright
red, she thought. Only if there was some pale pink. Or
perhaps clear.

"Come on," called Thomas, too loud. "You have to
see them."

Lily looked. She saw her mother's green station
wagon parked in the driveway, and behind it two
trucks belonging to the workmen who had begun to
convert their third floor. She remembered the last time
she had been lookout: she had seen Neal's van. They
had pretended that he was the enemy. And so he had
been, for a while. Lily could hardly remember herself
and the others as they had been that day: skulking
around the house, lining up to confront him as he left.

They hadn't known him then. Now they did. It had
never occurred to them that it was possible to know
him.

"Lily—"

"Watch out," she called. She started down. They
awaited her, disappointment clouding their faces. She
felt a moment of regret—of guilt, even—but honestly
she did not feel like playing. She wanted to get ready
for the party.

"I have to go in," she said. Perhaps she could find a
ribbon for her hair, she thought.

"Why?" said Thomas.

"I have to get ready. I'm going to Sandy's, remember?"

They did remember; they did not begrudge her her
party. But they thought that two hours was a very long
preparation time.

"But you can go on with it," she said. "You don't
need me. David's a better lookout than I am anyway."

"No," said David. "It's no fun with only three."

"Work on the tree fort, then," said Lily. She knew

that she didn't have to find something for them to do, but she felt that she was deserting them, she felt that she had to make some suggestions.

They struggled down the hill behind her. When they reached the house they saw Neal's van pulling into the driveway. He got out, called hello, and began to unload a few pieces of lumber from the back.

They ran over to see.

"Is that for the go-cart?" said Thomas; but they knew that it was, they did not have to ask.

"That's right," said Neal. "Wheels and all," he added, showing them.

Lily felt her heart sink. She wanted, very much, to help build the go-cart; she wanted, very much, to go to the swimming party.

Neal saw her face. In the past few months, as he had begun to be friends with all of them, he had felt that he had a special bond with Lily. He thought that she felt it, too. "What's wrong?" he said to her.

She explained about the party.

"All right," he said. "Don't worry about it. We're going to measure and cut the wood today, that's all. Tomorrow we'll begin to put it together. So go ahead, and you can help tomorrow."

She was grateful to him for understanding, for solving the problem—grateful, but not surprised. He had turned out much better than any of them could have hoped, given their difficult beginning.

She ran into the house to get ready, leaving the others to help Neal. Despite the fact that she was going to a swimming party, she decided to wash her hair. And perhaps, among the treasures on Peaches' dressing table, she would find a lipstick that would, if she applied it very sparingly, make her look not like a child dressing up, but someone almost twelve going on, say, sixteen.

58

⌇⌇⌇⌇⌇

THE GO-CART WAS BRIGHT RED WITH A BLACK
stripe along each side. It had two seats, one behind the
other, and whitewall wheels powered by pedals, and a
small black steering wheel. It was low-slung, like a racing car; Neal had engineered it so that it seemed to
ride as smoothly as a racing car, too. It was a spectacu-
lar piece of work; even though the children had helped
Neal to make it, and had painted it all by themselves,
they had no idea what it would be like when it was
done. No one in the neighborhood had anything near
as good; David and Lily had a busy time of it, for the
first weeks, organizing rides for their friends so that
everyone had fair turns.

Thomas had the first ride. Around the corner from
their house was a short dead-end street: the perfect
place to ride, and, indeed, the only place that Margaret permitted. He eased himself into the front seat,
placed his feet on the pedals, grasped the steering
wheel with both hands, and set off. They cheered him
as he pedaled harder and harder, picking up speed. He
felt a rush of air cooling his perspiring face; as he kept
his eyes on the way ahead of him, he was conscious of
the scenery flying by. This was better than cowboys

and Indians, better than Star Wars; it was the best game they had ever had.

On the second ride, Peaches sat behind him. They could not believe that the go-cart worked so well. If you pedaled really hard, you could go almost as fast as on a bicycle—or so it seemed.

They rode and rode all summer; they never tired of it. They could go forever on it—they could travel anywhere, they could imagine that they were driving not only a racing car, but a train, or a jet, or a space craft: anything at all.

And when it got dark and they had to put it away in the carriage house before they went to bed, they could imagine themselves to sleep, thinking about what it would be tomorrow.

Once in a while, at such times, they would hear the grown-up voices from downstairs: company, perhaps, or just their mother and Neal, laughing. They didn't mind him now. His laughter, his deep voice counterpointing their mother's, sounded familiar to them now, comforting to hear in the quiet night.

And if, some day, he came to live with them forever—if their worst fears were realized—well, they would deal with it when it happened. They were not going to waste their summer worrying, they were not going to spend their vacation time trying to anticipate disaster that might turn out not to be disaster after all, when it happened. If it happened.

David was glad he no longer had a notebook to keep up; Neal was around so often now that keeping a record on him would be a tremendous amount of work.

Lily wondered if Margaret's stomach went queasy when she saw Neal, the way Lily's did when she saw Brian Lansing. She had encountered Brian several times since the end-of-school party; he did not live in

their neighborhood, but his house was not very far
away, either. It was surprising, Lily thought, how often
she ran into him. He came over on his bicycle a few
times to see the go-cart; they let him drive it, and although he enjoyed himself Lily could see that he did
not—could not—throw himself into the imagination
part the way she and the younger ones did.

No matter. Once in a while that summer, in fact,
Lily thought that playing their games, imagining that
the four of them were what they were not, was not as
enjoyable as it used to be. Once in a while, in fact, she
began to be bored—impatient, as if she was being de-
tained on a journey that she was making to some other
place—a place she had not yet visited, but one that
she knew awaited her. As the summer passed she had,
ever stronger, the sense of existing between the two.
She was leaving the one; she had not yet arrived at the
other.

But she knew that sooner or later she would get
there: everyone did. Some days she could hardly wait.

59

❦❦❦❦

"Marry me."

She smiled at him, and he saw in her eyes not only love but something else. Trust, he thought. Confidence. But mostly love, more love than he ever could have hoped for.

"Yes," she said. She was still smiling when he kissed her.

It was a night like any other—a cool September evening, the first fire in the fireplace, dinner cleared away, the children done with their homework and long since in bed.

And yet it was, now, a very special night, and they both understood that. It was a turning point: nothing, now, would ever be the same. Neal had never imagined that he could be so happy.

He kissed her some more and then he pulled back a little. "Wait a minute," he said. He reached into his pocket and brought out the small black velvet box that she had refused to open last winter. Now she did. It contained a diamond solitaire—not an extravagant one, but big enough to be impressive. She slipped it on and turned her hand so that its facets caught the light from the fire.

"All right?" he said. "Is it—would you rather have something different?"

"No. This one is just right." As you are, she thought.

She expected him to kiss her again, then—wanted him to—but instead he took her hand, her ring hand, and held it for a moment. "When do you think you should tell them?" he said. "Or perhaps we should both—"

"No. I'll tell them. But I won't have to, you know. They'll see the ring. They'll know. But of course I'll tell them anyway."

"And what if they say no?"

"They won't."

Neal was not so sure. He had come a long way with them over the summer, but even so, this was different. This was the real test: everything else had simply been the preliminaries.

But he understood that just as she trusted him, she trusted them as well.

He kissed her again, loving the small, warm feel of her in his arms, loving the way she responded to him, the way she gave herself to him. He had earned her trust, he thought. And he would never fail her. Not even if the children did.

In fact they did not; they took her news very well.

They held a War Council to consider it. This was, they understood, their last chance to keep Neal out of their lives; from here on, events would go forward inevitably and there would be no turning back.

They thought about saying no. They thought about raising such a ruckus that Neal would go away—permanently. They did not want him to do that. They had become accustomed to him; he was part of their lives. Then they thought about their mother, and about how much they loved her and wanted her to be happy. They

made her happy, but so did Neal. It seemed not such a
terrible thing to move aside a little and let him in. And
so, without much discussion, they voted yes. He was a
good person. Probably he would be a good stepfather.
If he wasn't—well, they would deal with that when
they had to. They didn't have a crystal ball; they
couldn't possibly tell the future. The future had a way
of surprising you, their grandmother said. There was
no way to know whether the surprises would be good
or bad.

By the time the wedding day arrived, some weeks
later—a home wedding, the best kind, their grandmother said—Peaches was wild with excitement.
Never had she had such an opportunity for dressing
up. Their grandmother bought her a dress that was
almost more beautiful than their mother's, or so
Peaches thought: a pale gray velveteen—*velveteen!*—
which, they all said, set off her pink-and-gold-and-
white coloring to perfection. Peaches didn't care about
that; she liked the luxurious feeling of the fabric, and
the ecru lace collar and the black taffeta sash. She had
never expected to have such a dress. It hung in her
closet in a plastic dress bag, and every day she tried it
on until her mother, laughing, warned her that she
would wear it out before she had a chance to really
wear it.

So then Peaches begged Margaret to try on her
wedding dress, but Margaret, obscurely superstitious,
hadn't wanted to. "It fits all right," she said. "I don't
need to try it on, and I wouldn't want to tear it or rip a
seam or anything."

It was, she thought, quite a pretty dress—pale tur-
quoise, with an embroidered bodice and full sleeves
and a dropped waistline. She had been amused at
Peaches' disappointment when she saw it.

"Why isn't it white?" Peaches had said.

Margaret could see that Peaches was crushed. "Because," she said. "People don't wear white the second
time around."

Peaches had struggled to adjust her fantasy about
what her mother's wedding would be like. She had
imagined something like the wedding of Prince Charles
and Princess Diana: thousands of people cheering, a
huge cathedral, and, for her mother, an extravagantly
beautiful wedding dress, long and flounced and ruffled
—and white.

"But *why*?" she persisted. "Everybody gets married
in a white dress."

Margaret did not feel prepared to undertake an explanation of the symbolic significance of the white
wedding dress. So she ended the discussion by deflect-
ing Peaches' attention to the question of the menu for
the reception.

Peaches had consoled herself with the thought that
at her own wedding, whenever it happened, her dress
would be the proper color. Meanwhile she immersed
herself in every detail of the planning: the guest list,
the food, the champagne, the cake, the flowers. It
seemed that they would never have enough time to
prepare. Now here she was, standing at her mother's
side, and Lily, too, and the boys opposite with Neal,
and it was happening.

"I do," she heard them say.

"I do," she whispered to herself: "I do I do I do."

And then they were pronounced "husband and
wife" and it was real, it *was* happening, and it was time
for Neal to kiss her mother. He threw his arms around
her and kissed her very hard, and everybody ex-
claimed and laughed and came up to congratulate
them, and it was all so exciting that Peaches thought
she would burst.

But before her mother and Neal dealt with anyone

else they turned to the children and gathered them for a big hug, all together, and Peaches took the dare that she had made to herself and reached up on tiptoe and kissed Neal on his cheek.

For a moment he looked surprised. Then he smiled at her and gave her a special hug all to herself and kissed her in turn, and Peaches was glad she had done it.

And then everyone crowded up, and the party was under way. People began to move around, eating, drinking champagne, and Peaches was suddenly very busy. As her grandmother had said, these were her guests as well as her mother's, and she was to see that everyone was happy and well taken care of. There were more than fifty people, many of whom she didn't know. The house was filled with flowers, and a lot of people had brought presents, and in the pantry was a wedding cake more beautiful even than Peaches could have imagined—three tiers, with real flowers on the top and around the base. And in the dining room the table had all the leaves put in, stretched to its full length, and there was more food than Peaches had ever seen in her life. But not for long, she thought: fifty people could eat a lot.

"Hi." The speaker was a short, thin, bespectacled man, not handsome at all but with a nice smile. "I'm Jason Goodrich."

Peaches shook his outstretched hand and introduced herself.

The man nodded. "You look just like your mother."

Peaches knew that; people said it all the time.

"Well," said the man, very cheerful. "Good luck."

And he moved on, leaving Peaches to wonder what *that* meant.

Lily was overseeing the table, replenishing empty platters. She liked having something to do. She wished that she could take her shoes off—her first "heels," about two inches, very uncomfortable—but otherwise she felt fine. She had wondered how she would feel on this day, but they had been so busy with all the preparations that she hadn't had time to worry about it.

She glanced at her mother and Neal, standing with a small knot of well-wishers. They looked very happy, arm in arm; they looked right, Lily thought, as if they belonged together.

Which was Margaret's feeling exactly. She belonged with this man. She felt a little giddy—the warm room, the champagne, the excitement—but at the same time she felt calm. Settled, somehow; clear-eyed, as if, all these years, her vision had been slightly blurred, and only now was suddenly clear and sharp.

Neal was saying something to Ellen Lafferty that made Ellen laugh. Ellen liked him; all her friends did.

"You're sure?" Ellen had said when Margaret told her, several weeks ago, that she and Neal were going to be married.

"Yes." She did not resent Ellen's question; it came, she knew, from loving concern.

And she *was* sure: confident. And confidence, as Neal said, came from knowledge. We have seen each other through bad times, she thought, and so we know each other as many couples do not. We are dependable friends as well as lovers. We have given to each other what neither of us could have achieved alone.

And then she thought: but we are lovers, too—and better lovers, at that, for being friends.

She watched him now, standing close beside her. He turned to smile at her; he had a look in his eyes that made her heart turn over and sent a little shiver up her spine. Yes, she thought: this is right, this will last. I will grow old with this man, and every day I will know, just as I know at this moment, that he loves me.

Then a new crush of people came up—Barbara Kimball and her husband, and the Olsens, and several others—and she lost contact with Neal for a moment, but it was all right. He was still there, he would always be there.

"Mother of Four Marries Again; All Well . . ."

About the Author

Nancy Zaroulis' other critically acclaimed novels include CALL THE DARKNESS LIGHT and THE POE PAPERS. She lives with her family in Massachusetts.